"You can't say no to me now, Joy. You're mine for always and have been from the first moment I saw you."

Jake's warm eyes reflected a brief flare of desire before they narrowed to scan the beauty of Joy's naked body. He found it impossible to tear his eyes away as his gaze dropped lower, viewing a narrow waist that tapered to rounded hips above long shapely legs.

"How could I refuse you now? I think I'm being seduced by your eyes alone," Joy replied in a throaty assertion. "Your glance is as arousing as your touch."

"Hmmm..." Jake growled, moving closer to her, "We'll soon see about that...."

Dear Reader,

It is our pleasure to bring you romance novels that go beyond category writing. The settings of **Harlequin American Romance** give a sense of place and culture that is uniquely American, and the characters are warm and believable. The stories are of "today" and have been chosen to give variety within the vast scope of romance fiction.

In *Branded Heart* Alice Morgan takes us into the exciting world of rodeo—a subject that is dear to her, having raised and shown champion quarter horses. The magnetism between Joy and Jake is intense and will draw you in from the very opening of this novel.

From the early days of Harlequin, our primary concern has been to bring you novels of the highest quality. **Harlequin American Romance** is no exception. Enjoy!

Vivian Stephens
Editorial Director
Harlequin American Romance
919 Third Avenue,
New York, N.Y. 10022

Branded Heart

ALICE MORGAN

Harlequin Books

TORONTO • NEW YORK • LONDON
AMSTERDAM • PARIS • SYDNEY • HAMBURG
STOCKHOLM • ATHENS • TOKYO • MILAN

Dedicated to the memory
of my charismatic brother

Published December 1983

First printing October 1983

ISBN 0-373-16035-6

Printed in Canada

Chapter One

"See this photo, Rena?" Joy handed a torn-out, vividly colored magazine page across the table. "Could you have an erotic dream about that man?" she questioned her best friend, curiously intent on her opinion about a stranger whose image had haunted her mind since first seeing the advertisement two weeks earlier.

"Sure. Why not?" Rena shrugged, spearing a flaky piece of barbecued salmon and dipping it into a side dish of tartar sauce before raising it to her mouth. "He's got a cute tush, but too slender in the chest, and I don't really care for blond hair."

"Not him," Joy pointed out, pushing a fresh-baked square of cornbread aside. "I mean the brooding guy in the background."

"You're missing the point, sweetie. We're literally being blitzed with these notices lately. I've seen them on billboards and in most magazines. Believe me, they're not advertising either the model's sexy rear or your brawny demigod."

Her glance lingered on Joy's expressive face, intrigued as always with the stunning beauty of jade-toned eyes fringed with thick obsidian lashes she knew were natural.

"You're supposed to be so overwhelmed by the designer boots you'll insist your lover, or husband, whatever the case may be, will wear nothing else on his feet."

Joy reached for the candid sheet, drawing it back to hold in both hands. She was unaware Rena watched her closely while she scrutinized the advertisement for the umpteenth time. She stared at the model posed in midstride, his upper

torso turned toward the camera. He was strikingly handsome, his western clothing impeccably neat, but he looked
like a model and she hadn't given him a second glimpse.

From the first glance, her thoughts had been filled with
the tall cowboy in the background. The lens had captured
his enigmatic expression clearly. He stood alongside a
smaller, younger man, which added to his look of strength.
Both arms were raised, elbows resting along the rough-
hewn boards of a faded white fence. A shaped western hat
was pulled over his forehead, partially shadowing narrowed
eyes. Lean, hollow jaws and straight, well-defined masculine lips intensified his look of boredom.

A plain chambray shirt was stretched taut across the
width of broad shoulders, hugging his chest and tapering
along his rib cage to narrow hips encircled by a leather belt
with an oval buckle. One knee was raised, the boot heel
hooked on a fence rung, the other leg supporting his weight
on the dirt. Plain leather chaps hugged his limbs, outlining
their lithe shape. Their waistband was taut below his regular
belt, emphasizing his male contours with explicit detail.

Joy had never seen anyone like him before. He was so
different from the men she had dated and worked with, it
was astounding. Yet, she hadn't been able to blot him
from her consciousness. He exuded an earthy virility that
wrought a staggering unbidden response.

Joy raised a well-manicured hand, trying vainly to smooth
a wayward chestnut curl that had come loose from the
shiny chignon resting on her nape.

"Would you be shocked to know I've dreamed several
nights in a row that—that he's making love to me?"

Rena chuckled, leaning back in her chair to smile at Joy's
hesitant confession. "Not in the least, considering you're
the only twenty-seven-year-old virgin I know. I suspect it's
your underworked hormones burgeoning for expression.
You'd better find the man."

"Do you think he'd make love to me?" Joy asked seriously, uncaring her dinner was getting cold.

Rena threw her hands up in resignation. "What man
wouldn't? I've watched all my boyfriends drool over you
for years. One glance at you and I look like a stick figure."

"Hardly," Joy scoffed. "Your height gives you a regal appearance that I could never have." She handed the illustration back when Rena reached for it, nervously toying with her wineglass.

"I want this man to be my first lover."

"Seriously?" Rena quizzed.

"Absolutely," Joy declared emphatically. "I feel kind of like an overaged groupie, but I intend to find the man. If he's not married, I'll—"

"What?" her friend interrupted. "Ask him to hit the sack with you? Don't be a fool. You're the one who receives proposals, remember? I'm the one who gets propositioned."

"I'll do the propositioning," Joy blurted out, knowing her disclosure surprised Rena. They were the best of friends, though their paths rarely crossed since Joy lived permanently in Seattle and Rena traveled around the world for her travel agency.

"I think you've had a little too much wine tonight. I'm a staunch feminist, but I still hesitate to suggest a woman go to bed with a man she doesn't know. To deliberately seek an unknown man whose photo turns you on is even more ludicrous."

"Not to me it isn't." Joy's voice lowered, becoming unconsciously sensual. "We've both dated since we were fourteen. In all that time I've never found a man I could respond to. No matter how pleasant they are, I freeze when they touch me. I can't tolerate being handled. You've never hesitated to tell me you've been intimate with many men and right now I feel as if I have several years to catch up on."

Rena filled their wineglasses, took a slow swallow, and set hers on the table. "You better talk to one of the doctors you work with, honey. He or she could better explain the facts of life. It sounds like you think going all the way will release the touch-me-not attitude you've engendered for years."

"It's not that really," Joy explained, then hesitated until the waiter had deftly cleared their table of plates and silverware.

"After all this time to find a man who can enter my bedroom, even if it's through a fantasy, seems worth pursuing."

"But that's the problem. You're living a fantasy!"

"Yes, but a wonderful one. Believe me, in my dreams I don't have an inhibited bone in my body."

"Bells ring and all that hogwash, I suppose?" Rena mocked.

"Isn't that how it is?" Joy queried, widened eyes filled with innocent curiosity.

"God, no! I've yet to see stars flash and I've tried too many to remember. The American hero type, Latin lovers, expressive Frenchmen, and one or two gregarious Greeks."

Rena shrugged her shoulders, lighted a foreign cigarette, and inhaled in easy fluid motions. "Keep your memories as they are. A beautiful fantasy. The cold reality is often hard to bear. The morning after can be totally disillusioning for both partners, no matter how romantic the night before has been. Take it from one who knows."

"You sound bitter."

"I am. My head was filled with dreams of Mr. Right when I was twenty·one. Now I find a gorgeous wardrobe, world travel, and a growing bank account much more satisfying than most male companionship."

"You think I'm crazy, don't you?" Joy was reaching into her purse for her billfold when Rena stopped her.

"I'll pay this time." She took out her VISA card and laid it on the dinner check before answering the question. "Yes and no. I think you need a man to make love to you—"

"This man only." Joy looked at the advertisement. She could feel her heartbeat increase and a tremulous sensation in the depth of her abdomen—a physical reaction that occurred each time she looked at the stranger's likeness. "No one else will do."

"Okay," Rena agreed complacently. "You need *this* man to make love to you, but I also must warn you if he's anything at all like most of my lovers, one sample will be ample."

Rena's ·calm reply didn't surprise Joy. She hadn't expected any reproof from her liberated friend. They had always discussed the most intimate facts without embarrassment. Rena's honesty in expressing her dissatisfaction was disconcerting, though. Surely some of her relationships had brought her pleasure?

"Well, at least you didn't tell me to take two aspirin, go to bed, and call you in the morning, like my boss would," Joy teased.

"Since you work at your uncle's clinic I doubt if you'd dare mention this sudden urge for sexual intimacy. He's such a cold and aloof man it never surprised me he and your aunt were childless."

Joy knew her friend felt sorry for her. Rena's parents had been loving, her home filled with laughter and happiness, while Joy had lived a childhood stifled of any emotion. She never recalled seeing the slightest hint of physical affection between her aunt and uncle.

"Your upbringing is probably the cause of your frozen attitude to men and this impulsive desire to go off the deep end with someone as unlike your ordinary boyfriends as night from day."

"They can't help it, Rena. They're good people. Raising someone else's child couldn't have been easy on them. I've never lacked for anything," Joy said in defense of her only living relatives. She loved them and would always be thankful for the home they provided.

"Nothing but affection," Rena complained. Joy knew Rena never liked her aunt and uncle, yet adamantly refused to listen to any criticism about them despite their close friendship.

Rena glanced at her watch, then stood up and motioned to Joy. "I have exactly thirty-five minutes to board my plane for New York. Since you're driving me to the airport, let's get moving."

Joy grabbed her purse, slipped into a cashmere jacket, and followed Rena's slender figure from the dining room. They chattered nonstop on the short drive, knowing it would be at least three months before they saw each other again. Rena's admonition to take care and not expect miracles rang in Joy's ears long after they waved good-bye.

A light mist began to fall, filtering the glare from oncoming headlights, as Joy drove home. Seeing Rena always made her restless. She enjoyed her work managing her uncle's medical practice but it seemed so staid in comparison with traveling worldwide.

She remembered as a child longing to be a registered nurse. One year's training had convinced everyone involved she was too compassionate to continue. She had felt the pain of each patient, brooded helplessly about it as if it was her own. She knew it would be unbearable if it was someone she loved suffering and she couldn't bring them immediate relief. Someone she loved! Like her cowboy? Was it possible to feel genuine love for a man in a photo? she wondered.

Joy eased into the basement garage and parked in the assigned space of the towering building where she had rented a small, one-bedroom apartment for seven years.

Entering the privacy of her fifth-floor corner unit, she scanned the room with a critical eye. For the first time her carefully selected furnishings failed to elicit a favorable response. Even knowing she had a clear view of the Space Needle, Lake Union, the busy seaport, and constantly changing oceangoing vessels on Puget Sound didn't raise her spirits.

Not only was she aware of the emptiness of her personal life, but the lack of challenge at work added to her moodiness. Perhaps it was time for a total change in life-style, she reflected, turning on the radio to break the silence of the room.

With casual ease she prepared for bed, neatly hanging her jacket and dress in the crowded closet. A luxurious bath using an overabundance of expensive scent failed to soothe her unsettled nerves.

"Darn you, cowboy!" she grumbled, annoyed she couldn't dismiss the stranger from her mind. Seated before the dresser mirror she released her hair from the heavy coil, brushing the strands with unhurried strokes. Watching the vibrant tresses respond with an apparent life of their own, she admitted it was her one vanity as they tightened up in deep waves that fell below the small of her spine.

With a satiny swathe held in one hand she brushed the ends, openly contemplating as they curled back time after time. Only Rena knew how long it was since she habitually wore it in a heavy coil on her nape. She felt so sensual with the weight caressing her bare skin.

"Freud could explain better than I why I prefer to keep it hidden from everyone but my best friend," she spoke aloud, knowing full well her senses were heightened erotically with it unbound.

Would her cowboy like it? she wondered silently, staring at his picture on the nightstand. She touched it reverently before climbing into bed. The silk gown clung to her full breasts, its lacy bodice exposing more than it concealed. She adored sensual underwear in vivid colors, often paying outrageous prices for custom-sewn lingerie.

Propped against the ruffled bed pillow, she picked up the magazine page and stared unashamedly at the stranger's picture. An unknown man who had become infinitely important to her from the initial sight. First thing in the morning she intended to start the expected lengthy process to track him down. She had been perfectly serious when she had told Rena she wanted him to be her virgin lover. Her vacation began in one week and she was determined to pursue her quarry without thought of moral consequence or expense.

A smile raised her soft mouth, touching her face with an innocent beauty that belied her plans—wanton schemes that were as sensuous as her actions in her dreams.

Joy laid the picture on the nightstand, shut off the bedside lamp, and relaxed into a comfortable position in the middle of her bed. Erotic thoughts tumbled through her mind. She wanted to dream, wanted to lose all sense of reality and lose herself in the fantasy of the previous nights, yet she shook with dread that her stranger might not reappear.

Her last cognition was of the insanity of yearning for sleep to overcome her, to seek oblivion in a fantasy that Rena had warned her could never compare with the cold facts of reality....

Joy tossed restlessly, eyelids flickering but remaining

closed, mouth parting as a small whimpering sound of excitement escaped.

He came to her, arms outstretched, eyes filled with love and tenderness. With gentle regard for her pleasure he pulled her into his hold. She could feel the warmth of his nakedness pressed against the length of hers. Her body became supple, seemed boneless as she yielded to his superior strength. His hands threaded through her hair, stroking through its silken length, while words of love spilled forth in continuing reverence.

She gloried in his touch, raising on tiptoes to reach lips that were beautiful in their masculinity. From the first touch her head swam with the passion engendered. Their hunger knew no bounds, he as eager to be consumed by her as she by him. She held him tightly, aching to be as close as humanly possible to the man she loved.

As if rehearsed and directed by the finest choreographer, she felt herself swung up into arms that cradled her slightness with delicate care. Lips that took hers with a magic never experienced before continued to claim her responsive mouth with increasing hunger.

She made no protest when she was laid down on a soft bed of tall grass and drawn the length of his body. Hands that were bold with intent caressed her supple form until she whimpered with the need to get closer, to become one with her lover in their velvety soft hideaway.

Words of love and undying devotion were exchanged over and over, each eager to reassure the other of their adoration. Her heart overflowed with love when he buried his head in the lustrous strands of chestnut-brown silk, telling her it was the most beautiful hair he'd ever seen or touched.

When she couldn't stand the torment of not being his, her hands drew his face to her parted lips. She begged him to make love to her again and again, she cried that she couldn't bear another moment without being his partner in the most intimate act exchanged between man and woman.

With the agility of an accomplished lover he eased upward. She never made the least objection when he prepared to possess her; she parted her limbs, accepting his great body with hands outstretched to clasp his biceps. Her thighs quivered, soft breasts heaving as he hesitated, waiting intently until she beseeched him, pleaded for his love. It was so beautiful. The most perfect moment in her life.

"Love me, darling. Oh, darling, please love me," she whispered, her voice a deep throaty murmur, heavy with sleep. She tossed feverishly, then woke—as usual when her illusionary vision came to the same point.

Joy sat up, head bowed in her hands in the darkened room. Her body was covered in a light film of perspiration. She couldn't believe it. Another night in the stranger's arms. Another night when she failed to find satisfaction on their grassy bed.

"I have to find him!" Her voice echoed in the small room. "Only by finding the man can I seek release from the torment he unknowingly inflicts on me each night."

She fumbled for the light switch to check the time. Six o'clock. In an hour she would prepare for work, but in the meantime she could start her search. In Texas the boot company office might be open. Surely they would know who the man was they used in their own ads?

Within moments Joy had checked information for the Fort Worth company and was connected to the main office. She waited impatiently until a soft southern drawl answered with a cheery good-morning.

"Hello," Joy replied pleasantly. "Could you possibly tell me how to contact one of the men in your current ad?"

"Well, I certainly don't know the man's name but I'll switch you to my supervisor. She's been here for years and handles any problems. They're all three fantastic looking, aren't they?"

Joy waited, amused by the secretary's youthful exuberance, though Joy found only one appealing: the stranger she shared such intimacies with in the privacy of her darkened bedroom, the one man she planned to volunteer the same intrinsic sensuality to at their first meeting. She answered briskly when her thoughts were interrupted.

"Hello, Ms. Erickson," Joy said, repeating the woman's name. "Your secretary thought you might be able to help me. I need to get in touch with the models in your current ad. I've an interesting proposition to offer. Could you possibly give me their names and addresses?''

"Definitely not, miss. My secretary should have warned you our company has been deluged with calls regarding those three. We've decided to discontinue using the ad. It's been disappointingly ineffective in promoting our new line of designer footwear, since public interest is drawn primarily to the models' physical attributes.''

"Really?" Joy murmured, not knowing what to do next. She groaned inwardly listening to the supervisor's following comment.

"Especially the dark cowboy in the background. It seems all my young staff and numerous other women are eager to know where to find him. He does project a certain animal magnetism, don't you think?''

"Er, yes," Joy answered. Her hopes plummeted at the thought someone else was intrigued with *her* stranger. It was almost as if he were being unfaithful to her to know other women wanted him too.

Damn! she thought, irritated she would have to join a queue to find her cowboy. Ms. Erickson sounded at least sixty years old yet her voice took on a schoolgirlish pitch citing his, *animal magnetism*.

"We don't handle public relations in Fort Worth," she advised resolutely. "And it's company policy the N.Y. firm stay confidential.''

Joy hung up the phone. She knew she had problems ahead. New York had numerous PR firms. Maybe a little ingenuity would short list them if she could just think.

She got up, showered, dressed in Givenchy underwear much too flattering not to be seen, and pulled on the white uniform her uncle insisted she wear though she worked in the office only. Deftly doing her hair, she clipped it into a smooth chignon, then applied the small amount of makeup she normally wore. Through it all the stranger invaded her thoughts. She decided to phone the company again, hoping another receptionist answered the phone.

Her fingers trembled. "I'm getting more paranoid each day," she scolded, again waiting the three rings. Breathing a sigh of relief, she listened to the pleasant unfamiliar voice say hello.

"I'm calling for Mr. Lieberman of Shatner and Lieberman Shoes in Beverly Hills. My employer asked me to double-check the public relations firm Ms. Erickson recommended he use when they talked last week."

Joy crossed her fingers, hating to lie, but she was determined to outsmart any competitors for *her* stranger. She waited, filled with anxiety that the woman might check with her supervisor.

"Did she tell Mr. Lieberman it was Misner, Hendrix, and Seldon?"

"Yes," Joy lied, praying she was correct on her assumption. "Their phone number, please? I'm rather in a hurry this morning."

"Area code two-one-two," the woman burst out, slowing to give the number.

Joy thanked her, broke the connection with one pink-tinted fingernail, then dialed the New York number.

After one brief ring she listened to a brisk hello and repeated her request, using the practiced hauteur reserved for indignant patients.

"Sorry, Miss Sanders. Those notices were delegated to an advertising agency. Our work for that boot company is mainly involved with keeping their current Ms. Bubbly Boots out of mischief on her nationwide publicity tours and seeing she arrives at retail chain store openings in time to cut the ribbon. Believe me," the secretary sighed, "that's a full-time job for two of our staff."

"I can imagine," Joy replied sympathetically, grimacing at the name Ms. Bubbly Boots. She immediately pictured a frizzy-haired, subintelligent female with huge breasts, skin-tight jeans, and a wide, toothy smile. If Misner, Hendrix, and Seldon picked *that* title for their Fort Worth client, she didn't look for them to be a successful public relations firm much longer.

"Could you repeat the name of the advertising agency, please?" She wrote the number down hurriedly, giving a furtive glance at the bedside clock. It was time to leave for work and her uncle demanded all his employees be punctual.

Stuffing the paper in her purse, she walked quickly to the elevator. The phone call would have to wait until her lunch hour.

The morning's work seemed endless, but Joy finally rushed into her apartment at twelve twenty. She normally didn't drive home for lunch but it was the only way she could assure complete privacy during her phone call to the ad agency.

Within seconds she was talking to a flirtatious young junior employee of Gantry's, Limited. A youth who appeared long on education and short on experience, he was gullible enough to believe everything she said and couldn't have been more helpful. In ten minutes she found out the photos and models had been secured from Alfonso's, Hollywood's most prestigious agency; had been told her West Coast accent was captivating; and was invited to spend an exciting weekend in a fifth-floor walk-up with Charles whenever she visited New York.

"Obnoxious young man, but things appear to be improving," Joy declared to the empty room, adding Alfonso's name to the bottom of the note paper. At least trades were getting closer to home, she surmised, reaching out to dial the Hollywood number. Her phone bill would be decidedly higher next month.

A moan escaped Joy's lips when she heard the aggravating recorded message that Alfonso was on location. If she left her name and number, he would see she was contacted when he returned.

"Darn it!" Joy exclaimed petulantly. She wanted to find out who her phantom lover was immediately, not when Alfonso took the time to answer his phone messages.

A piece of cheddar cheese and a crisp red delicious apple, constituted her meager lunch, which she ate while pacing the living room floor attempting to plan what she would do when she actually found out who her cowboy was.

Joy waited each day for Alfonso or his secretary to phone. Every morning and noon she placed a call, leaving increasingly irritated messages. Friday afternoon she became totally exasperated, telling him just what she thought of someone who used a recorder to accept long distance phone calls and didn't have the decency to either unplug the machine or answer the message.

Saturday morning at two o'clock she was awakened by the shrill ring of her bedside phone. After groping for the receiver, she picked it up.

"Hello," she answered, her sleepy voice husky and unintentionally sensual. She could hear loud conversation in the background mixed with strident rock music.

"Did I wake you, my pet? This is Alfonso, your errant *artiste.*"

"I thought you were a photographer and model procurer," Joy snapped. She was miffed about being awakened. Hearing his smug voice she instantly wanted to put him in his place even if he was an avant-garde *artiste.*

"*Procurer* is the wrong choice of word for anyone dealing in flesh in this city, love. Though I do admit to dabbling in the availability of a fair number of willing participants interested in the exchange of sexual favors when business warrants it. What's your hang-up, darling?"

Joy couldn't believe her ears as Alfonso droned on in a voice dripping with sugary sweetness. She hated to imagine what the party he was having was like. Did the vice squad know about this man?

"I am interested in—"

"I get it. By the number of messages on my recorder—some rather unladylike, dear one—it appears you're needing a man too."

Joy was speechless. It sounded so crude the way Alfonso put it, yet she really was soliciting the dark cowboy's name for sexual favors. Surely the beauty of her fantasy couldn't be placed in the same category with passion for pay. It made the act of love sound sordid. Nothing about her dreams of being with the cowboy seemed touched by baseness until she listened to Alfonso's flippant remarks.

"Sorry to disappoint you, but the blond god in the boot ad wouldn't be interested in your gender at any price."

"Nor I him!" Joy stormed back. "I want to know how to get in touch with the tall cowboy in the background."

"I haven't the faintest idea who he is. That was a location shot. When I handed the aristocratic beast my business card and asked him to get in touch with me anytime, he stared at me from his great height, took a match, and set fire to my card, then ground the ashes beneath his boot heel. Without a single word of apology to me or my blond Adonis archetype, he stalked rudely off.''

Joy gave a sigh of relief inwardly. At least that solved one of the problems Rena had warned her about single men over thirty. She could imagine what Alfonso looked like and wished she had witnessed his silent putdown by *her* man. Surely he wouldn't be a misogynist too?

Any comfort was short-lived. If Alfonso didn't know the man's name or address and he took the photos, how could she ever find him?

"Where did all this happen?" Joy quizzed hopefully. Maybe that could narrow it down a little.

"In the wilds of Nevada. Such an uncivilized state, actually," Alfonso elaborated.

"Where in Nevada?" Joy beseeched him. "It's very important I know."

"Outside Reno. I shot it close to pens filled with malodorous cows and horses. Really rather more primitive than I prefer."

"When?" Joy pleaded. Would he ever quit detailing his feelings? She didn't care what he did or did not prefer as a life-style.

"Last summer. Close to the end of June, just before the start of Reno's High Roller Roundup, I believe they called it. Anything else, love? The slobs here have emptied all my expensive bottles of Dom Pérignon, and the ungrateful ingrates are yelling for more."

"That's all I needed." Joy thanked him, smiling as he wished her luck in contacting the arrogant stranger. His final suggestion to tell him hello from Alfonso and the blond model was answered with a mischievous chuckle. It looked like her brooding cowboy was admired by both sexes.

Picking up the magazine page, she scanned her hero nonchalantly leaning against the corral. After listening to Alfonso she now felt she had an insight into his thoughts. Apparently that look of boredom on his sensual face was not contrived.

Turning the lamp off, she curled on her side, going over her conversation with Alfonso. Any outside help in her search had come to an end. Whether she found her wayward nighttime lover would depend more on a lucky break now than incessant ingenuity, it seemed.

Late Sunday night she was exhausted. She had spent a whirlwind weekend packing clothes, watering plants, cleaning out her refrigerator, and paying the few bills that couldn't wait until she returned.

She was dressed in a comfortable robe, bare feet curled beneath her, while she relaxed in her only armchair and sipped a cup of delicious hot chocolate made with the last of the fresh milk on hand.

Disturbed by the ringing phone, she took a long drink in case the call was lengthy, reached out, and said hello.

"Hi, Joy." It was Rena.

"Where are you?" She hadn't expected to hear from her friend for weeks.

"London, and it's too damned early to be awake so talk fast and let me get back to bed. I called to see how you're doing in your manhunt."

"I have it narrowed down to one state," Joy explained breathlessly.

"Good. Hope it's a little one," Rena trilled back.

"Nevada."

"Big state but light on population. Seriously," she questioned, her voice lowering, "what have you found out?"

Joy related all her news as quickly as possible. Rena was as stunned as she had been to hear her uncle had been dickering for months on the purchase of a clinic in California. The deal had closed the first of the week. He had moved already and asked his niece to fly to Sacramento with her aunt and organize his new office instead of taking her vacation as planned.

"That figures," Rena complained. "He's using you again. Why don't you tell him to shove off, fly to London and join my group for a couple of weeks?"

"Sounds good, Rena, but I've already promised my uncle."

"Well, at least California is closer to Nevada than

Washington," Joy was reminded unnecessarily. She knew to the mile how far Sacramento was from Reno. The first free weekend she intended to go there and continue her search.

"Any lascivious dreams lately?" Rena questioned mischievously.

"None since the night you left," Joy answered truthfully. "I've missed the, er, lovemaking on our bed of grass."

"In the grass? Ugh!" Rena shot back. "I got it on with one of those nature boys once and all I remember is getting my back scratched and bug bites on my bottom." Her voice was filled with disgust when she admonished Joy. "Forget it. Insist on satin sheets and a king-size bed with room service at the touch of a button."

"With a cowboy's wages?" Joy reminded her, amused by Rena's outspoken suggestions.

"Believe me," her friend continued, unchastened, "there's no romance in making love in primitive conditions. I don't know how women ever managed to procreate with prehistoric male beasts. If it had been me, no he-man in leather Jockey shorts with a wood pole over his shoulder, could have got within a mile of hauling me by the hair to a dark smelly cave to fool around in the dirt."

Undaunted by Joy's laughter, Rena kept up her diatribe about men.

"Another thing, love. Insist he bathe first, clean his fingernails, and shave."

"Rena!" Joy interjected firmly. "That sounds so clinical. He certainly looks clean in the photo."

"He's a cowboy, remember?" her friend shot back. "Cowboys spend all day in contact with horses and cattle, which are both dirty and stinky. Better take along some air spray also."

"Good Lord," Joy chuckled, enjoying the ridiculous banter. "Shall I buy a flea collar too?" Rena's droll advice was getting more ludicrous with each comment.

"Might not hurt, honey. You never know what he picked up wrestling around in the dirt. Insist he wear protection and—"

"Hush, Rena. You're beginning to turn me off to all men again!"

"You're a novice to the practical side—or any other side—so pay attention," Rena scolded humorously.

"Good-bye, Rena." Joy laughed, reminding her how expensive it was for an overseas phone call before breaking the connection.

Joy took her cup into the kitchen, poured the cool remainder of the chocolate down the drain, washed up, and returned to the living room. She was leaving early in the morning to pick up her aunt, would drive on to the airport for their nine-o'clock flight, leave her car in a paid parking area, and be in Sacramento by ten thirty-five.

Rena's promise to phone in three weeks filled Joy with excitement. By then she intended to have searched Reno for her unknown illusionary lover and have good news to relate. Could she really find him? If so, she intended the reality in his arms to exceed the beauty of her fantasy.

Chapter Two

Tall, dark hero, where are you now? Joy asked herself in jest when three cowboys swaggered from the front entrance of Reno Hilton and deliberately blocked her path. They were nice-looking, young, and neatly groomed but it was obvious they had already had too much to drink and were determined to indulge in some playful mischief-making.

Suddenly wishing she was not alone, she hesitated, her expressive eyes warning them she wouldn't be bullied. Not easily intimidated, she held her saucy chin high, surveyed them with one arched brow raised in inquiry and her diminutive nose at a haughty angle. She was used to dealing with men's advances. These were mere youths and should present no problem if handled with a cool mind. She would let them have their say, then continue on with her previous plans.

She had decided to give the town a cursory search before taking a taxi to the rodeo grounds. In her purse was a new copy of the advertisement she intended to show each contestant. Filled with optimism, despite not observing any man remotely similar during her three-hour walk along the busy sidewalk, she was eager to proceed.

Would she recognize him if they came face to face? she wondered, though he had continued to dominate her thoughts in the daytime and haunt her dreams at night. One thing was certain, he was nothing like the three scanning her with bold impudence.

Undaunted by Joy's hauteur, they continued to obstruct the wide sidewalk. Heads tilted back and bright faces filled with open admiration, they stared without embarrassment, pleased to find such a beautiful young woman alone.

In unison their eyes moved from the obvious allure of her feminine curves to brazenly stare at her face. Her look of innocence, enhanced by stormy green eyes showing a hint of wantonness in their luminous depths, was a temptation. The unusual color was momentarily concealed by dark lashes lowered to avoid their silent regard.

Since they made no sign to leave nor offered an explanation for their behavior, Joy drew back, unaware the movement caused her cinnamon-toned silk blouse to tighten seductively across the fullness of her high breasts.

Moving forward, they formed a half-circle around her.

"Can you believe our luck today, T.G. and Buck?" the tallest, thinnest one asked his friends in a drawling voice. "Did you worthless rodeo bums ever lay your eyes on a better-lookin' filly anywhere?" He stood straight, head cocked sideways, slender hands tucked into a fancy tooled leather belt surrounding his skinny hips.

"Looks to me like we hit the jackpot, Slim," another answered, his bright hazel eyes filled with mirth. He bowed from the waist, tipping his broad-brimmed western hat to Joy. "I'm T.G., the best-lookin'; the young one is Buck; and the tall lanky one, Slim. We'd be honored if you'd let us escort you around this here neon-lighted den of iniquity."

Their unforeseen appearance and unusual sense of humor fascinated Joy. She listened raptly while their spokesman continued without interruption. When they were finished with their tomfoolery she would ask them if they knew her cowboy.

"A pretty little filly like you shouldn't be runnin' around alone. Some of these cowboys around here can't be trusted," T.G. teased boldly; his eyes lingering on her figure with obvious appreciation.

Entertained by their manner, Joy laughed softly, good-naturedly going along with the playful bantering. Giving each one a friendly smile, she refused their offer to escort her around Reno, expecting them to leave as abruptly as they had approached.

The three pretended remorse, looked at each other, then talked among themselves, before proceeding to compliment her in an outrageous manner. Their rhetoric was unlike anything she had ever heard. Amused, she stood listening as they continued their conversation as if she weren't there.

"What do you think, Buck? Should we let her go?" T.G. asked, his bold eyes openly admiring her spirited expression.

"Nope! I think we should rope and hog-tie her right here on old Virginia Street. In fact, she'll be darn lucky if she ain't packin' some man's brand before the day's over." Buck spoke sincerely, knowing a cowboy's tendency toward impulsiveness when he was drinking and confronted with such an attractive young woman.

Slim and T.G. agreed readily, entranced by her lovely smile and willingness to listen to their impertinent banter.

"She sure does show good breedin', don't she, boys?" Buck insisted, looking at his friends roguishly. "Just look at those wide set eyes...so large and intelligent. That sleek, shiny, well-groomed chestnut coat. Those long slender pasterns and well-developed chest muscles."

Not dismayed by Joy's changing expression, Buck's eyes lingered on her figure with increasing pleasure as his descriptive speech continued. "I gotta admit though, she shows a might too much Thoroughbred in the hindquarters—a little too narrow for my likin'," he added bluntly as he proceeded to circle behind her, his eyes never leaving her slender hips clad in a stylish Mayan print skirt.

Joy's face flushed a faint rose as the trend of the conversation became too personal. No longer amused, she turned to walk away. It would be no use to ask those three if they recognized anyone.

Slim, having had more to drink than his friends, reached for her arm, grabbed hold of it firmly with his strong fingers, and playfully scolded, "Don't leave us, honey. We intend to show you a good time tonight." He looked back at T.G. and Buck for encouragement. Emboldened by their nod of approval, he continued to clasp her arm tightly, his eyes as bright blue as the clear sky.

Joy looked around beseechingly, trying without success to pull her arm away. Their actions had become increasingly boisterous, and she was suddenly alarmed. How could she get free without causing a scene?

Instinctively, as Joy tugged to get away, Slim pulled against her, triumphantly drawing her close to his tall, wiry body. "Give me a kiss for luck at today's rodeo finals and I'll let you go, doll," he cajoled, becoming aroused by the proximity of her softness and the heady aroma of expensive French perfume filling his flared nostrils.

"No...stop! Please let me be," she pleaded, making a helpless gesture. "I—I realize you're only having fun, but I want to look over the town by myself." Her voice rose in anger as their horseplay continued and she began to feel threatened. Darn young fools!

"Not until I get my kiss," Slim warned her adamantly, looking at his friends again. "How about you, T.G.? And you, Buck? You'll both need a kiss for luck too, won't you?" He turned back to Joy. "Three kisses and you'll be free. That ain't too much to ask."

He lowered his head, trying to place his mouth on the enticing beauty of her parted lips, while she struggled. A few people paused to watch, were momentarily amused, then continued on their way.

Without warning, Slim was wrenched from Joy's stiffly held body by a large tanned hand gripping his shoulder in a steel-hard hold.

"Let her be, boys. We don't want this little beauty to get the idea that cowboys are rowdy, hard-drinking womanizers," a stranger drawled, his husky voice smooth as velvet with the pleasing accent of a native Texan.

Joy remained still, stunned into momentary speechlessness by the sudden interference of a forceful cowboy as unlike the younger men as night from day. Her cheeks paled, his effect beyond her control.

She couldn't believe it. It was *her* cowboy! He was so big, so overwhelmingly sensual, that every nerve in her body responded shamelessly.

Totally bemused by his unexpected appearance and the entrancing timbre of his voice, she stared wide-eyed, watching as the three youths smiled roguishly, then offered her their profuse apologies.

Slim had released Joy's arm the moment he felt the paralyzing grip and heard his friend's authoritative command. His voice became sheepish as he explained, "Hi, Jake. I was just funnin'. I wouldn't have done nothin' to hurt her, for sure. We was sincere when we told her she was the prettiest little filly we come across since rodeoin'."

He looked at the older man's formidable expression, then motioned to his buddies with resigned tolerance, before adding pointedly, "Hell, Jake, you more than anyone else should know what a compliment that is, considerin' all the good-lookin' women hangin' around the arena these days."

Joy stared openmouthed with astonishment. She was surrounded by four strangers and unintentionally the source of discomfort for three of them. The one they called Jake didn't look like either man or beast would dare cause him displeasure.

Jake. That fit him perfectly, Joy thought, still dazed by his presence. Her stomach churned involuntarily. It was all she could do to keep her knees from buckling and collapsing at his large boot-clad feet.

She gazed upward at his taut face. She couldn't believe she found the stranger who was foremost in her mind the last few weeks. He looked huge, towering over her with intimidating strength. She felt tongue-tied, swallowing to ease the tightness in her throat. Hypnotized by the sound of his husky voice, she didn't want to move, feeling driven to stare at the jut of his lean jaw. The photograph didn't do him justice. He was too vital and absolutely radiated virility, she reflected, trying desperately to control her heartbeat.

His skin was tanned a deep bronze, so unlike the doctors' she worked for, it was startling. He was so many things they weren't. His hand was still raised to clasp Slim's shoulder and it fascinated her. It was not the skilled, pale, cared-for hand of a surgeon but a strong, lean hand, callused and obviously capable in a different way. Dark springy hairs were sparsely scattered across the back to the taut knuckles of long well-shaped fingers.

Jake suddenly turned his head sideways, his glance catching Joy's openmouthed stare. Warm brown eyes twinkled as mischievously as his friends', but the look of intense possessive interest was not that of a youth. He scanned her face lazily, his pupils black as pitch and dilating with mounting intrigue.

Joy couldn't tear her glance away as his keen eyes narrowed, his sensuously shaped lips raising in a smile that showed strong, even white teeth.

I'm mesmerized, she admitted warily. She had never been so conscious of a man in her life. It was as if they were the only two people in the world. She could feel her heart hammering furiously at the stunning impact of his masculinity and she wondered how on earth she had ever thought she would have the nerve to suggest he be her first lover. At no time could she imagine having the daring to proposition such a self-assured man. What should she do now?

Annoyed by her body's instant response to his compelling good looks—far exceeding the dramatic reaction when she first saw the advertisement—she made a futile attempt to act detached.

Noticing Joy's immediate receptivity to Jake, T.G. was filled with resignation, prompting his buddies unhappily. "Let's go. We don't have a snowball's chance in hell of makin' out with this little beauty now that Jake's set his eyes on her. See you later, Jake."

Tipping their western straw hats, adorned with brightly colored feathered hatbands, to Joy, they apologized for their behavior and left. They walked three abreast down the broad sidewalk, heads turning right and left to look for further mischief before the rodeo began later that day.

Shocked by the stunning turn of events, Joy turned to Jake, her revealing eyes filled with appreciation for his timely interference, mouth opened to thank him. She felt like a dolt.

She didn't know what to do next. Her bold plans had seemed so easy when she talked with Rena. The hardest part would be to find him, she had assumed. Telling this stranger he was the only man who had ever turned her on, that she had dreamed about him making love to her over and over, seemed totally impossible now. Suddenly the best thing seemed to be to forget her momentary madness and run from him as far and as fast as possible.

Without saying a word, Jake took Joy's slender arm in the broad palm of one hand as she started to walk away. He drew her into the plush Reno Hilton casino effortlessly. They walked past the slot machines and gaming tables, rode up the broad escalator, strode alongside the Fisherman's Bridge restaurant, moved across the street through the overhead covered walkway, with its carpeting and trees set in shiny brass pots, to the main interior, and into the Cameo lounge. With a firm hand on her waist, he seated her.

Joy was breathless, confused, and temporarily incapable of uttering a single word or offering a token protest. She stared at Jake, awed by his manner and the luxurious comfort of the quiet lounge with its deeply padded wine-colored velvet booths in Victorian styling.

Visible over the curved back of the wide seat was a broad foyer with deep-red patterned carpeting. Vainly trying to gather her senses, she watched people stop to drop silver dollars in the Pot O' Gold Carousel slot machines on their way to the registration desk.

With an effort, Joy pulled herself together, prepared to put this cowboy in his place. It didn't matter she had agonized over wanting to meet him for weeks. He was much too sure of himself. In her dreams he had been so gentle and tender with her. Words of love had spilled from his mouth, his eyes had been filled with worship, the grip of his hands so sensitive and soft.

Rena was right. It had all been a fantasy. Her arm still tingled from his beastly strong fingers. She swallowed, faced him defiantly, and glared, all in one motion. Her stormy eyes sparkled, heightened emotions adding luster to the dark jade color.

"I appreciate your assistance in helping me out of a ticklish spot—though I'm certain they meant no harm and wouldn't have troubled me any further—but the fact is, I want your company even less than I did your friends'." She lied, knowing something about him entirely overshadowed any man she knew or was likely to meet. Considering the speed with which he had swept her into the lounge and her momentary confusion when he had confronted her, she was pleased with her choice of words.

That insult should wipe the arrogant smirk off his handsome face! No one liked to hear that a person couldn't stand his presence.

She stood up, feeling uncomfortably small, raised her firm little chin impudently, and spoke in her haughtiest voice, "Thank you, sir. Good-bye!"

The same steel-hard grip that stopped Slim reached up and touched Joy's shoulder, pressing gently down. She winced, finding herself seated and controlled as easily as a young child.

To her annoyance, she was sharply aware of the warmth of his fingers through her thin blouse. It was a burning heat that filled her body with escalating cognizance. Her breath caught in her throat as she warily obeyed. She felt hypnotized, unable to withdraw.

Nor could any other single female, she reflected. Maybe it would be best to surreptitiously find out where he lived, then leave. A few more intimate talks with Rena might give her the composure she needed to bring up the possibility of them going to bed together sometime in the distant future.

Jake removed his hand, motioned to the bartender, casually ordered two drinks, and leaned back. He looked at Joy with amused indulgence, his shrewd eyes sparkling with awareness of her futile attempt to put him in his place.

She clasped her trembling fingers together in her lap, lashes lowered to shield the vacillating urge to stay with the dynamic male specimen next to her. No wonder Alfonso and his blond model were drawn. The dark cowboy across from her would be fascinating to anyone. His blatant masculinity sent a multitude of thoughts flitting through her mind. She swallowed apprehensively, common sense warring with remembrance of ecstasy in his arms. Did she dare stay?

"Relax for a while. I've ordered you a strawberry daiquiri. That was the one drink I knew that was close to the color of your beautiful mouth."

"I don't drink in the morning. It's not even noon!" Joy blurted out, her fingers nervously pleating the material of her skirt. She felt flustered, wanting to stare openly at Jake, to let her eyes scrutinize each portion of his brawny frame and memorize every minute detail for later introspection.

Their booth was enormous but Jake made it appear as cozy and intimate as a table for two. His thigh had unintentionally brushed hers as he sat down and she could still feel a frisson of excitement from the touch. What sparks would his mouth caressing hers ignite?

"Drink it, sweetheart. It should help you regain your balance. You looked frightened when I intervened. You're obviously an urban lady or you'd have realized that most cowboys are a lot of talk. Very few become objectionable if their advances are rejected."

"They only wanted to show me around Reno, not take me to bed," Joy informed him hesitantly, amazed that his husky endearment should sound so genuine and intimate. Just like it had in her dream.

"Don't be naive, honey. That's the first place any man would want to take you. Fortunately, there are so many women hanging around rodeos waiting to go to bed with the first contestant who appeals to them, they don't have to pressure an innocent-looking girl alone," he told her before bluntly adding, "Moreover, Nevada has legalized prostitution a few miles from Reno, and plenty of local talent available for a fee also, though not legally."

"The words of a depraved man with firsthand knowledge, no doubt?" Joy retorted impulsively in a chiding voice. She had been correct to assume that irresistible charisma to women came from their instinctive knowledge that he knew how to please them.

Jake's eyes gleamed with humor. A deep laugh escaped his throat as he deliberately taunted, "Of course! I readily admit to my share of wild oat sowing, though I don't consider myself depraved. Let's see," he teased, rubbing his chin in contemplation, "it must be about six, er—"

"Hush!" Joy scolded, upset at his mocking laughter. She certainly had no desire to know how long it had been since he had made love to a woman. Whether it was six months, six weeks, six days, or—surely he wasn't going to say six *hours*! Could it be some of his ad fans had found him first and wanted the same thing she did? And succeeded in getting it?

She studied his strong features when he took his hat from the seat between them and stood up to place it behind him. His thick hair was raven-black, wavy and tapered across the nape of his neck in engaging disarray. Low sideburns enhanced his taut cheeks and, though no longer considered fashionable by her men friends, fit his air of masculine bearing perfectly.

He was a ruggedly handsome man whose commanding presence caused her stomach to churn involuntarily, despite renewed determination to act coldly disinterested. His wide shoulders stretched a body-hugging navy-blue plaid shirt with pointed collar, V-shaped pocket tabs and yoke. Lustrous pearl snaps closed the shirtfront, sleeves, and pockets. His narrow hips were encased in low-riding bootlegged jeans, belted around a lean, flat abdomen.

Joy still couldn't understand why he attracted her so. She had never talked with a cowboy, been on a ranch, or even listened to country music. But she felt powerless to tear her eyes from his back. He appeared inches over six feet tall, though it shouldn't surprise her since she had barely reached his shoulder during her ungallant march into the lounge. A buckstitched leather belt with JAKE spelled out in ornate sterling silver letters across the back looked hand-carved and expensive.

When he turned smoothly to face her before sitting down, she caught a quick glimpse of his dazzling buckle. It was larger than the younger cowboys' and nearly covered with gold engraving plus two diamond-filled rosettes. Probably a championship award and worth half a year's salary, she estimated.

Annoyed because she couldn't read the year he had won it, Joy guessed his age at ten to fifteen years older than the three cowboys who accosted her. With reluctance she admitted his maturity gave him a look of sufficient experience that would threaten any woman's virtue.

The pain of wanting him for her first lover gnawed at her

trembling stomach. Instead of meeting his bold look and openly confessing her attraction, she lowered her lashes, as unable to voice her sensual thoughts as a frightened teenager. In fact, she shuddered nervously, the entire situation was fast becoming a nightmare. A faint rose tinged her cheeks when she raised her eyes to catch him scanning her features with the same thoroughness as she had stared at his ad photo, now hidden deep in her purse.

· Jake nodded as the waiter placed a frosted glass in front of Joy and handed him a glass of foamy beer. He took a long drink, set the glass down, and looked up with a broad grin.

"Beer right out of the can has a far superior taste." He leaned back, both palms flat on the tabletop, fingers widespread, before asking in a low voice timbred with thoughtful earnestness, "Now, my beauty, I want to know your name, your age, where you live, what you do, and why you're wandering the streets alone. Reno, when the rodeo comes to town, can get pretty lively."

Joy shifted, acutely aware she was acting ridiculous. She sipped the daiquiri, lowering her eyes from his penetrating gaze to stare at the frosted glass clasped in both hands. The drink was strong and with any luck would give her the composure she needed to stay and learn more about him. She had never found it difficult to handle uncomfortable situations in the past.

"Though it's actually none of your business, my name is Joy Sanders," she answered rapidly. "I'm twenty-seven years old and currently reside in Sacramento, California. I earn my living as an office manager and have been *un*successfully trying to enjoy my first visit to Nevada."

There was no need to add to his self-assurance by telling him she had come to Reno solely to seek his lovemaking. He would never believe her anyway. Deciding she had been coerced into staying and he deserved a firm set-down for dragging her into the lounge, she returned his bold look with one of unwavering hauteur.

"Frankly, I doubt if I would have come at all had I known the street would be filled with bothersome cowboys."

Enjoying Joy's alternating attempts to defy or placate him, Jake smiled before countering, "Not hardly filled, my Joy, since this is the end of June and the height of tourist season, but there are enough of us around to make our presence known."

He emptied the glass of beer in one swallow, unaware Joy's eyes were riveted on the fascinating tautness of his throat when he threw back his head. With the back of one hand he wiped the small amount of foam from his lips. His expression was plainly amused by the fact she didn't know how to take him.

A range of moods crossed Joy's face before she came to terms with her temper and decided to overlook his arrogance and relax in the comfort of the soft booth. He wasn't the least bit bothered by a single insult or glare of disapproval she gave him anyway.

She looked him straight in the eye, determined to see how he reacted to being interrogated.

"I know your first name is Jake. Are you entered in the rodeo?" Slender fingers playing nervously with the stem of her glass were the only obvious sign that she wasn't as at ease as she wished him to think.

"Yes, but my days of riding rough stock are long over. I leave that to the fearless young cowboys in their late teens and early twenties."

Joy listened to Jake, entranced, having decided not to leave. After all, she could walk away any time she wished. Decision made, she gave him a smile so tantalizing his eyes darkened to deep chocolate velvet.

My God, she's stunning! he thought, knowing she would run like a frightened doe if she had any idea what his thoughts were. When he had spotted her over the heads of a Japanese tour group as he pushed through the hotel doors, he had felt jolted, struck down by a force equal to that time when a rank horse had kicked him when he'd been obliged to cut it free of a barbed wire fence.

Damned if his palms weren't sweating just thinking of stroking her silky-looking skin, not to mention how uncomfortable his jeans were becoming as his body hardened involuntarily. It hadn't been *that* long since he'd had a woman! He ached with the need to tell her she was his and the desire to have her spend the night in his arms.

Too late now, my love. Much, much too late, he surmised with unwavering confidence in his ability to persuade her she was his woman.

"What do you enter, then?" Joy asked curiously, unaware her query abruptly intervened in his rapid plans for her future. She was anxious to learn more about any sport he participated in.

Her lashes fluttered. Jake's eyes had darkened again, communicating a profound fascination so exciting she was afraid to glance up for fear she had imagined it. If she didn't know better, she would think he had plans to seduce her more blatant than any she had dreamed for him.

"I'm a bulldogger," Jake drawled, one dark brow raised at Joy's look of inquiry. "Steer wrestler. The man who throws steers to the ground." His laughter boomed in the room as he explained further. "You are green, honey."

"Since I've never seen a rodeo, except on TV, I was uncertain at first what event you meant," she offered in explanation. Her chin tilted upward, stormy eyes boldly meeting his taunting gaze.

"I did notice all the attractive posters in the windows advertising 'Reno's Richest, Wildest Roundup in the West' as the richest six-performance rodeo in America." He didn't need to know how many hours she had spent planning her trip to coincide with the last day's event. Everything had seemed to go wrong from the moment she arrived in Sacramento. It was a miracle their paths had crossed at all.

"I also presumed the inordinate number of slim-legged cowboys walking about are contestants." No need for him to think of her as a complete dummy.

"Very observant," he complimented her, pleased she showed interest in his way of life and preferred form of recreation.

"What else have you competed in?" Joy asked, finding the western speech fascinating. Learning anything about Jake would get her undivided attention, she admitted truthfully.

"I've done it all. Bareback and saddle bronc riding, bull riding, calf roping, team roping. My size is a distinct disadvantage in riding events—the best riders are usually under six feet—but not in bulldogging, as the extra height and weight helps me throw the steer to the ground."

"Where do you keep your horse when you travel?" Joy questioned, hoping that would give her a clue to where he was staying.

"I don't haul one anymore. I borrow one of the other contestants' for a percentage of my winnings. It's a lot less hassle when you only enter a few rodeos a year," he told her, shifting his wide shoulders to a more comfortable position against the cushion back.

"Aren't you a full-time cowboy?" she inquired, wanting to know everything she could about him. She knew Rena would be filled with curious demands about every facet of life from the moment he was born.

"Full-time cowboy but part-time rodeo contestant," Jake related without any further explanation. "When I found out my old buddy Louis was in charge again this year, I decided to fly up, say hello to him and his wife, Jean, play a little blackjack, roll a few dice, and enjoy my favorite sport too."

Jake reached for Joy's left hand, staring at her unadorned slender fingers for a moment. "You're still a slick skin I see—not spoken for or married—which I find amazing," he remarked solemnly. "In my hometown you would have been branded, corraled, and kept stalled close to the house at least ten years ago."

His fingers stroked the top of her hand with soft, gentle motions. "Any commitments for your affections?" he inquired huskily.

"No," Joy admitted, her lashes lowering in a vain attempt to conceal the effect of his words. He was the only man she had dreamed, literally and figuratively, of conferring her trust to.

"Good!" Jake exclaimed, his astute eyes pinning hers when she looked up. "It will save me the bother of telling them they are wasting their time."

Each solemn word was eloquently spoken as he casually

turned her hand over to run one finger in continuous circles around her sensitive palm.

Joy's pulse quickened, resuming its furious beating at the serious tone of his startling declaration. Her hand trembled, the sensual excitement of his unexpected caress more potent than the perfection of her erotic dreams. Emotion churned between them as she responded to his unhurried touch. Perturbed that she calmly submitted to his seductive stroking, despite her desire to do so, she caught her breath, quickly pulling her palm from beneath his well-shaped hand.

Reluctantly tearing her gaze from Jake's, Joy looked at his fingers. She thought of Rena's advice about a cowboy's grooming. His nails were clipped short, clean, and cared for. Working around doctors had made her fastidiously aware of a man's personal neatness. She inhaled, catching a faint aroma of heady after-shave.

Raising her lashes, Joy's eyes were held by Jake's searching glance. As if hypnotized, she watched him raise his hand toward her, felt his searing touch when he cupped her trembling chin.

He held her face motionless, his index finger moving with slow, deliberate strokes over her lips until they pulsated beneath his touch to part in a soft, moist sensual invitation.

His forceful glance beseeched her to understand his desire to reach out and to enjoy the moment of first contact as he was. She responded unconsciously. It was doubtful if her trembling limbs could have carried her from the lounge if she had commanded them to.

Joy knew Rena would accuse her of lying. His featherlike touch exceeded any fantasy. *It has to be destiny we met,* she reflected, totally entranced by the stranger who had governed her thoughts from the moment she saw his photo as easily as he apppeared to influence her physical reaction with the slightest contact.

Jake's eyes narrowed, their compelling depths filled with candid admiration. Joy made no protest when he leaned forward, enabling his cool lips to possess her throbbing mouth in a gentle, heart-shaking caress so pleasurable it shattered her conception of any casual kiss she had received in the past. She remained inert, too bemused to move. His touch was everything she had dreamed it would be and she felt like crying out when he eventually pulled back.

"Oh, Joy..." Jake drawled in a thickened voice, his warm breath wafting across her flushed face intimately. His mood was pensive, as if he didn't believe the perfection of her dewy lips possible. "Are you real, or a touch of magic created by Reno's delusive atmosphere?"

He reluctantly moved away, a crooked smile tugging the corner of his mouth while his eyes lazily ran over her softened features. "I'll never tire of touching your sweet mouth." His voice was husky, the proprietorial assertion as unexpected as his kiss.

Joy's lips quivered. It was such a brief caress, the upheaval so devastating, she knew her life could never be the same. She stared with clear luminous eyes, meeting his glance without flinching, yet bewildered by her tumultuous response. He was a stranger. A stranger who had cast a spell over her emotions from the first glimpse. A spell she knew only he could release. It was frightening to realize that her dreams were beginning to come true. It seemed so unreal somehow.

Suddenly confused by Jake's continued observation and intensely intimate comments, Joy turned her head to shield her thoughts. She could feel his smoldering glance, knew he was staring at her profile and the silken strands of hair that had come loose around her ears. Her stomach continued to churn from the exciting warmth still remaining on her parted lips.

Jake was totally unlike anyone she had known. His self-assurance confused her. She had come to Reno to seek his attention and was unprepared to find that he was in command and appeared to have every intention of pursuing her. He made plans without asking if they met with her approval, warned her he would not tolerate another man's interest, then kissed her to emphasize his seriousness.

Jake's smile was tender as he watched Joy's fingertips reach upward to touch her mouth. He was aware of her

momentary bewilderment and recognized his own autocratic personality. He never vacillated when he saw something he wanted. From the first sight of her defiant little
face glaring at Slim, his intentions were never in doubt.

"Are you shy with me, darling?" he asked, the fire of
her mouth still raging inside his body. His hand reached out
to cup her chin tenderly. It was impossible to keep from
touching her.

Joy looked at the empty glass in her hands, uncertain
how to answer. She could no more think rationally with his
fingers spreading over her jawline than she could pull away.

"There's no need to be," he told her huskily. One fingertip traced the enticing curve of her mouth while the
others radiated their exciting warmth into her smooth
cheek. "Our hearts touched when we first locked glances
and today is only the beginning of a lifetime together." His
breath quickened as she responded to his surreptitious
lovemaking, informing her with explicit seriousness when
her unwavering glance met his.

"Tonight, my love, we shall marry."

Chapter Three

"We shall what?" Joy blurted out. Jake's prediction broke the magical enchantment surrounding them more than anything could have. It was obvious he was putting her on, perhaps even playing out a game of fantasy love of his own.

"You're crazy!" She started to scoot across the seat, intent on leaving Jake and Reno as soon as possible—not from fear of his blatant declaration or persuasive physical advances; she was more worried about his seductive charisma. It was possible she would begin to believe his comments were meant to be taken seriously and she didn't want any man to think her that naive.

Rena would never accept that Joy had received a marriage proposal within minutes of meeting her cowboy, despite her warning her friend always received offers of marriage while she was usually the recipient of casual propositions.

As she reached for her purse Joy felt her hand clasped, completely engulfed in Jake's broad palm. One brief squeeze returned her to her seat. Mutiny filled her stormy jade-green eyes when they clashed with Jake's. His glance was filled with amusement.

Her breasts rose and fell, stretching the fine silk of her blouse as she debated what to do. Equally breathless from his boldness and his continued touch, she faced him defiantly.

"Nobody proposes marriage within one hour of meeting someone!"

"It's a family tradition," Jake explained with complete

composure. His glance never left Joy's revealing features while his hand released the hold on her fingers.

"What?" she blurted out sarcastically, unconsciously flexing her sore hand. "Insanity?"

"No, my fiery tempered beauty." He smiled tenderly, his deep brown eyes alight with fascination. "I mean proposing and marrying the first day we meet our chosen partner." His voice slowed, thick with his native drawl. "My great-grandfather did it. His son did it. My dad did it. Today I shall follow suit."

"Not with me you won't!" Joy shot back, glaring at Jake's confident face across the wide table. How could she have ever managed to get herself into such a predicament? He really was crazy!

"Only with you," Jake's husky accent echoed slowly, warning her of his serious intent. "I've obviously taken you unawares but wait and see if I'm not right. A few more hours courting and you'll be willing."

"Hours!" Joy hissed, glancing quickly around to assure they weren't overheard. "That wouldn't be courting. That would be rampant seduction. Courtship should last for months."

"Why?" Jake asked with irritating casualness.

Suddenly at a loss for words, Joy lowered her face. She stared at her fingers, surprised to see her hands were trembling while she deliberated. Her eyes raised, held with Jake's by the force of his personality.

"Because, it's an, er, er, an inherited custom, that's why," she stuttered, annoyed by his continued composure and becoming more unsettled with each comment he made.

"So is the men in my family marrying on the first day. I'll do it and no doubt our sons will do it too."

Joy's mind reeled with all the reasons a couple should have a long engagement. About to inform him how irrational he was, she was stopped before she had uttered a single word.

"Hush, woman and let me get busy with a traditional courtship. First, my beautiful creature—"

"Creature?" Joy checked him in return. "This is my day

for strange names. I've been called a filly, told my pasterns— whatever they are—"

"Probably meant to say sexy ankles," Jake prompted matter-of-factly.

"—are long," Joy continued, giving him a defiant glare. "My hips are too narrow—"

"They're perfect for a maiden filly," Jake interjected, a smile of indulgent amusement raising the corners of his firm, well-defined lips.

"Maiden filly?" Joy raised one winged brow in query.

"Unbred mare," he answered, watching her soft cheeks flush as she understood his meaning.

"Not only that," Joy continued, her agitation mounting as Jake became more amused with each declaration. "I have wide set eyes, a good coat—"

"Healthy, shiny hair," he told her, patiently explaining his friend's rhetoric, uncaring he continued to interrupt.

"And even well muscled—" She stopped speaking when he laughed mischievously, his eyes flaring with sudden desire as they lingered briefly on her heaving breasts before returning to hold her glance.

"You're beautifully stacked."

"That's enough. That part of their speech I understood."

"You have an outstanding shape, Joy. Does my honesty embarrass you?" Jake questioned softly, leaning forward to clasp Joy's fingers when she raised her hands to the table-top.

"Every comment you make does. In fact, Jake, everything about you bothers me," she whispered, trying unsuccessfully to ignore the pleasurable warmth of his touch.

"Good. From the first glance I had of your expressive little face as you tried to fend off my friends, I've been pretty bothered myself," he teased roguishly, his lazy look of appreciation making her aware of his play on words.

"That does it, cowboy! I refuse to pander any longer to your perverted sense of humor and ridiculous statements." Her chin raised defiantly, matching her next words. "Obviously, you have been bucked off once too often!"

In a vain attempt to free her hand, Joy pulled with all her strength. Furious that any man could control her so effortlessly, she glanced around to make certain no one was listening, then hissed furiously through clenched teeth, "Darn you, Jake, let me go this instant. In the short time I've been in Reno, I have come to the conclusion that all cowboys are crazy. And especially you!"

Why on earth did he have to be the one man whose physical contact she craved? For years she had dated "normal" men—intelligent, successful, personable men with great charm—and she had been bored by and frigid with all of them. Obviously there was a quirk in her personality too, she admitted with reluctance.

"You're gorgeous, darling," Jake drawled huskily. "What an exciting relationship we're going to have in the years ahead. I've always found a young filly with fire in her personality more to my liking than placidity."

Jake ignored Joy's perplexed expression, continuing without pause. "Relax, honey, while I explain our itinerary for the rest of the day."

Not giving her a chance to object, he related his plans.

"First, I intend to show you around the greatest little city in the West. You'll undoubtedly want to try your luck on the slot machines, then we'll go to the rodeo for my last go-round in bulldogging."

As he still held her hand in a firm grip, his brown eyes were filled with warm indulgence, matching the softness of his slowly spoken accent.

"I'll introduce you to some of my friends, we'll have dinner, enjoy a dance or two, and after that, your wish is my command. By the end of the evening I intend to have you convinced that packing my brand for life won't be all that bad."

"Not a chance! You're much too autocratic for any modern woman."

"Probably," he admitted easily. "Since my only interest is in pleasing you, it makes no difference."

Joy jerked her hand free as Jake relaxed his hold, knowing she wasn't accomplished in dealing with anyone as used to having his own way as the man before her. A woman would either love or hate him, she admitted. His attitude was almost archaic.

He gave her a wide smile, tiny laugh lines crinkling at the corners of his keen eyes, then related the rest of his plans as if she hadn't given him her most intimidating glance.

"If you're ready to leave now and promise to quit flashing your gorgeous, angry eyes my way, I'll stake you with a little Texas money for the one-armed bandits."

"The heck you will," Joy mumbled. She gripped her purse with both hands, uncaring that several chestnut curls escaped her lustrous chignon when she shook her head adamantly no. "My own California money will do just fine."

Jake stood up, ignored Joy's verbal protest and outward sign of irritation and assisted her from the booth. He plopped his hat carelessly on top of his unruly raven hair, took her slender arm in a firm grip, and drew her toward the escalator. Not giving her time to look around the main-floor casino, he guided her out the side door.

Joy pulled back, stopping to scold him. "You're the most arrogant man I've ever had the misfortune to meet." Her eyes sparkled, reflecting her inherent good nature and impromptu surge of playful gaiety. The surprise of his unexpected pursuit after weeks of stealthy schemes to accost him was too humorous for her to continue acting affronted any longer.

"I must admit, some of your ideas are much too tempting to resist," she teased, her delightful personality bursting forth in a soft feminine giggle. "Be prepared, though, to hire an armored car to carry home my winnings, cowboy."

Concluding Jake's ridiculous proposal was just a lot of silly banter, Joy gave him a wide smile, her anger leaving as suddenly as it had come. She had gone to great effort to find her dynamic escort and wasn't going to let a little ruffling at his audacity prevent further time in his company.

Amused by her impudent acquiescence after numerous attempts to defy him, he asked, "Did you bring any jeans?"

"Not with me. Why?"

"Well, you look beautiful in your silky dress and strappy sandals, but jeans would be more appropriate and comfortable for the rodeo. It's normally dusty around the chutes, and I intend to keep you close to my side where I can keep an eye on you at all times."

"You're a hopelessly bossy man, Jake." Joy laughed indignantly, trying hard to keep up with his giant strides as he moved forward. "I don't know a thing about you, yet you're telling me what to wear, what I'm going to do the rest of the day, and, to top it off, you have the gall to suggest that I'm going to end the day as your wife!"

Joy halted abruptly, chuckling as she looked upward. It amused her to watch his eyes narrow as he contemplated what she would say next.

"I didn't bring jeans as I, number one: didn't think I'd be invited to attend the rodeo with an opinionated male connoisseur of western fashion or, number two: didn't think I'd be seated near the chutes instead of in the grandstand like any normal person would expect."

Hands on her hips, her chin tilted pertly, she went on. "Furthermore, cowboy, we haven't even been introduced!"

He didn't need to know she experienced the most intimate acts possible with him in the privacy of her bedroom or that it hadn't mattered in the least whether she knew his name or not. Her fantasies since seeing his photo were so perfect anything other than the beauty of their lovemaking often seemed mundane.

Jake looked down at her expressive face, a broad smile tugging his mouth into a mischievous grin. As the crowd surged around him, he tipped his western hat in a flamboyant manner, then held it clasped over his heart with both hands.

"Miss Joy Sanders, I would like you to meet me—Mr. Jake Travis, a thirty-four-year-old broken-down bachelor with a tiny spread in Texas that barely grazes a few head of scrawny beef cattle and a bog-spavined horse or two. Do you need to know any more than that?" he asked, his broad shoulder muscles rippling beneath the thin material of his shirt as he pulled her possessively against his side. He was totally unconcerned that several people lingered to observe his unusual behavior.

"No, I guess not," Joy whispered, looking away from

their audience. "That's proper enough now, considering we won't see each other after today."

"Don't you believe it, honey," Jake warned her.

Joy flushed at the attention they received, her eyes glimmering with fascination as she waited for his next assertion.

"I was never more serious in my life, as you shall see," he rebuked.

Joy conceded Jake was as imprudent as she was, finding it physically impossible to remain immune from his continued flattery.

"Maybe so, but your confidence is due for a set-down too."

Coming to a mammoth-size western store, Jake turned to go inside, tugging Joy after him, her slender fingers gently clasped in his broad palm. He pushed the glass doors open with his free hand, tilting his head toward her to offer a nonchalant explanation.

"Parker's Western Store will have everything I want to buy. Get prepared to be transformed from a chic little city slicker to a bona fide country sweetheart."

"I must be dreaming," Joy mumbled, trying ineffectively to separate their intertwined fingers. Her mind reeled at the speed with which Jake made up his mind to do something. Even faster was his accomplishment of that task. She scanned the vast interior, noticing an assortment of expensive-looking western clothing displayed in honor of the rodeo. Before she was quite certain what his intentions were, Jake had told the saleslady what he wanted and Joy was promptly ushered into a dressing room.

The saleswoman handed her a green western pantsuit, then left, only to return a short moment later with a flowered green and brown western-styled shirt in fine silk. Pearl snaps matched those she had admired on Jake's shirt.

Joy stripped to a décolleté bra and bikini panties, smiling at the saleswoman's awestruck expression when she scanned the soft ivory satin with sheer lace inserts hugging her rounded curves.

"Indecently sexy, aren't they?" Joy asked, slipping eagerly into the new clothes.

"Hmm...they're, er, quite lovely, dear," the older

woman agreed enviously. "Quite revealing too," she added hastily.

Joy looked at her reflection in the full-length mirror. Excitement had darkened her eyes to deep jade. Avoiding her flushed face, knowing her quickened senses were heightened by the tumultuous confrontation with her cowboy, she gave her slacks a critical glance. They were tight, clinging to her rounded hips and slender legs. The cut was flattering and definitely more sensual than her dress, she admitted, glancing over her shoulder at the snug fit across her bottom. The tabs and pockets were outlined with a western yoke matching the one on the back of her blouse. The shirt was tailored to cling to her narrow rib cage, emphasizing her breasts.

"My, that certainly looks pretty, dear. Everything fits you like a glove," the pleasant clerk told her sincerely "Try the jacket on and see how you like the suit. I'll call your husband in to see if he approves."

She turned before Joy could correct her and called, "Sir, come see your wife. Isn't she lovely in her western clothing?"

Jake leaned against the edge of the dressing room door, towering over the saleswoman. His great size dwarfed the small room even further. He stared at Joy, standing before him.

"Yes, ma'am, my *wife* looks lovely as always. We'll take the outfit, won't we, darling?"

Enjoying every second of Joy's discomfort, Jake continued to tease. "You really should wear tight slacks and fitted shirts more often, dearest. They highlight every inch of your delightful figure."

He turned to the saleslady, who was obviously pleased with the easy sell of her most expensive western suit and blouse, asking if she had a pair of boots in size five.

"Is that correct, honey?" he questioned. He stared audaciously, his dark eyes daring her to reprimand him in front of the clerk's interested gaze.

His forceful presence overcame her urge to defy him. "Yes, that's right," she whispered. She opened her mouth and then closed it without a sarcastic retort, wondering why on earth she let him intimidate her. Normally she had no trouble dealing with dominating men. He would never believe what an independent woman she actually was.

"Come now, darling," he requested tenderly, his roguish face warning her not to contradict their relationship. "We'll have your dress wrapped so you can wear the slack suit. It draws attention to your, er, finer points."

Joy glared at him, darkened eyes shooting sparks of annoyance at his continued mischief behind the clerk's retreating back.

"Quit taunting me, Jake," she hissed in a furious whisper. "Why didn't you explain you weren't my husband? That's a terrible thing to do to such a nice lady."

Checking to make certain she wouldn't be overheard, she persisted in berating him, her twinkling eyes belying her angry tone.

"Furthermore," Joy continued, enjoying her temper now, "I can't let you buy me this suit. I thought you meant a pair of denim jeans like you're wearing." Lowering her voice further, she whispered, "Just look at the price of this suit. It's much too expensive." She held the price tag out for him to see, but he ignored her request. "I've never worn anything that cost this much in my entire life."

"Hush. I've already won several thousand dollars in the first two go-rounds. The expense of one outfit isn't worth fussing about." He nonchalantly shrugged any further protests aside, telling her he was also going to buy her boots and that was that.

Jake grabbed Joy's elbow, smiling at her mutinous expression, then seated her in the boot department. He sat beside her, stretched his long legs out in front of him, and checked the clerk's choice through narrowed, heavily lashed eyes. He looked at the several pair offered then shook his head no, telling her what he wanted.

"Those aren't good enough, ma'am. I want something really special for my wife. Do you have any made of alligator skin?"

The clerk returned with a pair made of their finest leather and slipped them on Joy's narrow feet easily.

Joy enjoyed the unfamiliar feel of cowboy boots, her

feminine vanity delighting in the pointed toes covered with sterling silver tips. She adored pretty clothes and was delighted with her outfit, though too saucy to inflate his ego by acting overenthusiastic.

As the saleswoman tallied up the bill, Jake took Joy's elbow and turned her around in front of him. He put one broad hand to his chin, cupping it while contemplating her change in dress. Her cheeks flushed a pale rose as he deliberately made her wait for his approval.

"Well?" Joy demanded, too impatient to delay another moment finding out what he thought. She hadn't wanted him to purchase the things but since he had there was no reason he shouldn't compliment her.

"Well, what?" Taking his time about answering, Jake continued to look her over lazily.

"Not well water!" she sassed back quickly. "Do you like it or not?"

"Absolutely perfect, my darling wife. You're a constant joy to my eyes."

She felt better after receiving his admiration, but chose to ignore his continued reference to her as his wife. Her boot heels clicked loudly as she followed him to the counter, where she had to mask her gasp when she saw the total amount of the bill.

Jake removed an expensive leather wallet from his hip pocket, casually took out six one-hundred dollar bills, and paid for the cost of Joy's new things without question. He noticed her furrowed brow as she debated whether to let him buy her clothes or inform the saleswoman why she couldn't accept such an extravagant gift.

Leaving the store, Jake laughed gently, took her right hand, and raised it to his lips. He placed a lingering kiss across her palm and inner wrist while holding her widened gaze.

"Haven't you ever let a man buy you clothes before?"

"No. Of course not," she replied breathlessly, her palm tingling from the pressure of his seductive caress.

"Not from a lack of offers, I'm certain," he replied in surprise, his mouth continuing to nibble her skin.

Too disconcerted to answer for a moment, Joy smiled

uneasily. "Thank you for the clothes, Jake, although you shouldn't be spending any money on me."

She was perplexed, still undecided about accepting his generosity. His warm mouth against her hand raised such havoc she felt incapable of challenging his persistence. It would be easier to mail him a check when she found out where he lived.

"The cost is nothing to me, Joy," he told her truthfully. "I'll be buying your complete wardrobe from now on anyway."

Changing the subject, he flashed her a dazzling white smile. "Let's go feed the one-armed bandits, honey. Take your pick of places, from the local supermarket to the fanciest casino."

He placed a series of tingling kisses on each dainty finger before lowering them to his side and striding forward. Annoyed when she pulled back trying to jerk her hand free, he scolded, "Quit tugging, Joy. This is part of your courtship."

"People who just meet don't get courted or have their palms kissed like longtime lovers," she retorted, meeting his look squarely.

"Why not?" he asked, his tone filled with arrogance. Jake noticed the angle of her impertinent little chin. Curbing her sassiness would have been an easier job when she was younger. Yet he could imagine how beautifully responsive she would be secure in the knowledge he loved her as no other man before loved his woman. Another Travis tradition, he thought smugly. The wives were all adored.

"Well?" he prompted.

"It's, ah, er, I don't know." Darn him! "It's just not right." What an inane answer, she reflected foolishly.

"Do you like it?" he shrugged, his eyes sliding over her face.

"Yes," she admitted truthfully. It was useless to deny her receptiveness to his touch. She owed the man that much honesty considering she had spent night after night imagining them sharing the deepest intimacies.

"Good." He stopped, bent to place fleeting kisses across her forehead, then proceeded toward the main thoroughfare. "Touching you brings me profound pleasure, so relax and forget any needless inhibitions that might keep you from accepting the wonder of our meeting."

He guided her effortlessly along the street, his thoughts assured as he looked at her happy expression while she observed the glittering casinos and colorful people lining the streets. He knew she was unaware her fingers were clasping his hand or that she had moved closer as if seeking his protection among the vast crowds.

"Did you know the odds are all against the player, Joy?" he asked softly. "Casino owners admit to being out to break you for everything you can afford to lose. And, win or lose, they're ahead."

"But how could that be?" she inquired doubtfully, her face turning up to his to await his reply.

"The winners always return hoping they'll win again, and the losers come back intent on improving their luck," he pointed out philosophically. "Over two billion dollars was gambled and lost in Nevada last year, which is amazing, since legalized gambling was only started some thirty-odd years ago."

"I knew gambling was big business, but that amount of money is even hard to visualize." Joy was awed, listening to each word attentively. She knew very little about gaming.

"With that much money involved casinos have to keep a constant eye out for cheaters, either players or their own personnel. The odds are better that you'll win than your chances of getting away with practicing fraud."

"I wouldn't think of attempting anything dishonest. Not when there are jackpots paying nearly a million dollars for one lucky pull of the handle," she teased, adding impudently, "A quarter of a million dollars will be enough for my first trip."

Jake's laughter rang low as he hugged her to his side. "You greedy little devil, you'll find that most of the time you can't get near the progressive jackpot slots. There's usually a determined gambler sitting in front glued to a stool, with three or four hundred silver dollars in trays. It's nearly impossible to gain a turn without a long wait."

Joy strolled gracefully beside Jake, unaware of the glances her form-fitting outfit received from the many men about. Her excitement mounted as he drew her inside Harold's Club Electric Saloon with its giant lighted cowboy hat hanging from the ceiling.

"Stay here, Joy, while I get some change," Jake instructed. "This looks like a lucky machine to me."

She watched his commanding physique as he walked away with the arrogant swagger she found common to cowboys, noticing several attractive women give him provocative looks. A twinge of jealousy surprised her when a striking blond placed her hand on his arm. It was the first time she felt the desire to go forward and claim the exclusive attention of any man. "How dare she," she grumbled, moving closer in order to hear. Standing behind an unused slot machine, she listened unashamedly to the woman's words.

"Hi there, handsome," the woman cooed in a throaty voice. "Aren't you the sexy cowboy in all the boot ads?"

Joy peered between the machines, watching as Jake took the well-manicured hand from his sleeve. His look would have made a less secure woman quiver for days. "Sorry, lady, I'm afraid modeling's not my scene," he lied, brushing past her to approach the cashier.

Joy scurried back. Her heart beat wildly against her breast when he returned. He appeared oblivious of anyone else, his glance holding hers with a look of such tender affection she thought she'd cry.

Without conscious thought her hand raised and touched his arm, feeling the muscle tauten beneath the thin cotton of his shirt. Pride shone in her eyes, the visible pleasure causing him to smile in response.

Attentively he held out two trays filled with silver dollars. "Here, honey," he smiled widely. "This should do for now. We only have time for a small taste of Reno before the rodeo starts."

"No, Jake. Thanks anyway." She had plenty of money in her purse if she wanted to gamble. Her original intention to come to Reno had only been to find Jake. Gaming had never entered her mind. Her recurring dreams had been more sophisticated than trying to win some money. She had come seeking a fantasy, not a fortune.

"Don't refuse me, Joy," Jake scolded forcefully. "It was my idea to come to Harold's Club. This little bit of loose change isn't worth arguing about."

"Loose change! There must be at least two hundred dollars in those trays," she told him crisply. His idea of loose change was certainly more grandiose than hers.

"So?" He placed the trays on the ledge, his hands rising to spread over the fine bones of her shoulders. "Look at me."

She obeyed.

"I've won and lost thousands and thousands of dollars in Reno and Las Vegas the last few years. This is nothing to me, so use it!"

He shrugged her futile protests aside effortlessly, all the time gathering her jacket, purse, and the wrapped dress and sandals so her hands would be free. He waited patiently, his happiness increasing merely by watching her.

Joy reluctantly accepted his money. His firm chin had a more determined tilt than she could cope with surrounded by witnesses.

"Okay, cowboy. You win this time," she chuckled. "If I lose, don't blame me if you have to hitchhike home."

She smiled at him, her eyes sparkling with enthusiasm and anticipation. She took a deep breath, placed a dollar in the slot, pulled the handle, and watched the reels roll around, clanking as they stopped, one by one.

Disappointed at not winning, she looked up in surprise. "It happened so fast and I lost. I don't think I'll play this one anymore," she blurted out, turning to leave.

Laughing at her naive comment and woeful expression, Jake grinned, even white teeth contrasting vividly with his deeply suntanned face and black hair.

"Be patient, Joy. Surely you didn't expect to win each time, did you?"

"I hoped I would," she flared back impudently.

"Keep feeding it, honey, but remember, I warned you their appetite for silver is insatiable."

Another dollar slid out of sight, the handle was pulled,

and Joy lost again. Ten times, ten pulls and no wins. Her smile was wan and her expressive eyes were filled with disillusionment.

"I'm not very lucky, it seems," she moaned plaintively, annoyed to see people around her winning while she didn't.

"Play three dollars at one time," Jake advised her, amused by her petulant glance when she looked at her neighbor's success. "You'd have won a couple of times if you hadn't been so cautious, since all three lines pay off. Here, let me show you."

Jake took three dollars from her tray, placing them in the machine. "Now pull the handle, Joy."

She did as he said, squealing with delight as lights flashed and twenty silver dollars clunked loudly into the metal tray below.

Ecstatic, she reached up, standing on tiptoe to place her lips against the side of his mouth.

"That's almost worth the money," Jake teased, hugging her tightly to his broad chest. The packages lay across her buttocks, held close by lean fingertips spread over the curve of her spine.

He lowered his head, his husky voice fanning her ear between each featherlight caress. "I expect a lot better than that if you win a bigger jackpot. That brief kiss was much too platonic for my tastes."

"Why not?" Joy taunted impishly. "A man should be entitled to some reward for sharing his hard earned money."

During the next hour her exhilaration rose and fell as she gradually saw Jake's money disappear from the trays. She raised her face suddenly, catching a look of sensual desire mirrored in the velvety depths of his eyes as they lingered on her.

She lowered her glance from the obvious fervor of his unguarded gaze. It was identical to those he had given her in her dreams. With resolute purpose her thoughts returned to their noisy surroundings.

Her soft voice was filled with dejection. "I can't understand it. I won several ten- and twenty-dollar jackpots and all I have left is three dollars."

"Not surprising since the jackpots went right back into the slots also," Jake reminded her.

"I know. But I certainly never dreamed it was possible to lose so much money in such a short time," she wailed.

"You're priceless, love," Jake exclaimed indulgently. "Why don't you put your last three dollars in the slot and we'll pull the handle together."

He moved behind her, his powerful body towering above hers by at least twelve inches. The intoxicating aroma of her perfume invaded his nostrils. Despite his attempt to blank his mind of her closeness he could feel his body respond, harden instantly. He leaned forward against her and felt heat flood through his veins.

My God, but he wanted to make love to her. He ached to fill her with his manliness until she clung and cried out with pleasure equal to his. He had had many women and always there was something missing, a growing restlessness afterward, and now he knew why. None was the tiny bit of femininity glancing up at him like he was the answer to her dreams as she was to his.

Joy trembled in response to the contact of Jake's lithe body. She looked away uneasily. His eyes had a way of transmitting the most erotic thoughts without a single word being exchanged between them. It was unnerving to see raw desire mirrored in the shimmering depths. She was definitely not naive about the mechanics of a man's arousal, well aware the moment his had stirred. Instead of it causing her to freeze with a feeling of repugnance, she wanted to lean back, even wanted to move against him.

She had to force her attention back to her surroundings. Her fingers shook as she placed them on the handle beneath his broad palm. Together they pulled. The reels spun, rolling to a stop as three sevens lined up in the center of the machine. Lights flashed as silver dollars began to drop into the tray and envious people looked on.

Joy screamed ecstatically, her shining eyes wide with disbelief, before turning into Jake's arms. Her hands clasped his neck, trembling fingers spread through the thick, unruly hair on his nape. Her lips parted, intending to give him a brief kiss.

Jake lowered his head, placing his firm mouth directly over her open lips. His hands, filled with her purse and package, still managed to pull her upward to touch the full length of his body.

With practiced expertise she felt his lips move, the moist penetration of his tongue shocking her when it searched and found hers in the first intimate kiss she had ever tolerated in her life. Her mind whirled, temporarily forgetting anything but the touch of the one man she would never resist.

Joy's knees threatened to buckle until she squirmed from Jake's hold. She flushed hotly at the attention they were receiving, but his touch was so stimulating she hadn't cared where she was. Her body quivered, heated blood surging through her veins in tempo with her rapid heartbeat.

His kisses were those of a mature man, warning her his needs were as strong as the strength in his commanding body. His intimate touch was expert, his mouth moving with the persuasive skill of an accomplished lover. It was apparent his sexual knowledge was aeons beyond her limited wisdom.

Jake turned Joy around gently and held her at his side. He smiled fondly at her bewildered expression when she saw the filled money tray. Could the kiss they exchanged have been as devastating to her composure as his? He doubted if his heart would ever beat smoothly.

"That's only part of your winnings, darling. You still have two hundred dollars to collect from the cashier. Do you want cash or silver dollars?" he asked, enjoying the awakening sensuality visible in her shimmering eyes. The glowing promise was even beyond his demanding expectations.

"Silver dollars," Joy pleaded, intentionally trying to shatter the mounting tension between them. The middle of a busy casino was not the place to have her first love affair, she decided now that they weren't touching. Though when he was kissing her it had seemed perfectly appropriate, she admitted with some shame. "I want to fill my purse, spend all night counting it, then exchange it for bills to give you back before I leave."

She laughed at his raised eyebrow, demonstrative of resigned tolerance as he shot her a glance before going to the
cashier. After collecting her winnings, Joy followed Jake
from the casino, excitedly talking about their combined ef-
forts bringing them good fortune.

Jake walked Joy briskly across the street toward his hotel.
He checked the time with a sigh of relief, not wanting to
miss his last go-round at the rodeo.

Rushing to keep up with his long strides, Joy told him in
a spate of enthusiasm, "I can hardly wait to come back
tomorrow and see if I can win again."

"What did I tell you about greed, woman?" he reminded
her. "You're like all the rest of the gamblers. Never satisfied!"

"True!" She laughed up at him rapturously. "I'll remember this day as long as I live."

"Me too, Joy. Me too," Jake agreed, increasing his
stride. He knew his memories would remain because of
Joy. He didn't give a damn about any jackpot.

"Hurry up, honey. It's almost time to go to the rodeo
grounds. We'll eat later if it's okay with you?"

Joy nodded in agreement, noticing for the first time that
they had returned to the Reno Hilton hotel registration
area.

With Joy's package in one hand, Jake placed firm, propri-
etary fingers on her waist. He escorted her past the ornate
brass doors into the heavily paneled elevator with its plush
suede walls.

Sudden embarrassment tinged her face with the realization that he was taking her to the intimacy of his private
room. She had fantasized for weeks about being alone with
him. Now that it was finally happening she found her steps
lagging. She was afraid she might reveal her real reason for
coming to Reno.

Chapter Four

Jake opened the door to a sitting area so luxurious in comparison with her small motel room, Joy was momentarily speechless. Towering high above the streets of Reno, the snowcapped peaks of the lofty Sierra Nevada mountains looked like an artist's painting instead of the view from a broad picture window.

She let Jake take her heavy purse without comment, scanning the impeccably decorated room thoroughly. The color scheme was soothing: tan and orange earth tones that seemed to fit the man before her. Broad couches and lounge chairs looked inviting; lamps and tables had been chosen to please the most discriminating.

Through an open doorway she could see into one of the bedrooms. One hand went to her throat when she saw the quilted king-size bed. A frown puckered her dark winged brows, mirroring sudden restraint.

Noticing Joy's concerned expression, Jake easily voiced his intentions. "Looks much too big for one, don't you think, darling?" Ebony sparks filled the brown warmth of his eyes as they swept her enticingly curved figure. "We'll start our honeymoon there later tonight. Agreed?"

Jake's deeply accented voice was like a gentle caress across her sensitive skin, bringing a soft flush of color to her face. She deliberately turned away from his knowing glance, her softened voice sounding uncertain.

"Don't tease me, Jake. I'm uncomfortable being in here with you as it is."

She walked to his sitting room window, attempting to gain a modicum of composure. She needed a few moments avoiding direct eye contact for fear he would discern the unsettling effect his lusty talk engendered. His bedroom had brought forth vivid fantasies of him making love to her. She closed her eyes, picturing again their naked bodies entwined. She could feel his muscles beneath arms that were locked around his neck, could taste the mouth that covered hers.

What's the matter with me? Joy deliberated silently. Prior to seeing Jake's photo she had never visualized being intimate with a man no matter how often they dated. Now she ached to experience all the erotic pleasures possible between partners.

Until their meeting and his consequent pursuit it seemed her fantasies would remain that. Fleeting nighttime entries to her innermost mind, resolving conflict of her emotional needs that seemed insurmountable reenacted in the bright light of day.

Troubled by her inward reflections, she blurted out the first thing that came to mind. "This is quite lovely, but undoubtedly beyond my means." A stupid statement, she grimaced dumbly. She had a healthy bank account and had traveled to many plush resorts with Rena.

Glancing across her shoulder, she watched Jake remove his hat, throw it on the couch, and approach. Her breath caught at the sight of his tall, lithe frame. She had never seen a man who appealed to her more. It was nearly impossible to tear her glance away, despite knowing how revealing it would be. She was always terrible at hiding her feelings and Jake was a shrewd man.

She turned to face him, waiting until he stood close. How smug he would feel to know she found everything about his rugged masculinity and bold personality irresistible.

"The temperature's perfect," she blurted out, mentally tallying the number of idiotic remarks she had made that day.

"It usually is in an air-conditioned room," he returned, amused by her sudden uneasiness at being alone with him. One hand briefly rubbed his nape while he pondered her appearance. With a thoughtful glance he inspected her features more carefully, both hands cupping her shoulders to hold her still.

"We forgot something, Joy," he declared, his deep voice as disturbing as the continued scrutiny.

Without saying any more, Jake walked to the couch to pick up his hat and removed the narrow, carved leather hatband with its sterling silver and jeweled buckle, then returned.

Intensely aware of each move, Joy remained motionless as he threaded it through the tapered belt loops of her western slacks. It fit perfectly around her slender body, though the strength of his hands fastening the buckle was a torment to her senses until he finished. She had only to reach out her fingertips to touch him, a desire she found increasingly hard to control.

With his taut chin held between the thumb and fingers of his right hand, he remained still, staring at her with narrowed eyes.

"Still something missing and now I know what it is."

With steady fingers he reached upward to remove the clip from her hair, deciding to see how it looked unbound.

"No, don't, Jake! I—I only wear my hair down at night. It's too long to stay neat if it hangs loose."

Joy grabbed his steel-hard wrists, her strength unequal to his determination as he broke her grip and released her hair from its smoothly styled chignon.

The sound of Jake's quick, indrawn breath filled the room as he witnessed her glistening hair cascade freely over her shoulders and back to fall well below her waist in thick, shiny waves.

"Stay still!" he commanded hoarsely when she tried to pull away. "God, Joy! How could you? It should never be confined."

"Do you like it?" she questioned in a faint whisper.

"I *love* it." His fingertips brushed the disarrayed curls framing her face. "You're already stunningly beautiful, but when you wear your hair loose you must have every male you meet willing to worship at your feet."

"None of my friends have seen it down," she told him, her jewel-toned eyes alight with pleasure. She had no desire to have anyone other than the man before her appreciate it. The extra work caring for such abundance was worth it knowing Jake was awestruck.

"You're the first man to see it unbound," she answered honestly.

"Every man should be so privileged," he moaned, bending his head to inhale the sweet perfumed scent. He raised several strands to his lips reverently.

"I've always been partial to chestnut horses and your hair is the same rich color."

With gentle hands he threaded his fingers through her hair, running them down its length and back as if he couldn't bear to pull away from its heavy silkiness.

Motionless, Joy reveled in his touch. Her knees threatened to buckle as the physical magnetism flowing between them increased alarmingly. Her erratic breathing constricted when she caught sight of the possessive intimacy in his warm brown eyes.

With his fingers entangled in the satiny strands, Jake pulled Joy to him, winding a thick swathe about her throat in a primitive caress. His mouth moved against the silky curls beside her brow. Hungry to taste her lips he raised her chin, parting her quivering mouth easily.

"Oh, Jake," she cried out, drowning in his persuasive caress.

Jake stifled further comment by rubbing the tip of his tongue back and forth, tracing the edge of her teeth. Slipping between their even whiteness, he explored the moist sweetness of her inner mouth with demanding expertise. His hands trembled, moving down her back slowly before caressing her curves in a sensuous rotating motion.

Pulled ever closer to Jake's hardened contours, Joy clenched his neck, her fingers threading eagerly through his rough-cut hair. Warmth filled her veins. Her body softened, becoming pliant in his arms. After the first caress she had known she would never deny him anything. Eager to experience more, her stimulated feelings responded shamelessly, automatically pressing her closer to his aroused form.

Slowly, with great tenderness, Jake moved his mouth

back and forth over her parted lips. Damp from his deep, lingering kisses, they pulsated beneath his mouth as he deliberately nibbled her soft lower lip with tantalizing leisure he knew would end in her complete seduction.

Joy murmured a plaintive appeal to continue when Jake raised his head. Her lashes fluttered, passion-darkened eyes filled with inquiring ecstasy before he returned to continue the insatiable mastery of her trembling mouth. She answered instinctively to the tip of his tongue touching hers with a quivering motion. Her limbs trembled, weakened by the increasing eroticism of his intimate kiss. A moan escaped while his lips lingered, learning the shape of her mouth with exquisite thoroughness.

Jake's voice was deep, its hoarseness caused by the desire to share his surge of love with the entrancing young woman clinging to his waist.

"Joy, sweetheart, you've completely bewitched me. My mind's filled with the sensuality of your mouth, my body stirred with the anticipation of our honeymoon tonight."

His clean, warm breath fanned her face. "I love you." His mouth swept her hair aside to kiss the sensitive area behind her ear. "Never another." He tongued inside her ear. "Only you until eternity."

Joy thought she'd die, hearing the thickened, sensual Texas drawl. His words created a devastating onslaught to her fragile self-control. It was the sexiest voice she'd ever listened to. A direct projection of the man.

"Oh, Jake. You—you don't."

"I do." With warm lips he kissed her smooth cheeks and closed eyelids, then returned to nibble erotically around her ear.

"You—you can't," she murmured. Her fingers clung to his shoulders or she would have collapsed. Her limbs felt like putty.

"I can." His voice was muffled beneath the weight of her hair.

"You shouldn't." Her voice was fading as the magic of his mouth continued raising havoc over her delicate skin.

"I do, I can, and I shall love you as long as I damn well please!"

Jake's declaration burst out clipped and forceful, a clear warning he meant what he said.

"But, er," Joy stuttered, "it's much, much too soon."

Jake silenced her protest with a fiercely demanding kiss, delaying until he felt her shudder along the length of his body.

"Do you think I'd ever let any woman go whose mouth tasted like honeyed nectar? Or whose body fit up against mine like it was made for me alone?" His ardent mouth continued to play over her neck. "If so, forget it and let's get the hell on with this courting."

A surge of desire swept over Joy. She needed no further coaxing to surrender to his demands. She arched upward, her slender body pressed so tight to his she could feel the imprint of his heavy buckle.

Standing on tiptoe, she clung to his wide shoulders, perceiving his firm muscles quiver beneath the thin shirt. Her heaving breasts strained against the silk of her new blouse, suddenly aching for the intimate touch of his lean, work-hardened hands. It was a privilege she had never allowed another man.

There was no hesitancy now. Jake's legs shifted to balance her body, moving her more intimately between their long length, letting her discover the evidence of his desire.

Instantly aware of his need, Joy was exalted to know she could arouse so dominant a man to the point of losing control. She had felt his body shudder when she moved against him, squirming in ways she instinctively knew would heighten his pleasure. They couldn't continue.

Letting her arms slide from his shoulders, she clasped his waist with fingers spread over his belt. She rested her head on his chest, lying quiescent as their breathing slowly became even.

He held her close, his sunbronzed hands caressing gently as they ran over her tumbled hair.

"Oh, Joy, courting anyone as responsive as you should be illegal." He placed a kiss on the top of her head. "Better reconcile to getting married soon. Paying homage to you will be considerably easier on both of us after we're man and wife."

Joy raised her face from the front of Jake's shirt. "You aren't really serious, are you?" Her voice was barely audible. Rena was right, she had jumped into her first love affair feet first and wasn't certain she was ready yet for the deep end.

"No one earnestly proposes marriage to a woman minutes after meeting her," she scolded softly, her misty eyes lingering on the indulgent glimmer in his.

His callused hand cradled her nape with loving tenderness, matching the whispering warmth echoing against her forehead.

"I did," he assured her truthfully. "I knew I wanted you for my wife in the length of time it takes to ride a bucking bull at a rodeo."

Joy pulled away from his disturbing closeness and walked across the room on legs that were decidedly unsteady. She hesitated in front of the window, looking over her shoulder at Jake.

"How long does a ride take?"

"A qualifying ride takes eight seconds," Jake told her, his eyes unerringly tracing her outline silhouetted by the bright sunlight.

"Eight seconds?" Joy swung around to face him in disbelief.

"Probably would have been less if I hadn't had to scatter a group of tourists to get to you." He laughed softly, observing her startled expression with amusement.

"A man wouldn't last long working the range or rodeoing if he didn't learn to make lightning-fast decisions. They had better be correct ones too, because you don't always have a chance for a second."

Jake checked his watch, groaning as he saw the time. "Let's head out to the rodeo, honey, or we'll miss the start. We'll leave your money and other clothes here, then pick them up later tonight."

"Fine with me," Joy answered pleasantly. "The money is yours anyway. Could I wash up first? My hands feel dirty from the coins."

"Of course. Use my bathroom. It's through the bedroom to the right."

Jake watched as Joy walked into his room. His feelings were so intense for her he thanked God for the miracle of their accidental meeting. His father had always told him the Travis men were notorious for rushing their chosen mate to the altar. He had laughed aside the warnings that his time would come, that he too would find the one woman in the world who could change his life-style with one glimpse. Satisfied with his single way of life, he had scoffed at that prediction. *No* woman could ever affect him that much. No female had, until the one he'd found today.

Joy crossed the deeply carpeted bedroom to enter a bathroom with a tiled interior and luxurious sunken tub. She lathered her hands heavily with the fragrant soap provided by the hotel. Catching her reflection in the wide mirror, she hesitated. Masses of satiny hair cascaded around her shoulders in unaccustomed disarray. Her face was still flushed with sensual awareness, green eyes sparkling with new depths.

I like myself this way, she thought, staring at her changed appearance. *And, my Texas cowboy, it's all because of you.*

She entered the sitting room, silently scanning Jake's broad back as he stared out the wide window. His cotton shirt was stretched taut by rippling shoulder muscles, his strong back tapering to a trim waist and narrow hips.

He heard her empty the silver dollars from her purse, smiling fondly as she placed them in neat piles of ten dollars each.

"Let's go, honey. I want to introduce you to Louis and show you around a little before the bulldogging starts. If I get a good time today, I have an excellent chance of winning. After we fly home, I'll order you a western belt with your name in silver letters to match mine."

He grabbed up his hat and placed it on his head as he walked forward, his eyes scanning her narrow midriff. "You're so tiny one of my championship buckles will probably hide your entire waistline."

"Stop it, Jake! You're moving much too fast," Joy admonished.

"Honey, I'm not out for a slow walk. If I'd rushed you like I wanted, we'd have missed the rodeo, galloped through the wedding ceremony, and raced at full speed back here to start the honeymoon."

Dubious that Jake could be sincere, Joy turned away, checked through her purse to see she had everything she needed, snapped it shut, and faced him. She had regained some self-possession and wanted him to know her behavior wasn't always uninhibited or foolish.

"Your pacing is too fast, Jake. It's just not believable that a man would propose to a woman the same day they meet."

"I don't know why not. A man who takes weeks or months to decide he wants a woman for his wife either doesn't have much of a woman or isn't much of a man."

Jake grabbed her arm, ushering her out of his suite, unconcerned that she hadn't finished chastising him about his hasty decision to marry. His long strides found them quickly down the hall to the elevator. Inside he pressed the button for the garage, turned to Joy, and smiled roguishly. "Isn't that right?"

"No! You're just trying to rationalize your own impulsiveness," Joy rebuked. "It isn't normal and you'd better slow down!"

"You weren't listening too good. I told you I *had* slowed down. It's ridiculous to delay the inevitable any longer. This afternoon we go to the rodeo. This evening we look over the town. Tonight we marry."

Joy looked at him aghast. "You can't bulldog your way into a woman's life so easily, Jake." Her chin raised, darkened eyes flashing sparks of temper. "I couldn't fly home with you on such short notice, even if I did say yes. I have a job and family commitments."

"No problem," he told her, indifferent to anything she said. "We'll fly to Sacramento, I'll meet your family, tell your boss you quit, then we'll continue on to my ranch."

Joy threw her hands up in dismay as Jake grabbed her purse and hustled her into the garage. He refused to listen, having an answer for every protest she made. Still not finished with her reasons why he was acting absurd, she grabbed her purse back, put the strap over her shoulder, and faced him with her chin raised defiantly.

"What about your family? What would they think if you

brought a bride home whom you had only known for a single day?''

Undaunted, Jake escorted her through the parking lot, striding forcefully to his rented Ford Thunderbird car.

"Wouldn't surprise them a bit. It's a family tradition, I told you," he reminded her haughtily. "Besides, it's been many years since they've dared question anything I undertake. My parents are warm, loving people and would welcome you with a typical, generous display of Texas hospitality."

"You're all crazy. Every last one!" she mumbled beneath her breath.

"Hush! We've the rest of our life for you to scold me but only a little time before the rodeo starts."

Opening the passenger door, Jake helped her in, calmly shut it, then walked to his own side where he eased his long frame into the driver's seat.

"Come over here," he commanded, turning to draw Joy's unresisting body across the front seat. "I want you close to me while I'm driving. The feel of your thigh touching mine during our short drive is much too tempting to resist."

He lowered his head to the side, placed a brief kiss on her parted lips, then turned his entire attention to driving.

His competent maneuvering through the crowded streets didn't amaze her one bit. With trembling fingertips she touched her newly sensitive mouth. She was still bemused by the continued devastating actions of her escort.

Joy's excitement increased as Jake headed north of town to the Nevada State Fairgrounds. He had explained that there was an entire week of entertainment, from the largest carnival in northern Nevada, Rodeo Queen contests, parades, barbecues, fireworks, and exhibitions to top-name western stars entertaining nightly to a packed grandstand.

Thousands of spectators were already seated in the grandstand and bleachers enjoying the start of the Professional Rodeo Cowboys Association rodeo. Joy looked curiously at the vast number of pickups, campers, and horse trailers parked behind the arena. Cowboys and cowgirls were talking in clusters or exercising their mounts, reining them through groups of competitors.

Filled with growing enthusiasm, Joy stared wide-eyed. She noticed the inquiring glances Jake received when he slowly eased his car across the dirt parking lot. He brought it to a halt beside a large empty stock trailer.

As he assisted her from the car, Joy stood self-consciously alongside his broad frame. All eyes were pinned on her, curious to see whom their friend was bringing to the rodeo.

Jake looked down at Joy's shiny curtain of hair, placed an affectionate kiss across her brow, clasped her elbow, and pulled her forward. A group of cowboys called out, mischievously taunting him about having found a new girl.

"Hey, boys, it looks like Jake done it again," an older man yelled, motioning for them to come forward. "Been raidin' some fancy dude's horse pasture, Jake? The little filly at your side sure 'nuff shows good breedin' like I ain't seen on this circuit in a month of Sundays."

The man's kind eyes were filled with admiration as he watched Joy, at the same time reaching out a callused hand, with the tips of his thumb and index finger missing, to greet Jake.

"Ah, Jesse, you don't know nothin' 'bout women. Any man who competes in team ropin' where two big guys pick on one poor little cow and still loses his fingers dallyin' the rope should keep his mouth shut," declared a younger, red-haired cowboy wearing a loud-colored western shirt.

"You lucky devil, Jake," another cowboy just a few inches taller than Joy butted in. "You not only win the first two go-rounds bulldoggin', you catch yourself a fancy up-town city girl as well." His eyes scanned Joy with thorough appreciation.

They all crowded around Joy, their expressions showing admiration for her striking beauty and shapely figure shown to advantage in her new formfitting outfit.

"Introduce us, Jake," the shorter one insisted boldly.

Jake placed a possessive hand around Joy's waist as he made the introductions. Unable to remember all their names, she smiled, enjoying their healthy outdoor looks.

They were deeply tanned, relaxed yet vital-looking as true athletes are. All wore similar western clothing. Tight denims clung to their long legs and colorful shirts conformed to the outline of their upper bodies. They looked self-sufficient and proud of their unique profession. An earthy virility undoubtedly explained their fascination with women.

It soon became evident that Jake's accomplishments were not taken lightly; their respect for him was close to reverence.

"Tell us your secret," a handsome blond cowboy named Kenny Madden asked. "You not only win All-Around Champion five years in a row, but you also manage to find the best-lookin' women wherever we go."

His eyes never left Joy's figure while he continued. "I sure could have used your advice yesterday, Jake. I airplaned off Gravedigger before he'd hardly cleared the chute. I swear I'm goin' to take up steer ropin' if I ever draw that man-eatin' ton of bull-hide again," he complained dryly, one hand rubbing his forehead. "He's the rankest bull I ever wrapped my rope on."

"Anyone rides that bellerin' beast will win, for sure!" the smaller one drawled, standing with legs widespread and both hands cockily tucked into his leather belt. "Course it'll be me, y'all know."

Jesse interrupted, wanting to give his opinion gained from fifty years of ranch work. "It ain't his buckin' that throws a man to the dust, it's the spinnin'. His loose, old leather hide's like tryin' to sit on a bolt of greased lightnin', they say."

"It's the spinners you win the most money on," Jake spoke out, his hand unconsciously caressing the curve of Joy's hip.

"Maybe so," Jesse continued gruffly. "But I'd rather wrestle nine hundred pounds of steer on the end of a rope any day than try to sit on a ton of horned dynamite."

Joy watched their animated faces as they continued talking with Jake. She glanced surreptitiously at his strong, handsome features. He towered over the other men in every way, she thought, a feeling of wonder surging through her on learning he had been an All-Around Champion several times.

The steel-hard muscles of his arm tautened as he hugged her close. His strength was awesome to Joy, yet he had exhibited nothing but gentle protectiveness toward her. She reveled in his constant courteous attention. No man had ever treated her with such tender consideration—or such arrogance either, she reflected.

"I wish you all the best of luck today," Jake told his friends, before teasing, "except in the bulldogging, which I intend to win myself."

Their glances were envious as they tipped their hats to Joy. They watched until Jake led her out of sight, her sensuous mane of hair and clinging clothes adding to their enjoyment. No matter what their age they appreciated a woman's beauty with constant enthusiasm.

"Jake, what are they all chewing?" Joy inquired, stepping carefully across the dirt. She was trying desperately not to get her new boots dusty. "Everyone seemed to have a jaw full of something."

"That, my greenhorn, is cowboy candy. More commonly called a wad of chewing tobacco." He laughed, observing her shudder.

"Ugh! That sounds terrible. How on earth can they like it? The younger they were, the bigger the mouthful, it seemed." Joy stopped, looked up at Jake's rugged profile, and hesitantly asked, "You don't chew tobacco, do you?"

Jake's amused expression caused Joy a moment's worry, before he reassured her worst fears. "Didn't I warn you? I don't smoke. I don't chew. And I sure as hell don't date women who do!"

He reached for her hand, laughing as she stared at him to see if he was actually serious. "Haven't been around many cowboys, have you, honey? That remark is as old as these mountains west of town."

Joy pulled her hand free of Jake's hold, placed them on her hips, and faced him in exasperation. "My gosh, if all cowboys have your sense of humor it's no wonder they're considered a dying breed!" Then, curiosity getting the better of her, she asked facetiously, "Why don't you chew?"

"I tried it once when I was twelve years old and that was enough. My dad said if I wanted to act like a man I should chew like a man. He gave me an oversize wad of the stuff and like the dumb, cocky kid I was I put the whole fistful in my mouth at once. I damn near choked to death trying to chomp on it like our ranch hands did.''

"I wish I could have seen that." Joy chuckled, imagining how he looked as a tall, undeveloped youth. "How was it?"

"So bad I've never had the desire to try it again. My father nearly split his sides laughing as he watched my face turn a peculiar shade of green, before I rushed behind the bunkhouse and spit it out.''

His smile was broad as he recalled his adolescent experience.

"I was so stubborn that if Dad had refused me I'd have sneaked a chew every chance I got and eventually acquired a taste for it. His reverse psychology worked.''

Walking on, Joy noticed heavy green metal holding pens. Inside the closest were a number of horses used in the riding events. Her eyes widened as Jake stopped. She watched entranced as the horses milled about or ate from the huge piles of hay provided.

"They don't look mean," she commented, looking up curiously as Jake leaned his long arms on the pipe rails.

"Most of them aren't. For no particular reason some horses never will tolerate a man on their back," he explained calmly, at the same time letting his eyes run over the stock, an unconscious habit that sized up their good and bad conformation features.

"Most are gentle enough to handle from the ground. Horses are creatures of habit and soon learn the routine. Contrary to what some people believe, rodeo stock animals have an easy life.''

"Bucking off a cowboy is easy?" Joy questioned dubiously.

"Considering they're only ridden about eight minutes total time a year, yes," Jake expounded, smiling at Joy's look of disbelief.

"What do they do the rest of the time?''

"Eat, sleep, travel, relax, and eat some more.''

"That doesn't sound too bad." Joy smiled, imitating Jake's stance by placing her arms on a lower rail and raising one shiny boot to the lowest rung. "They certainly look well fed."

Jake watched her with tender regard. She looked like a doll peering through the fence with her glorious hair shimmering in the bright sunshine. He knew there wasn't a cowboy on the grounds who wouldn't give his most prized possession to have her. She was the most delectable-looking woman he'd ever seen. More important she was his. All his. Every last luscious bit. Body and soul!

Joy raised her eyes, catching Jake's unguarded glance. She shadowed them with a hand and stared into the scorching cinnamon-colored depths. The message transmitted was as arousing as the man. She was filled with a mixture of fear and anticipation, knowing he wanted her as much in a crowd as he did when they were alone. Feeling awkward, she walked on, making no attempt to pull her hand away when he took it in his palm and strolled with her.

"Doesn't it hurt when they pull that back strap tight like I've seen them do on TV?" She stared at the sleek horses with their ungroomed shaggy manes and tails, intrigued by their different colors.

"No. The flank strap's made of soft leather and lined with sheepskin. The horses are conditioned to bucking when it's tightened but believe me, they'd buck without it. A good stock contractor can't afford to mistreat his animals. They're his livelihood and need to be healthy to perform to the best of their ability."

"At least they wouldn't cost much since they can't be used for anything else," Joy presumed, interested in learning about Jake's life-style.

"Not true, honey." He pointed through the corral. "See that Roman-nosed bay mare in the corner? Louis paid over twelve thousand dollars for her. Few really good bucking horses come cheap."

"Why?" She drew her hair back when a gust blew it around her face.

"Because they're worth every penny. Cowboys like to win on a great horse who's difficult to ride." His eyes scanned the animals, a look of remote excitement mirrored in their depths. "To ride an animal that no one else has

managed to qualify on is the biggest thrill of all." He remembered past challenges, all eventually conquered.

His hand raised to cup her shoulder, the fingers caressing
her upper arm gently. "Look at me, Joy," he commanded
fervently.

Joy raised her face, one arm lifting to cradle his neck
when his intent was clear.

Jake bent down, his lips covering hers, lingering to seek
the sweetness offered. He shuddered when her dainty
fingers stroked his nape and she moved closer. He couldn't
get enough of her glistening mouth and answered the pulsating movement with increased demand. Without embarrassment he continued cradling her close as the pickup men
rode by and voiced their appreciation in blatant outcries.

Joy flushed, pulling away to look into the next pen. Jake
casually pointed to mature horned team roping steers with
bony hips before explaining the large feeder calves were
used for roping. Being caught kissing her hadn't bothered
him at all, Joy acknowledged, forced to admit she had not
objected either.

"There have been many cries of animal cruelty raised
against rodeo competition but I'll guarantee you the animals sure as hell get treated better than the cowboys who
ride them."

He hugged her to his side, unable to keep from touching
the full length of her body. "Having fun at your first rodeo,
Joy?"

She wrinkled her nose fastidiously, inhaling the pungent
dust from a nearby corral as a large pinto gelding rolled
back and forth.

"I love it so far. One thing for certain," she chuckled,
eyes shimmering, rose-pink mouth smiling impudently,
"I'll never forget the smell!"

Jake strode forward to a pen of sleepy-looking bulls,
stopping so she could look inside. Many had humps on
their withers and large drooping ears, a trait of Brahma
cattle inherited from their sacred ancestors in India.

"It may be true that there isn't a horse that's never been
rode or a cowboy that's never been throwed, but no one's
ridden that gray bull."

He indicated a massive bull standing away from the others. Lazily switching his tail at insects, he looked gentle, small eyes staring indifferently at the two figures watching outside the pen. Jake made clear the bull was biding his time with the others until the run into the bucking chutes. Then each would explode into action during rodeos' most dangerous sport: bull riding.

Sensing their enormous power, Joy snuggled closer to Jake, glad to have the reassurance of his hand around her waist.

"They're fascinating, yet scary too. Did you ever ride bulls like these, Jake?" She couldn't take her eyes off the gray bull. He was bigger than the others and uniquely marked with black around the massive blunt-tipped horns and his eyes.

"I've tried everything offered, honey. It takes more than one event to win an All-Around Championship title."

"Yes, I can understand that, but why pick on bull riding?" She glanced up, smiling as his warm brown eyes fondly returned her gaze.

"At the age of twenty, I thought bull riding was the only worthwhile contest in rodeo. The girls crowded around like bees to honey."

"I should have known women had something to do with it," Joy chided, twisting out of his clasp. "You have to have gained your arrogance and aggressiveness somehow." She tore her eyes from the shiny tips of her boots to meet his amused glance impudently. Her attention was drawn to his mouth. It was shaped so beautifully and she would never forget how it felt grazing hers. His expertise had to be learned. From whom? When? How many?

"Too bad your dad didn't figure out a way to use reverse psychology and curb your appetite for women as well as tobacco!"

Joy was appalled at the jealousy in her voice. It was none of her business how many women Jake had made love to in the past.

He grinned devilishly, his brown eyes filled with awareness, traveling over her from head to toe with lazy assessment.

"It wouldn't have slowed me down a bit if he had, honey." One broad palm snaked out to clasp her nape, a thumb raising her chin, then holding it still for a hard, insistent kiss. "Because I'd still be pursuing you." He kissed her again to prove his tenacity.

Joy's eyes grew enormous, fingers unintentionally working their way up to his chest. She gave him a tantalizing smile, not the least surprised by his revelation. He seemed so invincible.

"Haven't the years taught you anything?" she sassed, squirming closer until they were touching from breast to thigh.

"Yes!" He slapped her on the buttocks and stepped back. "That you're trouble with a capital T." He scowled, his narrowed glare not matching the mischievous twitching of his lips.

"I mean about the dangers of competing," she rebuked, rubbing one hand on her throbbing bottom. He was so strong, his playful slap still stung.

"Maturity brought with it the desire to live to be an old man so I quit riding the rough stock years ago. When it started getting harder and harder to get up in the mornings I gave up everything."

"Everything?" Joy chided, knowing he was putting her on.

"Everything but bulldogging and looking for you," Jake told her, easing her aside when a pickup driver honked for them to move so he could unload some hay.

"Me? You really are crazy." Would she ever understand his complex personality?

"Yes, you! You're my woman. Sooner or later I'd have found you." His eyes were alight with devilry when he taunted her in a low voice. "It's too bad I took so long to happen on to you."

"Why?" Joy questioned, knowing she probably shouldn't ask.

"Because I damn near wore myself out with your sex until I finally spotted you in dire need of my protection."

Joy swung her head back, her scorn filled eyes trying to

outstare the mockery in his. He was more impossible by the moment. It was no wonder he wasn't married.

"I expected you to say something that absurd," she grumbled.

Amused by Joy's belligerence, Jake drew her around the pens to a secluded area behind the bleachers. He ignored her blistering comments about his chauvinistic attitude and easily placed her arms around his neck. Before she could react, he stifled her sassy little tongue with the pressure of his mouth in a series of heated kisses until she arched against him, momentarily quiescent.

"Hold on tight, Joy," Jake whispered in contact with her parted lips. "I'm going to take the kiss of luck I denied T.G., Buck, and Slim." One hand lingered on her hip, keeping her close. The other came up under her shiny hair and clasped her nape with fingers that had every intention of holding her still until his lips had left no doubt she was his.

"Oh, Jake," she murmured, already talking incoherently. He would think she had a two word vocabulary if he kept on kissing her with each whim.

"How are your knees?" His mouth moved over her face.

"My knees?" Now he was talking in riddles. "They're, er, fine."

"Good." He parted his lips, placing a tender kiss on each rapidly closed eyelid.

"Why...why?" she stuttered, his touch raising havoc with her pulse beat.

"Because," he warned her huskily, "I'm going to kiss you until they buckle, and I have no desire to hurry."

Jake's fervent warning caused a tremor to run through Joy's body. She was already mesmerized by the man and wouldn't have objected however long he cared to caress her. She had a lifetime of affection to catch up on and had no intention of missing any proffered by the only man she had ever responded to. She decided to volunteer his lucky kiss.

Joy stood on tiptoe, her hands placed each side of his hard jaw. She placed her lips hesitantly over the firm line of his sensuous mouth and kissed him briefly, pulling her mouth away to taunt breathlessly.

"How's that, cowboy?"

"I'll need a hell of a lot more luck than that."

Stifling any further comment, he lowered his head, taking possession of her mouth with unerring purpose. His mouth opened, parting hers with it. He was eager to taste the inner moistness with his tongue. Aroused by the heady sweetness, he explored deeper.

Joy's tiny whimpers stopped the intimate investigation. A poignant sigh of relief escaped her mouth into his, only to change to excited cries when he repeatedly rubbed his tongue sensuously over and around hers until she could feel her limbs tremble. Rhythmically in and out...on and on.

Jake continued to kiss her hungrily, his mouth warm and zealously insistent, first over her lips then across her cheeks to the sensitive area behind her ear. He buried his face against her neck, his warm rapid breath fanning the delicate skin with erotic repetition.

She moved her hips, shifting to get closer, as his hand moved slowly from her nape down her spine to the small of her back. With gentle strength he forced her body against the full length of his hardened contours.

Clinging helplessly, she knew her knees were ready to crumple up if he didn't release her. Her limited composure was in total chaos, matching the wild beating of her heart.

"Oh, Jake," she cried out plaintively, repeating his name over and over. "You're unlike anyone I've ever known."

Her head lay on his chest. It had taken what little control she could summon to pull away from his ardent lips. She had felt them on her eyelids, her entire face, alongside her neck, and finally around her ear. When his tongue had probed inside, between breathless whispered words of desire she had slumped to his chest. Even with her arms around his neck it was still impossible to stand on her tiptoes.

"You win," she told him softly, her words muffled by the thin cotton of his shirt. Her arms had lowered to cling to his waist. She couldn't have stood on her own if she tried.

"Knees buckling yet?" Jake asked softly, his fingers running through her silky strands of hair. "If yours aren't, mine are," he admitted without reservation. He continued to cradle her close, satisfied for the moment to stroke her hair while they regained their breath.

"This isn't how I normally act with a stranger." Joy drew back, resting against the strength of his arms crossed behind her lower back. Her misty green eyes met his squarely, entranced by the lights flickering in his widened pupils.

"I'm glad," he told her softly, entranced by her admission.

"I've never been able to tolerate any man touching me."

His hands trembled, cupping her hips as much to steady her as him. Did she mean what he thought? Surely at twenty-seven she wasn't virtuous? Impossible! No one that passionate could be untouched.

"You must have a hypnotic effect on me, or I wouldn't act so receptive," she continued, intervening in his speculation. Someday she would tell him about her dreams. Maybe even explain in full detail about her fantasies. Describe his lovemaking, which had been so beautiful she had spent days trying to locate him hoping to change the fantasy into a reality. Then she would tell him the reality was even more perfect than the illusion.

A loud call from atop the bucking chutes interrupted them, breaking the acuteness of their embrace.

"Hey, Jake! You'd better get up front. Louis has been waitin' for you for over an hour. He wants to wish you luck before the bulldoggin' starts."

"Okay, Ken. I'll be right up as soon as I'm certain you wild, undisciplined cowhands will keep your hands off my woman. Joy has my brand permanently stamped all over her," he informed his friend gravely. "Pass my warning on to all your worthless cohorts, hear?"

"Sure, Jake, but you ain't goin' to be too popular with Marie at the dance tonight. She'll be jealous as hell when she gets a look at Joy." Ken ran his eyes up and down Joy. "I don't blame you preferrin' a sweet-faced little beauty over that blond-haired b—"

"Cool it, Ken. Marie's no affair of yours."

Jake took Joy's hand, aware she had listened intently to Ken's opinionated comments and found them disconcerting.

"Forget it, Joy. Marie's just a longtime acquaintance and need never concern you."

Joy knew by Jake's expression that he wouldn't offer any further explanation, though her curiosity was aroused along with jealousy, about the unknown Marie's relationship with him.

She was mature enough to realize his sensual expertise would have been gained through an active social life with experienced partners. She flipped back her hair, eyes stormy with temper. She certainly had no desire to personally meet any of his playmates! Just hearing the name Marie set her teeth to grating angrily.

Intent on seeing Louis, Jake hurried Joy to the announcer's stand above the bucking chutes. A husky, broad-shouldered handsome man in his early fifties greeted them, taking Jake's hand in a powerhouse grip. He was openly pleased at seeing his longtime friend.

Intelligent brown eyes looked curiously from Jake to Joy. His dark brown curly hair and attractive face were barely noticed above the brilliance of his wide, friendly smile.

"Joy, I want you to meet my best friend. This broken-down old football player is Louis Edwards and a finer person you'll never meet."

Jake turned his head to smile at Joy, placing his hand on the opposite side of her waist in the possessive manner she found so endearing.

"Would you believe I flew all the way from Texas to Reno just to swap a few lies and share a cold beer with this man?"

Joy felt her fingers engulfed in Louis's strong grip, his mischievous expression as filled with humor as his twinkling eyes. She returned his look, her eyes shimmering with excitement, her soft lips, kissed free of lipstick by Jake, raised in a friendly greeting.

"My God, Jake, you picked a stunning beauty this time," Louis told him, sincerely entranced by Joy's loveliness and the warmth of her bright smile.

Jake's voice was firm when he turned to Louis. "You think I hadn't noticed that by myself?"

Warily she glanced at Jake. It was embarrassing to be the main part of their discussion yet not included.

"Fortunately Louis is safely and happily married to a sexy-looking blonde because he used to be a skirt chasing devil." Jake looked down into her eyes with undisguised appreciation while relating confident details with roguish enthusiasm.

"When he wasn't knocking heads together playing pro ball with the L.A. Rams, there weren't many females he passed by. Meeting Jean and a serious knee injury promptly controlled his rampant debauchery," Jake chided, the two friends smiling at each other with complete understanding.

Jake's hand slid up Joy's arm, his fingers consciously caressing her shoulder while she listened raptly. It was becoming increasingly hard to keep his hands away from her body. She was so perfectly proportioned he ached to stroke her curves without the barrier imposed by her clothing. His thoughts were interrupted by Louis's deep laughter. His friend was well aware that he was more interested in making love to Joy than visiting with him.

"Rampant debauchery!" Louis exclaimed. "I never met a rodeo cowboy yet that couldn't give a football player lessons in the basic arts of female seduction." He reached out to touch Joy's shoulder. "And this one is the worst of all!"

"That's a foul thing to say, old friend," Jake retorted indignantly, reaching up to brush Louis's hand off Joy's shoulder.

"Especially when I was getting ready to tell her your compelling personality and diversified talents have made you a success in many fields." He turned to Joy, muttering in a devilishly loud disclosure. "Currently he's the best damned rodeo promoter and stock contractor in Nevada."

Embarrassed by Jake's praise, Louis scoffed. "Get going, you wild Texan. I'll see no harm comes to Joy."

Ignoring the presence of Louis and the other people in the announcer's stand, Jake turned Joy into his arms. With accurate precision he kissed her leisurely until she pulled away, her composure completely shattered.

The sound of Jake's laughter rang in her ears as he leaped down the steps, his mind intent on competing for another win. It came as no surprise that he was instantly the center of attention.

As he towered over the other men, she was able to watch him speak, his arms raised to emphasize a point.

"He's giving the younger riders advice, Joy," Louis revealed matter-of-factly. "It's a common practice, though each is often in competition for the same prize money."

Joy observed Jake openly, impressed by the respect his friends showed as they listened intently to his comments.

"Just when did Jake win All-Around Champion, Louis?" It seemed unlikely it had been recently since he mentioned he only competed for recreation now.

"Several years back but there's not a man, young or old, who doesn't respect his opinion 'cause they know darn well he could still beat them all in any event he chose to compete in."

A soft, dreamy look crossed Joy's face as she looked down at Jake. One hand rose unconsciously to her breast. She was so filled with pride in his accomplishments she couldn't take her eyes off him.

Without warning, Jake looked at the announcer's stand. Touching his fingers to his mouth, he gave Joy an exaggerated kiss. She pulled back flushing with embarrassment as his friends looked up. They smiled broadly before turning back to rib Jake about his new girl.

"You'd better sit over here, Joy, and let me shut the door or you'll have Jake so flustered he'll forget which end of the steer to grab," Louis teased, wanting to learn more about the enchanting woman who seemed to have captured his friend's elusive heart.

Chapter Five

To Joy's relief she felt no awkwardness with Jake's best friend, accepting the metal folding chair offered for a ringside seat. Louis's knowledge was keen, each instructive remark making the action-packed scenes in the arena come to life. With mounting excitement she listened attentively to each word.

"Watch the bronc riding closely, Joy. You'll enjoy the exhilarating energy as the horses duck and dive, flying high and hitting hard."

Beginning to discern much of rodeo's picturesque rhetoric, Joy commented when a contestant grabbed the saddle, "I'm surprised any cowboy would admit to needing help to stay on. They all seem so proud of their athletic ability."

"They have to have self-confidence," Louis concurred, clarifying the maneuver. "No one blames them since I have such an exceptional string of bucking stock. It's no disgrace to see a cowboy grab the rigging to keep from being slammed into the ground while trying to ride one of my animals."

Despite leaning forward to ensure she didn't miss anything happening in the arena, Joy listened attentively. Unaware of Louis's amused glance, she noted the thrilling performance with wide-eyed appreciation.

"Notice, Joy, how the rider's boots are over the point of the horse's shoulders on the first jump," Louis indicated as a saddle bronc rider burst out of the chute. "If his feet aren't in the proper position at the start, he'll be disqualified. You've really got to put the iron to them to score high."

"Do you mean spurring?" Each cowboy racked his legs back and forth continuously from the moment the bucking started. She had noticed some wearing blunt-tipped spurs strapped to their boots earlier and presumed correctly that was what Louis meant.

"Yes. It's also called laying the licks on them."

"Oh, look! He fell off," Joy exclaimed, as the young rider took a hard fall over the rear of his horse. Everything was happening so fast she was afraid to look at Louis for fear of missing a single feat.

"That's called coming out the back door. Over the head is airplaning," Louis revealed. He pulled up a chair alongside Joy. With both elbows propped on the wood ledge he observed the filled grandstand with a gratified smile. Each year's attendance was superior to the last.

"Some of the horses are quite attractive." Joy didn't know much about what were considered good and bad points but many were sleek with bright-colored bodies and flowing manes and tails.

"I've got a couple that groomed properly could easily place in a halter class."

"Halter class?" Joy asked, raising a narrow brow in question.

"Classes where horses are judged on conformation and way of traveling while being led by their handler."

Louis smiled at Joy. Her interest was genuine and he admired the way she never hesitated to ask him to explain what she didn't understand.

"Kind of a beauty contest for horses," she teased, listening attentively as they announced bareback bronc riding would be next. She searched the arena for Jake, disappointment clearly mirrored in her eyes when she couldn't see him. She turned to Louis, questioning him about the following event.

"Bareback horses are much smaller than the saddle bronc animals, which sometimes weigh over eighteen hundred pounds. They're quicker too and can spin three hundred sixty degrees with each buck."

"Jake told me a horse's most natural instinct is to rid itself of anything on its back," Joy interrupted, pleased she could contribute something to their conversation. She had diligently memorized each thing Jake told her during their walk around the corrals.

"Jake's correct and the finest stockman I know. Either with horses or cattle." Louis had long admired his best friend's inherent knowledge of ranching and admitted without jealousy that it far surpassed what he had gained in the last few years as a stock contractor.

"Jake also told me though rarely doing the same thing twice bucking horses and bulls do develop patterns," she added confidently.

She placed a hand under her hair, swinging the unruly strands over her shoulder. Her satiny complexion glowed with health, the creamy skin touched with color from the bright afternoon sun shining into the booth.

Joy watched the pickup men on their agile mounts move in at the sound of the eight-second whistle. They picked off the riders, who slid over their horse's hindquarters and walked back to the chutes, waiting to hear if they had earned the day's high score.

Calf roping, with fast ties of less than ten seconds, was followed by team roping. Joy watched Jesse heeling a special breed of Mexican cattle with splotchy colored hides and evenly shaped horns. Age was no barrier in this event; he and his teen-age partner handily won second place.

When bull riding was announced, Joy watched the riders lower themselves cautiously over the top of the chute onto the beasts' broad backs. The cowboys took their time, making certain their heavy bull ropes were wrapped correctly. Hitting them down into their gloves, they were aware their life could depend on the ropes coming undone quickly if thrown.

"One of the worst things that can happen to a bull rider is to get hung up in his rigging," Louis told her, his expression serious as he watched with as careful attention as Joy.

"It makes me shudder to think of it." She could feel a tremor of anxiety run up her spine. It would be unbearable to witness anyone being injured during her first rodeo. "I can see where it would be impossible to guarantee anyone safety in this sport.''

"The only guarantee in rodeo is you're going to eventually get hurt. Some cowboys are so superstitious about the ambulance, or meat wagon, as they call it, they won't even ride in one unless they're unconscious.''

Joy cringed inwardly hearing Louis talk about rodeo dangers. She was filled with sudden distress, afraid that Jake might get hurt while she watched. She knew she couldn't ever bear to see him in pain.

The huge bulls exploded out of the chutes, one after the other, leaping and twisting with bone-jarring force in an attempt to unseat the men on their backs. Swinging their massive necks sideways, they tried to hook the riders with blunt-tipped horns, at the same time twisting their massive hindquarters. Most managed to throw their riders easily.

The sturdy chutes shook as an enormous gray bull tried to leap over the top. Joy recognized his unique markings at once. In awe of his great size in the holding pen, she was amazed to see how agile his cumbersome body looked now. His wicked-looking head and blunted horns were visible above the tall chute as he refused to settle down. Her breath caught as the audience screamed with fear for the cowboys helping. They momentarily scrambled to safety, only to return the moment the bull fell back to the ground.

Louis placed a comforting hand on Joy's shoulder. He observed her slender shoulders quiver and leaned over to speak with concern.

"That's Gravedigger. There hasn't been a qualifying ride on him in the three years he's been in my string.'' Louis frowned, cupping Joy's shoulder when the bull bellowed, crashing his weight into the gate.

Joy looked at Louis briefly before returning her gaze to the chutes. She couldn't tear her eyes away from the bull. Even in the announcer's stand they could both feel the force of the animal.

"Jake showed him to me earlier. He's so much larger than the other bulls, his size made him appear dangerous though he was standing docile enough at the time.''

"Every bull rider wants to be the first to ride him.''

Louis looked thoughtful for a moment. "Someday one will, but he's injured too many young men and I've decided to sell him to a cattle breeder in Texas before he kills somebody."

Joy watched three men waiting in the arena by the front of the chutes, curious about their dress and purpose. "Who are they?"

"Those are the rodeo clowns and absolutely fearless when a bull rider gets in trouble. They're responsible for saving many lives." He pointed to the side. "See the man with the dented barrel?"

"Yes. He looks quite funny dressed in old faded-red long underwear and baggy jeans with wide suspenders. Why does he have a barrel next to him?"

"For good reason." Louis leaned toward her, his voice serious. "Bull riders have no pickup men and have to get off on their own. After a cowboy slides or is bucked off, the barrel man teases and taunts the bull with an old red cape. If the bull tries to gore the clown—after the beast's attention is intentionally distracted from the fallen rider—the clown hops into his barrel. The brunt of the bull's horns can savagely knock it across the arena."

"I imagine the riders really feel indebted to the clowns' bravery." She couldn't imagine anyone voluntarily going into the arena on foot when a bull was loose.

"Rodeo spectators also love the daring and excitement provided by these outstanding athletes," Louis expounded.

Joy concurred, her eyes never leaving the chutes. She was amazed when Louis told her cattle were color blind and only attacked the cape because of its movement. She had always thought they charged a red cape because of its vivid color.

T.G., the young cowboy who first accosted her in downtown Reno, had drawn Gravedigger. Finally satisfied with his rope, he pulled his hat low on his forehead, raised his right arm, and nodded to the chute man that he was ready.

With a loud clang the gate flew open and Gravedigger exploded into the arena with ground-jarring force. Twisting his body, the gray bull kicked his hindquarters high in the air. Immediately changing directions, he started into a spin, his lightning speed unseating his rider instantly.

Thrown over Gravedigger's shoulders, T.G. just missed being sideswiped by the bull's blunted horns. He staggered slowly to his feet, momentarily stunned by the heavy fall. Bellowing with rage, the huge bull lowered his head, front hoof pawing a spew of dust as he prepared to charge T.G.

Cowboys inside the arena climbed onto the safety of the heavy chutes, aware of the bull's lethal horns. Joy observed the clowns in action as they rushed in to distract the violent animal.

Gravedigger lunged forward, turning abruptly to chase the advancing, taunting clown waving a ragged cape. His horns sideswiped the barrel, knocking it several feet across the arena. The agile clown was braced safely inside, his last-second leap made amid worried screams from the spectators.

Shocked with fear, Joy jumped up, one hand clasped over her mouth. She watched, temporarily speechless, before slumping back into the chair. Her face paled with relief when Gravedigger was herded back to the holding pen, knowing she would never forget the animal's viciousness.

"That was horrible." Her shoulders trembled as she looked at Louis. "I was so frightened for T.G. Thank God he's safe!" she gasped compassionately.

"That's how T.G. got his nickname, Joy." Louis patted her shoulder with his broad palm. It was obvious Joy was too tender-hearted to ever be overly enthusiastic about bull riding.

"I don't understand."

"Every time he'd walk back to the chutes after being thrown, he'd say 'Thank God I'm safe.' Before long everyone started calling him T.G. and now most of the cowboys don't even remember his real name."

"My gosh," Joy sighed. 'Why doesn't he consider another occupation?''

"He's a rough stock rider by preference. They call bull riding a ton of fun, but I'd rather face the Washington Redskins' defensive line any day."

Louis spoke with enthusiasm, his keen brown eyes scanning the cowboys close by.

"Rodeo's a rough and tumble sport with lots of action, Joy. The contestants wouldn't want to do anything else. They're professionals; they warm up beforehand to stretch their muscles like joggers and other athletes do. One tenth of a second can mean thousands of dollars and the difference between winning and losing, so they have to be fit."

He glanced across at the grandstand and bleachers. Each seat was sold and filled with a wildly fascinated spectator, young or old.

"Rodeo has to be the finest family entertainment in America today." He couldn't think of any other form of entertainment that equally delighted people of every age.

Louis pointed toward the cattle chutes at one end of the arena, telling her Jake would be bulldogging soon.

Filled with anxiety, Joy watched one cowboy after another leave the box after his steer. She stared mutely, knuckles clenched, tension increasing as Jake's turn came close.

Mounted on a compact, red-dun quarter horse, Jake quietly watched the other contestants. The sleek animal appeared eager to give chase. His broad chest muscles bulged, veeing deeply into slender front legs. The hindquarters were bunched and heavy as he anticipated what was ahead. His small foxy ears were cocked forward, large dark brown eyes watching intelligently, his fine neck bowed in a graceful arch while waiting for Jake to give him a cue to move.

Jake looked at the announcer's stand, catching Joy's eye. She stared with open admiration at his wide shoulders and long lean legs. Her pulse beat frantically, reacting immediately to the physical magnetism of his athletic, virile good looks.

Jake smiled, tilted his hat to Joy, then reined his horse into the box alongside the chute. Spinning it around to set up, he leaned forward, waiting with undivided attention for the steer to be released. His horse's muscles strained, ready to leap from the box as soon as the steer had cleared the barrier. The hazer waited on the other side to race alongside the steer, keeping it running straight.

Released from the chute, the big horned steer charged, heading toward the opposite side of the arena. Carried to the steer's left side in three quick leaps, the fast quarter horse, borrowed to compete on, prepared to run on by.

With skill and accurate timing Jake eased from the right side of the saddle toward the steer. He slipped his right arm up the steer's neck under the horns and his left arm under its jaw. Legs forward, he dug his boot heels into the ground, stopping the steer and throwing it to the ground in 3.5 seconds.

The crowd rose in unison to cheer his near record-breaking speed as he released the steer and stood up.

Calmly brushing the arena dust from the seat of his jeans, Jake looked at Joy. He gave her a broad wink and walked to the side as the dazed steer staggered to his hooves and trotted away.

Joy, ecstatic over his good time, turned to Louis, exclaiming, "Wasn't he wonderful? Oh, Louis, do you think Jake will win again today?"

Deep laughter boomed from Louis's throat. "With less than eleven seconds on three go-rounds I would say he'd be damn near impossible to beat. Steer wrestling takes a big man on a fast horse and Jake had a tremendous run today. That red-dun stud horse is the best in the business, traveling around thirty miles an hour when his rider leaps off."

"It looked so easy," Joy said gravely. "If I had blinked my eyes I might have missed it entirely." She couldn't believe how rapidly it was completed.

Louis grinned. "Everything happens so fast; when Jake bulldogs it looks simple. Believe me, honey, it takes precision timing and tremendous skill. When you know my friend better, you'll realize how great a man he is in many ways."

I know already, Joy thought earnestly. Her mind lingered on the weeks of dreaming about meeting him. She'd never dared visualize he'd turn the tables on her with his heated pursuit. It still seemed unreal.

Without warning, Jake leaped up the stairs, burst through the unlatched door, and took Joy into his arms. He swung her around in the narrow confines of the announcer's stand, his lips seeking hers for a hard kiss until she squealed out in protest.

Both of his strong arms were still wrapped around her squirming body when he smiled mischievously at Louis. "How about that, Louis? One good luck kiss from my woman and an hour later I win over ten thousand dollars!"

Jakes's eyes glimmered, skimming Joy's flushed features with tender amusement. "Before today is over I'm going to put two wraps and half hitch around Joy and make certain she's packing my brand for life!"

Louis narrowed his eyes. He was stunned by Jake's exuberant announcement. It was impossible to believe he was serious about Joy, despite her beauty. He had seen him with many gorgeous women, inwardly acknowledging his manner had always been arrogantly aloof. With Joy he acted like a different person—free and easy yet possessively jealous, evidenced in how abruptly he had removed his hand from Joy's shoulder earlier.

"Congratulations, old buddy." Louis's eyes went from Jake's face to Joy's then back again, his deep voice warning devilishly, "To celebrate your staggering capitulation I'll expect you to buy all the drinks tonight." He clapped Jake on the back with a powerhouse grip. "Remember, no watered-down booze either. After all, it was my steers you won all that money on."

"Fair enough," Jake agreed, holding Joy close with long fingers spread over her curved hip. "With your capacity for swigging moonshine, I should have entered calf roping too," he teased, deep brown eyes filled with laughter. "We'll see you and Jean at the dance later on."

Turning to Joy, Jake commanded huskily, "Come on, honey." He reached for her hand, engulfing its smallness in his broad palm easily. "I'm going to buy you the biggest prime beef steak in Reno. I sure hope it's Texas beef, 'cause anything else is bound to be tough," he drawled emphatically, his tone filled with pride in his home state.

"Watch out, Joy," Louis retorted. "Some of the worst braggarts in the world are cowboys and Texans. A combination of the two can be totally unbearable." He bid them good-bye, watching with keen eyes as they left.

Brushing aside numerous congratulations from his friends for winning all three go-rounds, Jake clasped Joy to his side

He walked straight to his rented car, seated her with gentle courtesy, then lithely eased his large frame behind the steering wheel.

Breathless from rushing to keep up with his long stride, Joy relaxed against the soft leather seat. She laid her head back to observe his features. There was no comparison between looking at his photograph and seeing him in person. It was impossible to control the sudden quivering in her stomach.

She was amused by the speed with which he had rushed her away from his friends, and smiled. Wavy hair framed her face with a sheen of brown silk. Her lips parted sensually, enchantment lighting her eyes with jeweled shades of deep green.

"Where's the fire, cowboy?" Her whisper was throaty, the words a slow entreaty.

"In my heart, darling."

He turned to face her, his side touching the steering wheel, not making any attempt to start the motor. Keen brown eyes roved lazily over each feature of her lovely face, their soft color changing to black as his emotions heightened. His arms stretched to her and his strong hands were gentle on her slim shoulders.

"Come to me, Joy," he coaxed, his voice thick, a low sensuous whisper that brought goose bumps to her sensitive flesh.

Without protest she slipped into his arms, drawn forward by the wonder of his seductive persuasion. She melted against him, her body fluid and soft over his, her chin raised, her slender white neck arched backward to allow him access to the rapidly beating pulse of her throat.

Jake's head lowered, the invitation irresistible. His lips eagerly parted, to hungrily caress the delicate skin. Encouraged by her warm response, he trailed his lips to her face, each husky murmur of love blurred incoherently against her creamy skin. His mouth tasted, lifted, then lowered to touch again. Each movement became a mixture of pleasure and torture from holding his rising desire in tight check. He wasn't used to waiting and he wanted her like no other woman in his past.

With every teasing motion of his mouth, Joy became more aroused, unconsciously pushing forward to rest her pliant body as close to him as the narrow confines of the car would allow.

Weeks of yearning made her powerless even if she had wanted to resist him. In his presence she was a changed person. A startling passionate woman fiercely responsive to the man she knew she loved.

Low murmurs of protest escaped her throat as he made her wait for the possession of her mouth. Filled with impatience, she raised her hands to hold his face still, only to find them cradling his head as he lowered his lips to the soft swell of her throbbing breasts.

The warmth of his body invaded hers. His masculine scent; a mixture of good soap, arena dust, and healthy sweat heightened her emotions more than any expensive shaving lotion could. She gloried in the impassioned words spilling forth unrecognizably as he trailed kisses from her breasts to her face.

Joy's eyes closed slumberously, her trembling hands clasped tight around his neck as she strained to understand. After a lifetime deprived of verbal and physical affection she craved the most minute expression of Jake's concern.

"I love you so much, darling," he murmured against her neck. "So damn much, I could hardly stay in the arena long enough to bulldog my last steer," he reiterated in an increasingly heavy drawl.

"Really?" she questioned breathlessly. It seemed impossible that he was as ardent as she'd fantasized. "Oh, Jake..." She broke off, reeling when his breath wafted erotically into her ear.

"Each time I glanced at your sweet face, I ached to take you to the nearest preacher." He raised his head, his nostrils flaring as he inhaled her heady scent.

Their glances locked, his black as pitch, hers soft and luminescent. Tension mounted between them and escalated when his dark silky voice summoned, "Kiss me, Joy." His shoulders trembled. The promise in her eyes was more than he could stand. "Kiss me now!"

Joy's eyes closed, her lips raising the fraction of an inch it took to obey his forceful decree. Nervously her tongue darted out, leaving her mouth parted and damp, eager to receive his possession.

Jake kissed her so sensuously, she forgot everything but the overpowering need to be in his arms. The longing for his lovemaking filled her with dissatisfaction equal to the frustration of waking before finding release in her erotic dreams.

She felt his hand slide to her hip, its strength easily drawing her against the length of his body. She let her leg move across his, his steel-hard muscles contrasting with her feminine softness.

Their passionate embrace went unnoticed despite the brightness of the late afternoon sun. Jake's car was conveniently hidden by an empty cattle truck. Joy was free to revel in the touch of his hands as he stroked her back, and she made no protest when his fingers spread over the base of her spine to explore beneath her heavy mane of hair. Every lingering caress was tender, giving her pleasure while showing her how susceptible she was to his determined seduction.

Joy's lustrous hair spread over his hands as they raised, one cradling her nape, the other cupping one full breast. His face burrowed in waves soft as silk. Nibbling the lobe of her dainty ear, he slowly circled the inner cavity with his tongue while his hand fondled each breast as if memorizing its exquisite shape.

Joy pressed frantic kisses on his taut neck, inhaling the aroma of his heated skin and the smell of horse and cattle that clung to his clothes. She made no protest when his hand unsnapped her blouse to explore her naked curves. Deft fingers slipped inside the low cup of her bra, sensuously rubbing the hardening nipple into a taut crest. She arched her back, crying out longingly for him to accept the aroused tip into his mouth. Her actions were instinctive, the desire flooding her trembling body as old as mankind.

Jake shuddered, his senses returning with shocking suddenness. Pulling Joy's arms from his neck, he gently eased her away from his stimulated body after one trembling kiss to the tip of each thrusting breast. He cupped her chin, the taste of her skin lingering with tantalizing sweetness. A low groan of anxiety escaped hoarsely at the sight of her dilated pupils, shimmering with brightness from unshed tears of passion.

"Forgive me, darling." His fingers traced the fullness of her luscious mouth. "You're so responsive, I completely forgot I was making love to you in a car in broad daylight and barely hidden from several thousand people."

Joy pulled from his hand, fixing her blouse with fingers that had suddenly grown clumsy. She was so shaken from his lovemaking it would take all her concentrated effort to regain a modicum of composure.

"I love you, Joy."

His deep voice filled the car with echoing tension. The simplicity of his words filled her heart with overflowing tenderness. She turned to face him, one hand outstretched to touch his arm. His voice was serious, leaving no room for doubt despite their having known each other a matter of hours.

He placed his fingers over hers, drawing them forward to clasp between his hands. "Before dawn you'll be my wife as well as my lover, Joy. Does that frighten you?" he asked with concern, for he realized his courtship was rapid.

She examined his features intently, knowing she owed him an honest reply. "No, Jake. I feel as if I've known you all my life. I think we were destined to meet in a way." In the morning she would tell him everything, including her weeks of haunting visions and the search that followed. She withdrew her hand, clasping her fingers tightly.

"Are you a virgin, Joy?" His voice was harsh, filled with taut explicitness. He kicked himself inwardly. His question had come forth unbidden. Ever since she had said she had been unable to tolerate another man's advances he had been filled with tormenting curiosity.

She could see his knuckles tighten before his hand dropped to his lap. Aware he waited for her answer with indrawn breath, she asked softly, "Would it matter to you if I wasn't?"

His eyes had darkened close to the color of his raven hair as they held her questioning gaze.

"In all honesty, it would kill me to know another man had ever possessed you, though it wouldn't affect my love—if you can understand that reasoning."

He reached a hand across the seat back to cradle her nape with such tenderness she wanted to cry out. Before she could reply, he continued.

"Realistically, at your age, I shouldn't expect you to be innocent, nor with my experience should I deserve it," he told her bluntly. "Need I be jealous of any man, darling?" he persisted.

Her glance was clear as she answered candidly. "No, Jake. I've never been with a man before." She never hesitated. His comment that his love would not be affected by previous lovers touched her heart more than anything he could have said. He was a proud man and inherently possessive. His understanding that it was likely she had had previous lovers showed a tolerance that exceeded many of her previous men friends. She abhorred the double-standard for men despite no previous inclination for promiscuity.

Reverently he drew her forward to place a lingering kiss with trembling tenderness until unbidden tears trickled beneath her clenched lids, down her cheeks, and onto his face. Pulling back, he kissed them dry, cradled her to his side. Without comment he started the car and slowly pulled from the dirt lot to the paved road.

Joy was silent during the short drive to his hotel, immersed in the belief that it was really possible for two people to be destined for each other. There was no other explanation for what had happened. Their entire relationship had to have been foreordained by a higher power. His tender glance expressed the same profound awareness.

Breaking into the deep introspection shared in silence, Jake told her warmly, "I'm returning to the hotel to shower and change clothes before we go to dinner and the dance later tonight."

"I'll need to change too," Joy reminded him.

"Your new western suit is entirely appropriate for our evening's entertainment." Not wanting to be away from her for a moment, he was adamant that she not return to her motel room.

Shooting him an amused glance, she laughed softly. "Fine with me, Mr. Travis. I rather like the looks of my new outfit." The material was soft and the fit so excellent she had dreaded putting her dress back on.

"So do I." He smiled. "And so did every man in town who spotted you."

"It's not too tight, is it?" The pants did fit her legs and bottom snug. Even the blouse clung to her breasts provocatively.

"Not for my tastes, it isn't," Jake reassured her, his eyes taking in the perfection of her petite figure with the thoroughness of a man who can't see enough of the woman he loves.

"Here we are," he explained unnecessarily, coming to a stop in the hotel's garage.

Joy followed Jake into his suite without saying a word. She was still bemused by his tumultuous lovemaking and the excitement of the day's unexpected events.

Jake threw his hat on the chair and casually unbuttoned his shirt while walking toward the bedroom.

"Relax on the couch, honey. It won't take me long to get ready," he called over his shoulder, unconcerned that Joy could see him.

She watched his shirt come off with a quick tug, her eyes taking in the sensuality of his rippling back muscles as he laid it on the corner of the wide bed.

Suddenly nervous by the feelings aroused at the sight of his partially naked form, she walked to the window. It was all she could do to force herself to remain in the living area. It seemed so right to walk into his bedroom.

She felt the urge to go to him, to tell him of her desires, to undress and suggest they take a shower together. The image of their naked bodies clinging beneath a cooling spray of water was followed with the vivid impression of being kissed wildly, legs and arms entwined on the king-size bed—an inevitable conclusion if she allowed her inclinations to win over her better judgment.

With a deep sigh she forced her trembling stomach to settle. In a matter of hours she would be his wife and was well aware he wouldn't take long after that to claim her for his own. She could hardly wait, as bewitched by his kisses as by his commanding personality and appealing ruggedness, which had attracted her from first sight.

Apparently it had taken a dominant male to bring out her latent sensuality. Certainly none of her previous dates had elicited any response at all. Jake was a man who made a decision, commanded it be met, and had the power to follow through with his admonition.

Yet his strength was also in his ability to treat her with great tenderness, she reflected pensively. Her heart was filled with the wonder of his touch.

Jake entered the sitting room. Standing before her, freshly showered and shaved, his coal-black hair glistened with cleanliness. He wore a dark brown western suit styled with a shaped yoke across the back and front. Its cut fit his broad shoulders before tapering perfectly to his lean waist. Alligator dress boots shone with a high polish. His white silk shirt was immaculate. A braided leather string tie held at his throat by a silver and gold vee-shaped clasp added an elegant touch. The dazzling championship buckle, visible between the open lapels of his jacket, drew her eyes to his flat abdomen, emphasizing its masculine sensuality.

Joy stared openly, her shining eyes filled with admiration. Her nose inhaled Jake's pungent woodsy after-shave. She found herself responding shamelessly to his virile maleness.

"I'd like to wash up before we leave," she told him, forcing her legs to walk calmly across the room. It was all she could do to avoid throwing her arms around him. She was addicted to his touch although not certain she was comfortable with the knowledge that her future happiness depended on one man. Being contingent on another person after years of independence seemed too naive for a mature woman. At his nod, she moved to the bedroom.

Jake's dark eyes narrowed, watching her curvaceous figure outlined clearly against the walls of his suite. Her graceful movements filled him with desire, one he forced himself to tamp until she would be his wife.

"I'll mix two drinks to celebrate," he told her, going to the room's wet bar. He took a bottle of liquor from the cabinet and poured the whiskey into waiting glasses filled with ice cubes. He watched the amber liquid swirl before settling.

Muscles rippled across his wide back when he shrugged to ease the fleeting stiffness caused by his recent tussle in the rodeo arena.

Time to think of raising a few sons instead of flying all over the country bulldogging steers, he thought. His mind suddenly filled with the image of Joy pregnant from his frequent lovemaking.

Frequent? Hell, I'll be insatiable! he moaned in frustration.

Joy entered the bathroom, her glance held by his damp bath towel and splashes of water on the floor, the only visible signs of his recent shower. The room still smelled of his after-shave, causing her body to tense at the intimacy implied by their sharing the same room. She picked up his towel, holding it against her breast.

God help me, she cried inwardly. *I love him so much, I get pleasure from something that touched his body.* She drew air into her lungs, already familiar with his clean male scent.

After laying the towel down, she washed her hands and face. She scanned her reflection in the mirror, not the least surprised by the sensuous look of her softened mouth and dilated pupils.

Fresh lipgloss was applied with nervous fingers before she brushed her hair until it hung in long, shimmering waves below her waist. She rummaged through her large purse for the tiny vial of her favorite perfume. A dab behind each ear, the hollow of her throat, inside her wrists, and deep in her cleavage made her feel feminine. Refreshed, she entered the sitting room to see Jake standing before the window, the room lit only by the fading sunlight.

He glanced over his shoulder, asking softly, "Come here, Joy. We'll watch our first sunset together."

She walked forward, taking the glass he offered. She enjoyed the taste of the smooth whiskey. Its warmth spread through her body, reminding her of the many drinks she had consumed at Harold's Club. She wasn't certain which was more intoxicating. Straight whiskey or Jake.

Placing his arm around her, Jake inhaled.

"Hmm, darling, you smell good enough to eat. That's mighty sexy perfume you're wearing." He placed a feather-light kiss against the corner of her brow, his warm, clean breath wafting across her sensitive skin. "If you tell me what it is, I'll get you a gallon."

Joy raised her face, smiling mischievously. "I doubt it, cowboy. I have to save for a month to buy a tiny vial." She leaned her face into his shoulder, bemused by the pleasure of being touched solicitously.

"I'm glad you like it, since it's all I brought with me."

Jake leaned forward, placing a hard kiss on her parted lips.

"Sweetheart, your own fragrance is far superior to any I've inhaled thus far made by man."

Finishing his drink in one swallow, he took Joy's half-filled glass and growled in a threatening voice, "Come on, woman. I'm damn near starving to death!"

Within a short time he had driven her to a popular steak house, parked, escorted her inside, and they were seated at the best table, enjoying the attentive service of the maître d'.

Joy was bemused by the ease with which Jake managed. Her eyes scanned the large menu without interest. She had no appetite for food. Her only concern was in the man who had stolen her heart.

She briefly studied the seafood salad set before her, which Jake ordered despite her protest. Too wrought to eat, she watched him. She was satisfied with sipping the excellent wine while he enthusiastically consumed a succulent-looking steak.

Her dreamy eyes never left his face. Rena would never believe she had won the heart of her Texas cowboy in one day's time.

"Were you ever hurt?" Joy questioned, her fingers clenching the wineglass uncontrollably. Just thinking about Jake lying injured caused her pain. The thought of his strong body damaged and bleeding made her face pale. She reached for his hand, and her fingers clasped his tightly in involuntary compassion.

"A few broken bones. Nothing serious," Jake replied

matter-of-factly. "Eventually everyone pays the price of competing."

His eyes scanned her face, recognizing her concern for his safety. "Oh, honey," he exclaimed in an attempt to reassure her, "you need never fear for me. I'm older now and hopefully wise enough to realize that like all sport and athletic competition, each year a new crop of men and women come along, a little younger and often a lot more talented. Bull riding, especially, is a young man's event that I wouldn't think of entering anymore."

Jake raised her pink-tinted fingers to his mouth. He was awed by her solicitude.

Tears unexpectedly brimmed in her eyes. Dabbing at them with her free hand, she smiled. "I feel like a big baby." She stared with misty eyes, trying to laugh off her emotional outburst. "I don't think I could bear it if you were hurt."

Jake leaned back as the waiter cleared their table, waited until they were alone, then soothed her fears.

"Don't worry about me getting hurt, honey. I'll be so busy being a devoted husband, I'll probably never set my boot heels inside an arena again."

"I very much doubt that." She chuckled, her somber mood forgotten with his easy assurance. "Louis told me you're hopelessly addicted to bulldogging and—"

"And?"

"Chasing women."

"I'll have to have a long talk with him tonight. I may wrestle a few steers in the future but I have a definite feeling that you'll be all the woman I'll have inclination to handle."

Jake's ready humor brought forth a responsive chuckle. Slowly sipping several glasses of the excellent wine, she gradually shared her interests with him. They were too enthralled with each other to waste time talking about their pasts. Only the immediate future seemed important.

Joy's heart responded to his continued homage. She hadn't known she was so in need of a man's affection. Her love escalated, building up until she was shaken with the intensity of such deep emotion.

After dinner Jake took her in and out of the casinos, at each one insisting she place several dollars in the slot machines, which she promptly lost. They viewed the gun collection and western memorabilia at Harold's Club, shared shrimp cocktails at the El Dorado, admired Fitzgerald's and Harrah's luxurious interiors. Joy stopped Jake long enough to watch curiously as a scruffy old man walked Virginia Street with a sign over his back and chest advertising he'd cash checks and make change. He looked out of place among the glitter.

When Joy pointed in awe toward a group of Japanese women playing blackjack at tables with a thousand dollar minimum bet, Jake mentioned that was where he sat.

"Every couple months or so I fly a few friends of mine up just to spread a little Texas money around," he explained casually.

"On a rodeo cowboy's salary?" she questioned, not believing him one bit.

"Certainly!" His chin raised arrogantly, deep brown eyes narrowing at her look of skepticism.

"Rodeo cowboys can earn many thousands of dollars a year, though I assure you competition takes its toll, with long flights and determination. Most crisscross the United States several times a month in order to hit all the bigger rodeos."

"I wasn't aware of that," Joy answered. It seemed she had a considerable amount of learning ahead of her.

"You've had enough sight-seeing, Joy." Jake grabbed her hand, striding out of the casino with determined steps. "We're going to spend some time enjoying a little country nightlife."

"Doing what?" Joy questioned impishly. She had never felt more exhilarated in her life.

"Honky-tonkin', you little city slicker," he drawled smooth as velvet.

"Lead on, cowboy!" Joy exclaimed, her eyes gleaming with happiness as they returned rapidly to his rented car. It appeared her western education would continue throughout the night.

Chapter Six

Jake drove to nearby Sparks, Nevada, easing the big car to a stop across from the Red Rose Saloon and Dance Hall in a parking area packed with pickup trucks. Joy could hear the muffled sound of western music as they walked toward the unpretentious building with its yellow neon sign.

"This is one of our favorite watering holes when we rodeo in Reno," he explained, letting his gaze sweep slowly over her animated features.

"Watering holes?" she teased back. Tilting her chin upward to easier see his sun bronzed face, she gave a low laugh. "That sounds like something from the lore of the old West."

"Touché, sweetheart. I keep forgetting you're a"—his glance trailed up and down her figure with devilish thoroughness—"fancy, uptown city girl, as my friend so aptly mentioned earlier."

With a gentle grip Jake retained his hold on Joy's arm as he drew her inside past the observant security guards. He paused, towering above most of the other men. His eyes narrowed, searching the darkened room for Louis and Jean. Not spotting them, he looked down to smile at Joy. His breath caught at the revealing look in her glorious jade-green eyes, elated that she appeared to have relinquished her heart into his care. She was so beautiful, he was torn between wanting to introduce her to his friends and rushing her back to his suite to stow away for his exclusive pleasure.

"Stay close, honey."

"I intend to," Joy answered, scooting nearer. She had no

intention of becoming lost in a dance hall filled with strangers.

Jake's hand cupped her shoulder, protectively hugging her to his side.

Spotted by a crowd of enthusiastic youthful cowboys unwinding after the end of a long rodeo, they were welcomed boisterously. While congratulating Jake on his lucrative win, they noticed Joy's wide-eyed, besotted look. Her expressive eyes glowed with love as she watched him shake each outstretched hand with friendly enthusiasm. None was the least surprised at her interest, knowing Jake's charisma aroused as much admiration in men as it did women.

Joy's heart pounded with excitement as she held on to Jake's arm firmly. Her ears filled with the echoing sound of an electric steel guitar solo. She looked around the vast dimly lit room. Unaccustomed to hearing pure country music, she found the beat compelling and easy to listen to. It was a rousing sound, as intriguing and individualistic as the cowboys' and cowgirls' dance steps.

With casual ease Jake placed his arm around Joy's waist, his fingers spreading beneath her hair to clasp her hip bone intimately. His deep drawl caught his friends' attention, the words filling them with glee.

"Drinks on the house tonight. This has been the best day of my life and I need help celebrating." He lowered his head to place a hard kiss on Joy's mouth before returning his gaze to the crowd around them.

"Since you all got slickered up for a little rompin' and stompin', you might as well get all likkered up too!" His voice was husky, each word clear, the rhetoric emphatically western.

Joy smiled, her entranced face lifted to gaze at Jake. She could still feel the touch of his mouth over hers. Even a brief kiss was devastating. Keenly aware of it from her lips to the tips of her boot-clad toes, she knew he was the most sensual man she had ever met.

His gentle teasing and fun-loving personality complemented her own sense of humor. He and his cowboy friends seemed to converse in a language all their own. Entertaining, earthy sayings, bluntly spoken and as individual and varied as their spokesmen.

Laying her head against his sleeve, she could feel the strength of his hard muscles beneath her cheek. Her long, flowing hair was swept aside as he lowered his head to place a lingering kiss over her ear. Her soft flush, along with his whispered declaration of love, went unnoticed in the shadowed, noisy dance hall. She lowered her lashes, uncertain how to respond to the desire in his voice and the blatant need showing in the depths of his darkened eyes.

"I want to share my fortune with all you freeloading, rodeo-riding riffraff," Jake announced, motioning for the cocktail waitress. He told her to take his friends' orders for the rest of the evening and give him their tab.

"Hot damn!" T.G. blurted out, dressed in a new wine and gray striped shirt and creased western slacks. "Now I can quit drinkin' the mix and start on straight whiskey, thanks to old Jake." He eyed the waitress boldly. "Hey, pretty lady," he called, taking a step forward. "Bring me a bottle of Jack Daniel's. I'm goin' to find a dark corner, sip some hundred-proof heart-starter, and seduce the first good-lookin' female that gets close enough to grab."

"Gravedigger must have rattled your cage when you bit dirt, T.G." Buck teased, one hand slapping him on the back. "You know you ain't allowed to have a bottle in here." He looked at the others with his chin held cockily. "You can damn well drink it glass for glass like we, more gentlemanly, sophisticated, bareback bronc riders, do." He ducked agilely when two ropers feigned punches for his tall story.

"Cool it, cowboy," the pert waitress chided when T.G. reached out to touch her. "I'm well aware that you guys thrive on fast times, fast horses, fast music, and fast women."

"Well, then, sweetie, how about me takin' you home later?" T.G. suggested, not in the least put off by her attempt to set him in his place.

"Fine with me," she laughed back. "Just check with the biggest security guard at the door. Since it's our first wedding anniversary tonight, he might have plans after work."

With one thumb casually hooked in a carved leather belt

while his eyes scanned their immediate area, Kenny laughed at T.G.'s sudden mood change and sheepish glance toward the entrance.

Spotting a girl alone, Kenny blurted out with confidence, "Observe my expertise, y'all. I found me a woman who looks hotter than a brandin' iron and prettier than a new-born foal. It's time I show her that I'm not only the best bull rider here, but beyond compare at dancin' too."

"Hell, Ken," Slim scoffed, "I've seen you tryin' to do the Okie Stomp and you dance like a stove-up, ring-boned old geldin'. If you want to see some fancy footwork tonight, watch me."

Standing with some difficulty, Slim braced his legs to balance his tall, thin frame. He had continued drinking during the day and it was definitely taking a toll on his equilibrium.

Kenny left the group to return seconds later. His arm was around the slender young girl in tight blue jeans who had drawn his eye. A bright low-cut sweater emphasized her small breasts as she stared up at his handsome features as if he were her dream come true.

Having heard Slim's derogatory remarks about his dancing, Ken scoffed raucously. "Watch you? You've already tripped down the steps twice and ran into each of the four pillars just tryin' to walk to the bar."

"Not my fault, Ken," Slim returned without embarrassment. "It's too damn dark in here for a cowboy bucked off on his head twice in the last two days."

Buck interrupted, bragging loudly, "I could teach each of you." Making certain they were all listening, he continued, "I figure dancin's just like bareback ridin'. You keep one leg each side and your mind in the middle!" Ignoring their loud gibes, he looked around searching for a girl as cute as Ken's.

Jake laughed, amused by his young friends' bantering and Joy's rapt attention while she studied them to see if they were serious. Their talk would go on for hours along with blatant flirtation with any willing woman. He had done it himself when he was their age.

His hand shifted, placed on the small of Joy's back beneath her heavy swathe of chestnut hair. He stepped sideways to stand directly behind her. Protected from the milling crowd by his size, he was able to ease her down the stairs to the tables, intent on finding Louis.

"Are all rodeo cowboys like your friends?" Joy asked, smiling at Jake over her shoulder.

"Most of them," he told her truthfully. "They're generally pretty aggressive and as competitive at a dance hall as they are in the arena."

"There's plenty of women to pick from," Joy returned truthfully. She had never seen so many attractive women or men intent on having fun. "This is a huge hall, Jake." It seemed to ramble on and on.

"I've been told it's the biggest dance hall in Nevada. It doesn't equal Gilley's in Pasadena, Texas, but it's a damn good substitute." His inherent pride in his home state unconsciously brought forth a quick comparison.

Jake recognized Louis standing at a table near the bandstand, his raised hand holding an empty glass. Guiding Joy along the edge of the dance floor, he worked his way forward to the table, with two empty chairs saved for them.

Louis smiled widely, his even teeth dazzlingly white against the deep tan of his face. Permanent laugh lines crinkling by his eyes attested to a ready sense of humor.

"It's about time you two got here, Jake. I'm dying of thirst." One large hand reached out to shake his friend's in greeting. "Since you promised to pick up the tab, I told the waitress to stay away until she saw me talking to a big obnoxious-looking Texan, then come running with her most expensive booze."

Louis had one heavy arm draped around the shoulder of a striking blond woman at his side. His broad frame dwarfed her tiny curvaceous body as he smiled at Joy before making the introduction.

"Meet the woman who keeps me on the straight and narrow, Joy. My wife, Jeannie. Pretty classy-looking old broad, isn't she?" he teased, leering at his wife's shapely figure displayed in a tight-fitting black sweater. "Too bad she's so jealous or I'd steal you from Jake." His voice lowered in a conspiring whisper. "I have to humor her or she's liable to boot me out and keep all my money."

Jean laughed at her husband's mischief and good spirits. After twenty-five years of marriage, she wasn't surprised by anything he said. Smiling at Joy, she scoffed his remarks aside.

"Ignore him, Joy. Louis loves to tease. Unfortunately he'll also get worse as the evening progresses and he gets a few more drinks under his belt."

She looked at Joy, remarking with flattering sincerity, "You have the most gorgeous hair I've ever seen."

"Thanks, Jean." Joy turned her head, aware of the lustrous strands waving around her shoulders. "I'm not used to wearing it hanging down my back like this. I keep wanting to confine it in a chignon again."

"It's certainly appropriate at a western dance," Jean assured her, looking at the many young women with loose, flowing hair, though none as long or beautiful as Joy's.

"Louis told me this was your first rodeo. How did you like it?"

"I loved it!" Joy exclaimed with enthusiasm. "All except the bull riding," she added as an after thought. "It scared me to death when T.G. was thrown by Gravedigger."

"I agree, I prefer reading or watching television now, having seen enough rodeos to last me a lifetime."

Jean eased away from Louis, smiling at the way Jake kept Joy close to his side, despite his carrying on an earnest conversation with her husband.

She agreed with Louis that it seemed impossible Jake was serious about any single female. She had watched women vie for his attention for years. He was so sensual and ruggedly handsome, they pursued him despite his aloofness at their overtures. Since his appearance in the background of the boot ad, he'd stayed on his ranch in a deliberate attempt to avoid their pursuit. She knew he was a man who liked to do the chasing and thoroughly enjoyed his bachelor life-style.

"Are you from Nevada, Joy?" Jean asked curiously.

"No," Joy answered, leaning into Jake's jacket-clad arm. "I live in Sacramento. Do you and Louis live in Reno?"

"No way," Jean spoke quickly. "We're avid anglers and

have a new home in Boulder City overlooking Lake Mead."

"That's near Las Vegas, isn't it?" Joy questioned.

"At the Arizona border and Hoover Dam actually," Jean pointed out.

"I'll bet it's beautiful by the lake." Joy had never traveled through the desert country, though the many photographs she had viewed were intriguing. It had been an interesting contrast with the lush green countryside around Seattle.

"It is, though I'm in the process of decorating now. I decided to leave our son, Jeff, and join Louis for a change of scenery. It's good to be by ourselves, though we both miss him, much to his consternation, I'm sure."

Joy's eyes turned wistful. Her childhood had been lonely and she had regretted being raised alone. "I always wanted a brother but my parents both died shortly after I was born and my aunt and uncle who raised me were childless."

Overhearing her conversation, Jake raised his fingers to Joy's gleaming hair, stroking the silken waves with loving tenderness.

"You won't miss a brother now, darling. I intend to supply you with a bunkhouse full of little cowboys of your own. About one a year ought to do it," he teased audaciously. He slanted her a daring look.

Joy covertly nudged his shin, warning him to behave. She knew her flustered reaction had amused him.

"Don't blush, honey," Jake asserted bluntly, bending to place an affectionate kiss across her brow. "Anyone with eyes in his head can see you're my woman."

Joy flushed at Jake's outspoken declaration. Her lashes lowered to avoid Louis's and Jean's silent observation. She could imagine how awkward they felt too, conscious that she had known their friend only a day. Jake, of course, was totally unperturbed by his hasty resolution.

The band members returned from a brief intermission and were a highly welcome interruption for Joy. She turned to watch them, fascinated by their flashy western clothing.

Immediately starting to play, their lead singer burst out with a nostalgic Hank Williams song.

Jake looked down at Joy, his brown eyes glittering with sparks of devilry. "Can you dance?"

"You bet!" she confirmed, tilting her head to smile at him.

"Ever dance country before?"

"No. I don't even listen to that kind of music."

"Quick learner?" he teased, reaching for her hand.

"Certainly," she shot back, enjoying his light banter.

"Good! If you're not a country music fan you'll be unfamiliar with the steps and I intend to trip the light fantastic tonight."

"With those feet?" Joy chuckled, eyeing his large boots.

"Of all the nerve! Now I'm really determined to show you some fancy footwork." Jake scowled, telling his friends to stand aside while Joy helplessly looked over her shoulder at them.

"Let's go, kid, your suburban education continues, starting off with some good old Texas Two Step!"

"You really are a braggart," Joy scolded, smiling at Jean and Louis before following without protest as Jake excused them. He tugged her onto the large dance floor, wasting no time to show her he was deadly serious.

Suddenly finding herself enfolded within his steel-hard arms, she melted against him, easily following his lead. With easy grace he circled the floor, his great body cradling hers intimately.

With the cry of "Your Cheatin' Heart" throbbing in the background, Joy's soft form became even more pliant, fitting the curve of Jake's hard masculine torso as she kept in step. His natural smoothness was not unexpected. Each motion of his body was performed with the agility of a top professional athlete.

She doubted if there was anything he couldn't do well if he really wanted. A soft blush tinged her cheeks when she thought of the sensual expertise of his lovemaking. His touch had been sure, knowing exactly how to give her pleasure during every embrace no matter how brief. Even in her fantasies he had been the perfect lover, she reflected humorously.

The band played continuously, each western song telling

a sad tale, sentimental, emotional stories of broken hearts or unsuccessful love affairs.

Joy never missed a step, smiling mischievously at Jake's look of consternation as they paused between songs.

"How am I doing?" she asked, her chin raised impudently.

"Fair," he told her, refusing to tell her she was like a feather in his arms. She followed his lead as if they had danced together for years.

"There's nothing to it, cowboy," she taunted, miffed by his refusal to compliment her instantaneous mastering of the steps.

"Think so, woman? Then prepare to get a quick comedown."

With Jake's warning still ringing in her ear, Joy concentrated on his back as he sauntered off to the bandstand. He had a fleeting conversation with the leader, handed him some money, and returned with a smug look on his face. After placing his jacket on a chair, he caught her hands.

Joy waited curiously, excitement welling in her breast when the heavy, pulsating beat of "Memphis" started. The floor filled rapidly, cowboys and cowgirls anxious to dance to the throbbing rhythm resounding through the huge hall.

Determined to show Jake that she could match his most intricate steps, she relaxed. Any inhibitions were overshadowed by her intense desire to prove she wouldn't be outshone on the dance floor by anyone.

As the drummer continued to pound out the heady beat, the steel guitarists picked up the tone with increasing volume and incessant rhythmic swing.

Joy's body became fluid, her long hair flowing out in a cloud of chestnut brown silk, radiating brightly in the overhead lights. Her sensual dancing drew all eyes as Jake's friends pulled back in open admiration to observe.

Each provocative movement of Joy's curvaceous figure was a delight to watch. Her jewel-toned eyes glimmered with happiness and the heady, teasing delight of proving she didn't need Jake's tutoring in everything. The hard, driving beat seemed to pulsate throughout her body, transferring its hypnotic effect to her feet. She was exhilarated, feeling there wasn't a song she couldn't dance well to.

Jake was stunned. With his years of practice he was barely able to match her nimble steps. There would be no teaching Joy to do the country swing or any other wild, dizzying traditional western dance. He became aware of the undivided interest they were creating and the extreme desirability of Joy's sensual body and motioned to the soloist to stop. Damned if he was going to outfit her in a formfitting blouse and skintight slacks so his libidinous young friends could get a thrill.

When his friends resumed dancing, after congratulating him and Joy on their electrifying exhibition, Jake drew her back into his arms as soon as he had eased his jacket back on.

"Showoff!" he scolded, bending to nip her earlobe.

"Me?" Joy clung to his arms, catching her breath while answering his gibe. "You're the one who paid the bandleader to keep playing that song over and over." She gave him a pert look, not fooled for a minute as to what his intentions had been. "Undoubtedly with the sole purpose of proving you could dance and I couldn't!"

Jake laughed, agreeing without shame she was right. "I must admit that for a city slicker you do a pretty good imitation of country-style dancing."

Joy swung her head back, glaring at him while thoroughly enjoying their exchange.

"Imitation? Why, you...you—"

Jake silenced her protest effectively by placing his mouth over her parted lips. It had been far too long since he tasted their honeyed sweetness.

Of their own accord her hands raised, clinging to his strong shoulders as she scolded that he never let her win a single argument.

"Hush, woman. Don't you know you're not supposed to interrupt a man intent on kissing?" His breath brushed her lips, interchanging with hers while she squirmed from his tight hold.

"Kissing?" Joy railed back, feeling him nuzzle her forehead. "It feels like you're trying to eat me."

"Hmm, you wanton female, that's one hell of an idea,"

he husked, raining kisses across her brow and down the side of her face. His whispered words of how he wanted to make love to her made her oblivious of anything but his touch despite their being surrounded by hundreds of dancing couples.

With both strong hands under Joy's waist-length hair Jake fondled her back seductively. He could feel her petite form tremble before her hands rose to clasp his nape.

They danced slowly, their bodies touching intimately in the darkened dance hall as one slow, pulsating song after another was played.

Joy responded to Jake, lulled by the plaintive music as well as the continued seduction of his mesmerizing personality. It was so heavenly being held close to this strong, masculine frame she wished the night could go on forever. With her face lying against his chest, the warmth of his body and clean male fragrance invading her nostrils, she knew complete contentment with a man for the first time in her life.

Listening attentively as the singer's husky words broke into her consciousness, her pulse throbbed in time to the unfamiliar beat of "Help Me Make It Through the Night."

Joy paid rapt attention as Jake pulled her closer and whispered in her ear. His heavy drawl caused her stomach to churn with emotion. Her heart pounded uncontrollably, blood speeding through her veins as each word cast a spell of love to the depths of her soul.

"Listen to the words, darling," he murmured, his voice muffled beneath the weight of her hair as he slowly let his tongue trace the entrancing shape of her ear.

"Which—which ones?" Joy asked, shivering as she felt the warmth of his tongue start to probe the sensitive interior.

Laughing huskily at her sudden confusion while she deliberated whether to pull away or strain to get closer, he raised his head.

"All of them. They explain exactly how much I need you with me tonight."

Joy's glance lingered on Jake's face. She could still experience the torment of his tongue erotically circling her ear.

It had wrought havoc with what little control she had left, causing a tremor from her neck to her toes.

"You've already managed to take the ribbon from my hair," she reminded him unnecessarily. Awareness escalated the moment his hand threaded through the luxuriant strands streaming down her back.

"True," he admitted, adding with assuranace, "though I have yet to enjoy its chestnut silkiness lying soft upon my skin."

He stroked her back, bending low to whisper, "I want to feel it on my naked body, Joy. Across my chest, my abdomen, and my thighs. With you above me, then me above you."

Joy buried her face against his chest. She couldn't meet the blatant need showing in his eyes. She felt hypnotized...by the setting and by the music...but most of all by the man.

"Who—who wrote the song?" she stuttered, vainly trying to break her trancelike state. Everything he did or said heightened her sensitivity to his continued seduction.

"Kris Kristofferson," he answered smoothly. "My favorite rendition is by Jerry Lee Lewis. Until I met you, it held no meaning other than the appeal of the poignant lyrics. Tonight I realized it was written solely for us."

Jake kissed her face reverently, his hands cradling her tight to his hard male form as they slowly circled to the sensuous beat of the band. The singer's deep voice continued into the microphone, the amplified sound reverberating around the hall in increasing volume. Jake's hand slid to Joy's rounded hips bringing her ever closer to his aroused body.

"Will you lay down by my side till the early morning light?" Jake drawled harshly. He shifted his hips to mold her figure like a second skin, from her soft, feminine curves to her shapely limbs.

Joy was too entranced to answer, knowing it wouldn't make any difference what she said anyway. Jake could sweep aside any protest with a single tender touch or expressive glance from thick-lashed brown eyes that could see straight to her soul.

She lowered her hands to grasp his lean waist, reaching beneath his open jacket until she felt the imprint of his silver and gold buckle. Pressing her breasts against the thin silk of his shirt, she could feel her nipples harden erotically.

Jake's back muscles rippled beneath her fingertips and a shudder ran up his spine the moment he felt the erect tips against his chest. The stimulation of her body touching his was the most stirring experience he had ever endured.

"Only you can help me make it through this night and all the nights from now on," Jake warned her, drawing a deep breath in an attempt to control his desire to rush her straight to his suite.

"Hush, Jake," Joy hinted in a weak voice. "I'm trying to listen to the words of the singer."

"Forget the vocalist and listen to me. I'll translate the most important phrases," he insisted, his warm breath fanning her forehead.

"She sings explicitly clear," Joy pulled back to explain when Jake lowered his head, breaking off her words with a searing, openmouthed kiss that left her knees trembling as she clung to him for balance.

The vast hall closed in on them, seeming filled with their love as, enfolded close, they danced. Jake's lips pressed tender kisses across the silky hair over her brow as she burrowed into the strength of his chest. Unperturbed they could be observed, he continued to make gentle love on the dance floor while indulgently whispering his approval of her heightened response.

Joy listened to Jake's intimate verbal expressions spoken softly into her ear. They caused a spasm of desire deep in her abdomen. His physical presence had cast a spell over her emotions even more mesmerizing than his photo hidden deep in her purse.

She listened to the last verse of his favorite song, agreeing silently that it was sad to be alone. Never, never would he have to plead for her to help him make it through a night. She was his. Body and soul.

Bowing to the audience, the lead vocalist put the microphone down before motioning to the band to switch to a faster, upbeat tune.

"Come with me, Joy," Jake commanded, breaking into her profound thoughts. "We've barely got time to get to the Marriage Bureau before it closes."

"Oh, Jake," she whispered, trying desperately to regain her senses. She gave up instantly. His appeal was so overpowering she couldn't have protested if she wanted.

"If you mean 'Oh, Jake, *no*,' then forget it," he warned firmly, taking her silence for dissent. "You can't say no to me now. You're mine for always and have been from the first moment I saw you."

He guided her through the crowded dance floor. Stopping briefly at the front bar, he handed the cocktail waitress a thick wad of bills, telling her it should cover his friends' tabs and give her a generous tip besides.

Without a single good-bye they slipped unnoticed from the dance hall. Jake tugged her across the vacant street, uncaring she had to trot to keep up with his long strides.

"If you don't love me now, my wife-to-be, you damn well will by morning!"

Bemused by his actions Joy remained silent as she was placed in his car and driven to downtown Reno. Surely there wasn't another man in the world like her cowboy. No other man she knew would have even fantasized about carting her off to get married the first day they met, much less carried out the plan without the least hesitation.

When he had completed the affidavit, Jake handed the clerk twenty-five dollars, took the envelope into his palm, placed it inside his suit jacket, and ushered her to his car. In moments he was stopping before a small house on the edge of town.

Jake's fingers never left her waist as he raised his left hand to knock loudly on a heavy wood door badly in need of paint.

The porch light came on before the door was opened to reveal an old man obviously awakened from his night's sleep. He peered at Joy for a moment, then looked up at Jake.

"Hi, Jake. Nice to see you again, thought it's pretty late for a visit, isn't it?"

"Not this time it isn't, Judge," Jake explained, making no apology for waking his friend. "I'm here to get married.

Today I found the woman I want for my wife and I want her wedded before dawn.''

"Okay, lad. Whatever you say. You always were an impatient cuss. Your request don't surprise me none at all.''

The old man scanned Joy over the top of his glasses. His pale blue eyes were intelligent, set deep in a face lined with character.

"Can't say as I blame you, Jake. You've picked a beautiful young lass to make your wife," he added kindly. "It's a good thing my brother's visiting me, young man, as even you'll need a witness to make it legal.''

Joy was completely bewitched by Jake's dominating personality, dazed by the about-face of the situation and his consequent pursuit. She barely listened as the judge performed a lightning-quick marriage ceremony.

On the way to Jake's suite all she could remember clearly was how comical the two old men looked with their sparse gray hair standing on end and their untidy nighttime attire. She snuggled into Jake's large body, leaning her head sleepily against the width of his shoulder. He parked the Thunderbird, smiling indulgently as he supported her slight form. From the garage they were whisked soundlessly to the upper floor. As the elevator stopped her legs trembled. Both hands clung tight to his waist using his strength for balance.

Joy was suddenly scooped into his arms and tenderly cradled. Slender fingers tightly clenched around his neck to accept his heated caress with an overpowering hunger that surprised them both. She was melting inside, aching with the need to express her love.

"Do you love me?" Jake questioned urgently, prior to claiming her ardent mouth again and again. Awed by her obvious physical pleasure, he shuddered in response. Her receptivity was stunning. The blazing message when her vivid eyes locked with his made him euphoric.

"Aren't you going to reply, Mrs. Travis?" he groaned against her lips.

Instead of answering, Joy reached up and kissed him with all the passion she had longed to express from the moment she first saw his photo.

"My God," Jake moaned intensely. "Your mouth was

shaped just to tell me what you feel in your heart." His hands trembled with the force of love surging through his body. "Your message spelled out 'I LOVE YOU' in capital letters."

Shifting her slight weight so he could open the door, he gave her a hungry look. "If I don't get you inside our room we're liable to be arrested. I can't take many more of your eager little kisses."

Joy blushed a faint rose, watching as Jake opened, then closed, the door before deliberately turning the bolt so they wouldn't be bothered.

"I love you, sweetheart," he whispered against her sensitive neck. "Are you prepared to help me make it through the night?"

At her shy nod, the need to communicate his feelings physically as well as verbally was fast becoming unbearable.

Without answering, Joy slid down the length of his body, holding his arms for balance when her knees started to buckle. She glanced upward, her eyes filled with the wonder of her feelings before standing on tiptoes to kiss his chin.

"I love you, my darling cowboy," she whispered tenderly.

She let him ease her jacket from her shoulders, curiously wondering when he gently pushed her into an armchair. She watched him, admiring his broad shoulders and glistening black hair as he pulled off her new boots, setting them one by one on the carpeting. Standing up, she intentionally avoided his arms when he reached out to enfold her.

"No. Not yet, Jake. Let me take a bath first, before we..." Her voice faded away, a tinge of pink coloring her cheeks at his careful scrutiny and amused look. Hiding her thoughts behind lowered lashes, she continued. "I feel dusty from walking around the rodeo grounds and dancing." Turning away, she whispered, "I won't be long, darling."

Jake's husky laughter followed her as she walked into the bathroom. He turned to mix a drink, a deliberate ploy to force his body to relax while anticipating making love to his young wife.

Chapter Seven

Joy leisurely stripped off her new clothes and wispy under-wear, annoyed at how unsteady her legs were. Her balance was precarious when she reached up to tie her long hair off her nape with a ribbon from her purse. An amused giggle burst out when the room began to whirl as she eased her body into the deep sunken tub rapidly filling with warm water.

My gosh, I'm drunk! she thought with self-disgust, re-calling how much liquor she had consumed since meeting Jake. *My husband will never believe I rarely drink. That I find overindulgence revolting, in fact.*

Opening a new bar of scented soap, Joy rubbed it into the washcloth until it was frothy with suds, contemplating her wanton behavior with serious concentration.

She loved Jake, there was not the slightest doubt about that. Possibly from the first moment she had seen his photo. The most unique, wondrous thing was that he re-turned her love equally. She could hardly wait to contact Rena and tell her the marvelous news.

Eager to be Jake's wife in the fullest sense and receive the ecstatic pleasure of his lovemaking, Joy vigorously scrubbed her naked limbs. There would be no waking be-fore fulfillment tonight. Erotic realism faced her, not tor-turing fantasies.

When she was finished, she rinsed the washcloth before splashing water over her back and shoulders. At the sound of Jake's footsteps crossing the bedroom carpeting, she hesitated, looking up when he opened the bathroom door. Instinctively she raised both hands to cover her breasts, her expressive eyes filled with intrigue, waiting to see what he would do.

Jake paused in the doorway, a brief flare of desire shimmering in his warm eyes before they narrowed to scan the beauty of her naked body for the first time. He stared openly, stroking with a fiery glance each golden toned curve with slow deliberation. She was gorgeous to him, her silky skin glistening with cleanliness, soft breasts high and taut with the beauty of maturity.

It was impossible to tear his eyes away. His loins ached to find release between her satin-smooth thighs. Unconsciously wetting his mouth with his tongue he was eager to take her lips again and again, to lower his mouth and taste and linger on every inch of her virtuous body.

With a trembling hand he set his drink on the tiled countertop, grabbed a fluffy bath sheet, and reached down to release the bathwater. No words were needed. His fine eyes expressed his thoughts explicitly as he bent to draw her slender body from the tub before wrapping her in the soft towel.

Joy's glance lingered on his face. She delighted in the touch of his hands as he picked her up and carried her easily into the adjoining bedroom. It made no difference to either of them that she was still soaking wet from her bath.

The silence was electrifying while she was slowly lowered to the carpeting. She stood barefoot, holding the towel over her breasts while watching with passion-filled eyes when he bent to pull back the plush bedspread and top sheet before turning back to her.

Innate shyness left when their eyes locked, his a warm earthy chocolate, hers a jewel-colored jade-green. The heady wonderment of finding the man she loved overpowered any thoughts of hesitation.

"I love you, darling," she whispered, unable to contain the words any longer. She reached her arms to him, entwining his neck within her loving clasp. The bath sheet fell unnoticed around her feet. Arching upward, her rounded body was soft and receptive as she clung to the man she had cherished for weeks.

"I should hope so," Jake crooned. "It'll make what I intend doing to you a lot more tolerable. The many ways I intend to express my love might shock you if you didn't.''

Joy pulled back from Jake's clasp, her fingers stroking his nape seductively while she slanted him a courageous glance.

"I'm old enough to not be easily outraged, darling," she pointed out softly. "Don't mistake lack of experience for lack of knowledge."

Jake planted a hard kiss on her parted lips, his voice filled with laughter. "Honey, unless you were tutored by a Texan you're totally unprepared for the loving you'll get. We're just getting started when most other men are finished."

Joy scoffed, her eyes alight with mischief. "Louis was right, my husband. You are a hopeless braggart."

"It's the truth!" he swore, his eyes drawn to breasts that were lush. They were full and satin smooth, thrusting enticingly upward. The rosy nipples slowly hardened to taut buds when he gasped at such arousing perfection. All humor left in a rush, changing to a carefully controlled, burning eagerness. He had never seen such flawless elegance.

His gaze slowly lowered, viewing a narrow waist that tapered to rounded hips above long shapely legs. He ached to rest his head on the flatness of her satin-smooth stomach, wanted to kiss her navel before lingering until mindless on the silky triangle of hair. With gentle fingers and searching lips he yearned to probe until she was on fire with the same needs that had tormented him since first touching her that morning.

"I think I'm being seduced by your eyes, darling," Joy told him in a throaty assertion. "Your glance is as arousing as your touch."

"Hmmm, woman," he growled low. "We'll soon see about that."

"Fair enough," Joy remarked, tossing her upswept curls aside to give him a pert glance. "I'll give you my honest opinion afterward."

She slipped her hands under his jacket, pulling his shirt out of his waistband eagerly. She could hardly wait to touch the velvet smoothness of his back muscles. She laid her head against his heaving chest, knowing her questing touch was the cause of his trembling.

Inhaling her sweet scent, Jake scolded huskily. "You're talking too much again, sweetheart."

With gentle fingers he removed the ribbon from her hair, his senses heightened further by the silky chestnut-brown strands cascading down her back to end just above the enticing beauty of her firmly rounded buttocks.

"Oh, Jake," Joy cried out, overcome by the pleasure of his hands stroking through her unbound hair.

"Shush," he drawled huskily. "I have much better uses for your mouth than words."

She moved closer, her lips raised upward in a gamine smile. Rising on tiptoes, she reached forward to touch his mouth, agreeing readily that kissing was much more important now than talking. He took her lips with such finesse, her breath caught in her lungs and her knees threatened to buckle. On and on he searched until her hands lowered, zealously helping him undress.

She gloried in his intense virility. It was what had attracted her from the first. She had dreamed of this moment for so long. There was nothing he could do to her she wouldn't accept with fervent eagerness, nothing humanly possible she wouldn't delight in. He was the one man in the world she sought passion from.

She stared openly at his broad chest, heavily covered with a mat of black hair that veed downward to his fully aroused manhood.

Joy pressed her body against him, delighting in the feel of his naked form. Every caress across her skin was a new experience, making her eager to receive them over and over again. She felt herself drawn to his bed.

Gently laying her on the cool sheets, Jake lowered his body beside her. As his fingertips cradled her nape, his mouth trailed a path over her sensitive skin.

"I know what arouses a woman, Joy," he murmured against her throat. "But I want to learn how to satisfy the woman I love...to give you pleasure and release. Tonight will be my first lesson in pleasing you."

"That sounds beautiful," she spoke softly, her breath warm against his bronzed skin. She loved it when he talked of his love; it was arousing.

"Loving you feels so good, Joy. So good."

"Hmm, it feels wonderful being loved," she gasped, his lazy exploration across her sensitive skin unbelievably exciting. "I never dreamed it would be like this, Jake."

She murmured Jake's name over and over while his hands roamed at will. There wasn't a part of her body that he didn't touch, each inch sensitive to his stimulating, unhurried stroking. She never dreamed such strong hands could be so gentle on a woman's body. It was a miracle the way he touched her hard where she wanted yet swept her skin with a featherlight touch in overly sensitive areas.

Her breasts burgeoned when he cupped them in his broad callused palms, tenderly lifting their weight upward to meet his lowering head. A tremulous gasp was torn from Joy's throat when she felt him take one nipple between his lips.

"Beautiful," he moaned. "Beautiful to look at and heaven to taste."

The moist pressure of his mouth alternated between breasts and increased as his tongue flicked back and forth. At that her stomach muscles clenched uncontrollably. She could feel the hot, exquisite pleasure flood into her loins, her aching for fulfillment increasing at an alarming rate.

His hands and mouth were driving her wild. She needed him. The body that had ached for his touch for long weeks held nothing back. Her hands and limbs seemed to have a life of their own as they sought the closeness of his. She gloried in his contrasting hardness.

Answering his touch with one of her own, she pushed closer when his hand left her breast to stroke the outer length of her limb. When his return route became more intimate, her heart lurched, palpitating in increased excitement. She tried ineffectively to still her quivering muscles when he explored her inner leg, ankle to knee, upward along her silken thigh until his hand reached the apex of her femininity. His fingers found each sensitive area, stroking gently to rouse her to the highest possible ecstasy.

With a deep moan, he lowered his head to touch his tongue to her trembling stomach. His mouth trailed a path lower, ever lower, until it replaced his exploring fingers.

Joy's fingers clasped his shoulders as she felt flood after flood of rapture spread throughout her body. The excitement of his mouth worshiping her body, the continuous flicking of his firm tongue, were almost more than she could stand. This was beyond anything experienced in her most stirring fantasies, far beyond any pleasure she'd ever dreamed.

Jake was driven by an urgency never endured, compelling urgency aroused by love for the woman beneath him. Moving with complete ease of motion, he entered her, slowly, patiently, despite his aching hunger.

"Jake! Oh, Jake." Joy's breath came in short gasps. His driving motions seemed endless. The most rhythmic, acutely sensory movement she'd every experienced.

"Oh, Joy, you feel so good." He shuddered when her body arched upward, silken thighs clinging to his hips as she cried out his name again and again in a final release.

Joy's mind swam, becoming hazy as she tried vainly to stop the overwhelming dizziness, until she was unaware of either time or place. With eyes closed, she released her grip on his arms, succumbing completely to the inevitable faintness she'd been holding back since her bath.

Jake's own body, damp with desire, still possessed hers. He felt her slender limbs gradually slacken in his passionate hold. Shock filled him at the realization that his wife had lost consciousness.

Easing away from the warmth of her body lying below him, he stared with love-filled eyes. Her lids were closed, heavy lashes making dark crescents on her flushed cheeks, visible in the dimly lit room. He watched wordlessly as her breathing slowed, him name murmured incoherently as she relaxed into a deep sleep.

Jake shifted his body away gently. He had planned to make love until dawn. She was the most sensual woman he'd ever been with and he wanted to make love to her over and over until they both succumbed to ardent fatigue.

He covered her soft, flawless body tenderly, his glance lingering on her voluptuous curves. Gritting his teeth, he rose and walked into the sitting room with firm determination. He stood at the bar, downed a double shot of whiskey, and shuddered as it hit the back of his throat.

Pacing the sitting room, he rubbed the nape of his neck

with one hand in a vain attempt to ease his tension. Several minutes passed before he went into the bathroom to stand beneath the cold spray until his heated body had cooled enough to allow him succor in sleep.

Briskly rubbing his sinewy body dry, he laughed bitterly. "This will be a tale even Louis wouldn't believe."

As the first light of morning dawned, Jake eased from Joy's languorous limbs. She had spent all night cuddling close in peaceful contentment.

The hours of frustration had taken their toll on Jake. His eyes were haggard. A stiff beard covered his firm chin with a dark shadow. He knew his endurance and patience had been tested unbearably. His control was stretched beyond limits he had felt capable of surviving throughout his long, sleepless night. He had wanted her more with each passing moment.

He rose, stretching to ease his stiff muscles before walking wearily into the bathroom. Within fifteen minutes he was showered, shaved, and dressed in clean jeans and a freshly laundered long-sleeved shirt.

Entering the bedroom, he looked down at his wife. Her tumbled, brown mane of hair glistened, partially covering her lovely face. He reached over to kiss her soft cheek, inhaling the sweet scent.

"I love you, Joy."

Jake checked his watch. Six o'clock. He left the suite and rode an empty elevator down to the lobby of the hotel. "Too damned early for what I want."

Jake was intent on finding a jewelry store open. He found a pay phone, cursing at the irritating amount of time spent calling until he found a jeweler to fit his needs. He was only interested in one that handled the finest stones, determined to purchase the most beautiful emerald and diamond engagement-wedding ring set available. He doubted seriously if it could match the shimmering beauty of his wife's wondrous green eyes.

His mind so filled with thoughts of Joy, Jake was startled to feel a hand on his arm. Looking up irritably to see who dared stop him in the deserted lobby, he scowled.

"Where are you going, Jake honey? I missed you last

night. By the time I got to the dance, the guys told me you had already left.''

Thirty years old, tall, and boyishly slim, Marie Thornton was an accomplished barrel racer who followed the rodeo circuit year round. Her brittle personality and promiscuous ways had turned Jake off from the first moment he met her, ten years earlier. Through the years she had made it clear she wanted to share an intimate relationship with him. Jake, never interested, had repeatedly avoided any situation where they might find themselves alone.

Marie looked at Jake, smiling invitingly as she moved closer. One hand reached up to stroke his muscled forearm. She had always coveted the thought of being Jake's wife. Despite being unsuccessful thus far, she was determined to get him. She refused to believe any man wouldn't be aroused by her charms.

Jake pulled his arm roughly from her clasp. Planting both feet firmly, he rose to his full height, arms crossed in an aggressive stance. He stared aloofly, his eyes turning hard and indifferent.

''Why should you care whether I was at the dance or not, Marie? You know damn well I've never been the least bit interested in your advances.''

His words were cruel and brittle, but he didn't care. He couldn't stand Marie and the sooner they parted company the happier he would be.

''I'm in a hurry,'' he pointed out rudely. ''I've been phoning for the last hour to find a jeweler open.'' He checked his watch, then declared, ''I have an appointment in ten minutes to purchase my wife's wedding ring.'' That should end her pursuit, he thought smugly.

''Your what?'' Marie screamed in shock. Stepping forward, she clasped his arm angrily. ''When did you get married and who to?'' she demanded furiously.

''None of your business,'' Jake told her bluntly, roughly shrugging free of her grip for the second time.

Undaunted by his behavior, Marie continued her diatribe. ''The guys mentioned you were hanging around some woman. My God, not one mentioned you wanted to marry her!''

Looking him over with disgust, she taunted, "After all, Jake, you never had to get married to get what you wanted in the past." She placed both hands on her hips, raising her chin in scorn. "What's the matter, cowboy, wouldn't she come across without a marriage certificate?"

"Shut up!" Jake warned her.

Marie's laugh was bitter. She glared with glittering blue eyes, her thin lips a red slash spitting vulgar words as she released the venom his constant rejection had aroused.

"You dare to give me the cold shoulder for ten years and then marry some cheap trollop within twenty-four hours of meeting her! I'll see you in hell for this!"

Jake's jaw firmed, his eyes dark and icy cold as he faced her with barely controlled anger. If she had been a man, he would have flattened her the moment she opened her mouth.

His manner was contemptuous as he furiously admonished her. "Don't ever dare call my wife a gutter name again or I'll forget you're a woman!" With a last chilly look he spun around to leave.

Marie clasped his sleeve, all pride leaving as she cajoled, "Please, Jake, don't leave me. It's such a shock to hear you're married. You always enjoyed women in the past without permanent ties. What's so different about this one?"

Her face had paled to a deathly white. Upset by his scorn, she felt sickened by the havoc his announcement had made to her normal composure. She desired him more than any man she'd ever known.

Giving her an autocratic glance over one broad shoulder he pointed out brutally, "I love my wife. That's what makes 'this one' so different. Joy's the only woman I've ever told I loved and the only woman I've asked to marry me," he challenged coldly.

Stunned by Jake's firm assertion, Marie faced him scornfully, her body tense with anger and her own frustration.

"I suppose you had that decrepit old alcoholic friend of yours, Judge McClellan, perform rites?"

"That's also none of your business," Jake added dryly. "You're forgetting the judge is my friend and I won't tolerate him being maligned." He gave her a searing look, a fist clenched at each side of his denim-clad hips. Arrogant and forbidding, his voice lowered to a deep explosion. "I find both you and the conversation equally distasteful."

Ignoring his warning, Marie cried out, "You fool! I would have given you anything!" Strong hands rested on her narrow hips. Short blond hair lay smooth around her nape, contrasting vividly with the wild fury in her eyes.

"How well I know," Jake chided cruelly. "The only problem was I never wanted it, did I?"

He brushed her aside and his long strides took him through the entrance without a backward glance.

Marie watched him, her features flushed with rage. She walked to the registration desk, her thin body taut with anger.

Giving the clerk a thin lipped smile, she inquired the suite number of Mr. Jake Travis. With the room number echoing in her brain, she took the elevator to his floor. Her mind was feverish with hatred for the unsuspecting Joy.

Determined to hurt Jake as he had hurt her, Marie knew the easiest way would be to cast doubts in the eyes of the woman he loved. Her strides were long as she walked to Jake's door. She was eager to confront his wife, then leave before he returned, well aware how dangerous his wrath would be.

Joy awakened slowly. Stretching her limbs across the comfort of the wide bed she was momentarily surprised to find herself in Jake's bedroom. She lay quietly, her mind in a turmoil of frustration trying to remember everything that had taken place the night before.

She eased carefully into a sitting position, moaning when intense pain pounded across her temples. Rubbing her throbbing head with cautious fingertips, she mused over the past twenty-four hours.

"Jake," she called in a throaty voice. Pulling the rumpled sheet over her nakedness, she found it hard to believe she was married. Only the day before she had thought it impossible she would find her fantasy lover.

"Jake, darling," she repeated, certain that he would come to her from the sitting room. The continued silence told her the room was empty. She got out of bed and looked through the suite and second bedroom. Wondering where he was, she returned to the bathroom.

She stared at her reflection in the mirror. Her hair was tousled, her eyes shadowed, and she had a terrible headache, but memories of Jake's lovemaking still filled her with pleasure.

Joy took a leisurely shower. She wanted to be fresh and clean when Jake returned. Letting the warm water ease the tension from her body, she turned slowly around as it ran over her smooth shoulders. Careful to see her hair didn't get wet, she had tied it high off her nape with ribbon.

She was drying off when she heard a hard, impatient knock on the outside door. Assuming Jake had forgotten his key, Joy wrapped herself in the soft bath sheet and rushed to the door. Her heart beat a rapid staccato against her breast in delight at seeing her husband.

She opened the door cautiously, peering around the edge to see a tall blond woman staring back at her. Taken aback by the obsessive hatred in the stranger's eyes, she hesitated, her hand on the knob.

Marie burst into the room, easily pushing Joy aside before slamming the door shut behind her. She glared enviously at the astonished young woman standing before her.

"Who are you?" Joy asked, her chin raised. She felt no danger, just curiosity that any woman would push her way into a stranger's room. Perhaps it was someone Jake knew.

Filled with loathing, Marie spitefully blurted out, "Jake's mistress!" Jealously taking in the outward composure, she waited.

Joy's eyelids flickered, a sudden paling of her face the only sign that the woman's words had pierced through her heart like an arrow.

"That puts me one up on you then. I'm his wife." She knew Jake was attractive but she certainly didn't expect to meet a former lover the day after her wedding.

"You stupid little bitch," Marie chided cruelly. "You're no wife! You're nothing but the victim of a deception that Jake pulls in every town he rodeos in."

"Would you like to see my marriage license?" Joy

taunted. No loudmouthed cowgirl was going to get the better of her despite her inner heartache. It was all she could do to keep her chin raised and meet the hatred with a glare of equal arrogance.

Taken back by Joy's self-possession, Marie spat forth, "What's a piece of paper? Judge McClellan will do anything for enough money to buy a bottle of wine, including a mock-marriage ceremony, Joy."

The impact of the woman's words hit Joy with the force of a bullet. How could she possibly know her name? She tried to gather her thoughts together in order to question her intelligently, but faltered, giving Marie the impetus she needed to continue her diatribe.

Thin lips clenched in a straight line, Marie jeered, "I can see you're still stunned by a night of Jake's lovemaking. The man's insatiable as I should well know, considering he just left my room after an hour's continuous passion."

Joy swallowed, the sound of her wildly beating heart nearly drowning out the shocking declaration. She had no idea how long Jake had been away. No man could be so base, especially the one she loved with all her heart. Holding the towel tightly to her breast, she waited. Better to let the woman spew forth her lies then calmly ask her to leave. Eyes shutting briefly, she prayed for Jake to return and end the nightmare of the past few minutes.

"Jake could seduce a marble statue if he set his mind to it," Marie continued with relentless persuasion. "I forgive his extra-curricular affairs. Years ago I found out no one woman—even one as experienced as I am—can satisfy his sexual needs. Women can't wait to get into bed with him, and men think he's some sort of god."

Joy suddenly remembered Kenny Madden's comment at the rodeo that a woman named Marie would be unhappy when she heard Jake had another interest. She had been so entranced by Jake, Ken's warning was soon forgotten. Inherent pride temporarily overcame the trauma of the bitter announcement. Straightening her shoulders, she held her chin high, refusing to be intimidated by anyone's vicious taunts.

"Get out, Marie!" Joy demanded, knowing she had correctly guessed her adversary's identity. Her eyes turned cold as ice, hoping she could outstare the older woman.

Ignoring the demand to leave, Marie's voice was filled with loathing.

"Jake's quite a vigorous lover, isn't he? It's been years now that we've been together," she lied, lowering her short lashes as if remembering intimate moments in the past. "Yes, making it with Jake spoils a woman for a more 'normal' man."

Shock waves tore through Joy's trembling body as she listened to Marie's blatant outcry.

"Since you appear to be finished explaining your indiscreet life-style, I'm ordering you to leave. What Jake and I did is none of your business," Joy stated with surface bravery.

Joy stared boldly into the hard face across from her, appearing outwardly in control as she reached for the doorknob.

"Don't think you're the first woman he claimed to love, or the first he asked to marry for that matter. Sex to him is just a game," Marie blurted out.

Marie turned as if to leave, then spun around to add an additional vicious thrust. "Only I know what's in the man's mind at night. He always thinks he's in love. Once possessed, he loses all interest."

Impaled by the cold blue eyes, Joy listened in silence. Would the pain never end? She was desperate to be alone and gather her thoughts together. Where was Jake? Why didn't he appear and assure her of his love in his soft-spoken drawl? Even convince her it was Marie's idea of a horrible joke. She pulled the door open and stood aside.

"It's nothing but a fantasy," Marie interrupted her introspection. "When morning comes, Jake always scurries back to me without a single thank you to the woman he's left, pleading remorse and begging my forgiveness."

"Get out of this room now!" Joy reiterated. Enough was enough. She refused to listen to another word.

Marie laughed. "He may look like a giant among men, but under that sleek, tanned skin with its single blemish, he's a jumble of insecurity and mental problems."

"Out!" Joy demanded, moving a step closer.

"You never had a chance holding him, with your dewy-eyed innocence. His kind of man needs a woman of experience." Her smirk was knowing.

'Then obviously you don't fill the bill either, Marie, if, as you say, he's constantly seeking diversions wherever he travels!"

Joy swept forward, anger giving her added strength as she pushed the larger woman out the door. She received little satisfaction in having had the last word. Turning the bolt securely, she leaned against the cool panels in a brave attempt to gather her senses.

The effort was futile as Joy fled to the bedroom. She covered her stricken face with fingers that refused to quit shaking. Her tightly held composure fled in a rush as she collapsed across the wide bed. Convulsive sobs racked her petite figure, the resultant tears streaming unchecked between her tightly clenched eyelids.

She was torn apart with indecision, not wanting to believe the horrible insinuations against the man she loved. Marie's evidence was too damaging. She knew so little about her husband, while the other woman detailed knowledge of their marriage that only Jake could have confided. Most damaging of all was her reference to the small scar in the crease of his groin. Joy had noticed it, had been surprised it was the only one after years of rodeoing. She had even touched it with her fingertip while they made love. Only a person in close intimacy would know of its existence.

She rose, wiping her eyes with the back of her hand. "God, help me," she cried pitifully. "Jake's not even my husband!"

Filled with shame at the way she had responded to each sensuous caress, that she had actually pursued him, sought him relentlessly to be her first lover, she prayed that time would blot out the burning memories of his perfidious love.

With fingers made clumsy by haste, it seemed to take forever to dress. She slipped into her sandals, grabbed her shoulder purse from the living room table, and prepared to leave.

Common sense warred with the strong desire to confront him. If he was with Marie, he wouldn't even return, she sobbed to the empty room. Vulnerable, she let increasing waves of doubt poison her mind until Marie's vicious lies completely overshadowed Jake's continued declarations of love. His intimate, passionate promises whispered such a short time before seemed a horrible fabrication from a depraved man when put in their proper perspective now.

Joy knew that even if he did appear she wasn't emotionally able to face him with the horrifying accusations reeling in her mind. She decided to leave.

Driven by the need to escape in haste, she glanced tearfully at her western outfit and expensive boots. She remembered how proud she had been to wear them, how smugly self-satisfied she felt to be Jake's woman.

The neat stacks of silver dollars lay untouched on the table as Joy fled the room. Her body was racked with unbearable pain. Nothing in God's world could ever force her to return to Reno. All her happy expectations had turned to bitter mistrust.

She had gambled for love. To her abject sorrow she found that, deprived of Jake, she was the most tragic loser of all time.

Chapter Eight

Joy glanced at her desk calendar, wondering how she had actually made it through the last thirteen traumatic months.

Whoever said time heals all wounds must have meant the physical ones, she thought wearily, knowing the passing months had not eased her feeling of remorse over Jake's perfidy. *Or my love,* she cried inwardly.

Her self-analysis was interrupted by the buzzing intercom on her desk.

"Joy, come into my office please," Brian requested.

"Certainly, Dr. Stevenson," she responded agreeably, walking from her small office to his luxuriously appointed private consultation suite. He was the newest partner in the prestigious offices of Tilson, Matthews and Stevenson, prominent greater Los Angeles area neurosurgeons.

Joy ignored Sally's questioning look. Her friend was busy in the receptionist's office and could learn what Brian wanted later. It was eleven fifty and Joy knew Sally would be irritated if her conversation with their employer lasted into their lunch hour.

She knocked once, then entered through sculptured oak doors. The plush interior, professionally decorated with bona fide antiques, was as affluent as many of their famous clientele.

"Yes, Doctor?" she inquired, stopped by his abrupt admonition.

"Brian! When we're alone call me by my first name."

"Brian, then," she agreed, standing just inside the opened doorway. "Did you want me to take dictation?"

"No. I wanted you to take pity on my insatiable need for your company and share lunch with me today. I've made reservations for two at Perino's," he told her, a hopeful smile tugging the corner of his mouth.

"Perino's! I don't have a dress in my wardrobe elegant enough for that restaurant," she exclaimed with surprise.

"You underestimate your beauty, Joy. One look at your exquisite face and you'd be admitted anywhere. Well?"

Joy looked at Brian's handsome features, but they failed to cause the slightest increase in her heartbeat. He was tall and slender with sandy blond hair and keen blue eyes. Despite his being articulate, a brilliant surgeon, and excellent company, she was unmoved by him emotionally.

Will I ever snap out of it? she wondered. *Am I doomed to compare all men with Jake and find them lacking?*

Joy shifted uncomfortably, aware that Brian desired her. They had dated occasionally the last few months. Whenever he pressed for a more intimate relationship, she had stopped him. She never offered an explanation, nor had he asked what her problem was.

"I can't, Brian. I've already promised Sally that we'd eat together."

Disappointed by her refusal, he complained roughly. "You have lunch with Sally every day, Joy. I'm certain she would survive if she ate alone this one time."

Noticing her haunted look, he hesitated. He had curbed his needs, hoping by biding his time she would respond to him freely. It wasn't working and each day it became harder to keep his feelings to himself.

"I can't break my promise," Joy explained adamantly.

Aware of her stubborn determination, Brian made an alternate suggestion. "I'll cancel our lunch reservations...if you agree to have dinner with me tonight."

"Sorry, Brian. I can't," she told him softly. "I'm going to wash my hair, then go to bed early."

"Your hair is sparkling clean, Joy. Other than having a headache, that's the most overworked excuse a woman uses."

Brian walked around his desk to Joy. He could smell the scent of her perfume and it stirred his blood.

"I'll be there at six o'clock," he said, refusing to take no for an answer.

His sharp tone surprised Joy into placating him temporarily.

"I'll give you my decision this afternoon, Brian."

She glanced at the time, frowned, then told him if she didn't leave, Sally would be furious and snap at his patients the rest of the afternoon.

Joy ducked out the door, sensing that Brian was about to take her into his arms. She knew she couldn't stand to have him touch her today. She hadn't been sleeping at night and was becoming increasingly irritable. Things that normally never bothered her were beginning to get on her nerves. She was well aware it was unlike her usual even disposition, especially with someone she liked.

She couldn't seem to help it, having to bite her tongue constantly to keep from telling Sally to shut up. Her constant chattering seemed to drive her up the wall lately.

Sally rushed down the hall, scolding Joy irascibly. "Jeez, I didn't think you were ever coming. Now we probably won't get my favorite booth or have time for dessert and I'm an absolute wreck I'm so hungry."

Not bothering to comment, Joy grabbed her purse and followed Sally's short, stiff-legged strides to the elevator for the smooth ride to the mezzanine floor.

They walked side by side from the air-conditioned medical building to be hit with a blast of hot air. Despite it being the end of July, it was unseasonably warm.

Hollywood, California, might be a world famous city of glamour and excitement, but, Joy thought, at noon it wasn't much different from others of comparable size across the United States. Its wide sidewalks were packed with people rushing to their destinations. She watched as they trod across brass-outlined stars set in ornate concrete, unconcerned the symbolism contained names of illustrious motion picture personalities. She agreed without remorse that the movie-capital mystique rarely lasted long.

An avid people watcher, Joy looked around her with interest. A few chic beautiful women elegantly dressed and coiffed, with deep tans and eyes concealed by wide, designer sunglasses, walked with practiced grace to expensive boutiques or exclusive restaurants.

The majority earned their living in shops or the prestigious office buildings towering over the street, dressed conservatively, and ate hurried, inexpensive lunches at franchised eating places.

Some professional men wore custom-tailored suits and clasped expensive, status symbol attaché cases in their manicured hands. They contrasted vividly with the profusion of sauntering youths, dressed in skintight jeans, outrageously printed T-shirts, and scuffed designer sneakers.

"Why so glum, Joy?" Sally blurted out, annoyed by her friend's silence and the fact that she hadn't volunteered what Brian said.

"Actually, I was thinking that I've never seen a movie star in person," Joy smiled, hesitating as they approached the intersection.

"Well, I haven't either, but I don't care. I've got a heck of a lot better chance of spotting one in Hollywood than I would in Modesto, where I spent most of my life."

"True," Joy admitted as they stepped down from the curb. She and Sally were caught in the middle of Hollywood Boulevard when the traffic light facing them flashed DON'T WALK in bright red. Embarrassed, Joy ignored the blaring horns and raucous comments and dashed to the safety of the crowded curb. Undaunted by the irritated drivers held back by her presence in the intersection, Sally made no attempt to hurry, a cross scowl furrowing her freckled brow.

Joy smiled at her refusal to be intimidated by anyone, waiting until she rejoined her before walking toward the coffee shop where they ate lunch together five days a week.

They passed several storefront windows, Joy's eyes scanning the familiar displays with detached interest. Suddenly grabbing Sally's arm, Joy stopped without warning before a fine art gallery's lone exhibit. She was unaware of the hasty steps taken around her.

"That painting!" she exclaimed. "Wait a minute, Sally. I have to look at it closely."

"Come on, Joy," Sally grumbled, jerking on her arm. "That's only a stupid western picture. You told me you can't stand anything to do with cowboys or rodeos." Peeved by Joy's behavior, she told her sharply, "You've already made us late for lunch."

"Go on, Sally," Joy told her, tugging her arm free without looking away from the painting. "I'll only be a moment."

Joy's eyes were held by the compelling oil painting of a bucking bull and fallen rider. She continued to stand in front of the fashionable gallery, staring at the single display. It was huge. At least three feet by four feet, she estimated, the heavy oak frame adding its own beauty.

Disgusted with Joy's attitude, Sally gave a flip of her short, curly red hair and continued down the sidewalk. Her only interest was in trying to get a booth in the busy café.

Joy stared, her eyes darkening, the green hue more vivid as her face paled. Bright midday sun reflected off the marble building, silhouetting her trim, shapely figure through the thin material of her white uniform dress. Her chestnut hair glistened, tiny tendrils escaping from the smooth chignon to frame her face and ears with delightful curls. She blinked back tears, her damp lashes momentarily hiding the pain visible in her haunted eyes. Memories of the past became lucidly clear, flooding her body with piercing torment.

That's Gravedigger! It has to be. Oh, Lord, please let me forget! she wept in silence. Her stomach muscles clenched, churning in raw, aching discomfort. The sight of a bucking Brahma bull had caused the hurtful images of the past to return with startling clarity.

I have to forget... for the sake of my sanity... I must! She reproached herself, recalling the long nights of torturing meditation while she tremulously prayed for sleep to release her from thoughts of the past.

She drew a deep breath, quivering lips soundlessly pleading for composure. Unbidden tears trickled down her face. She wiped the moisture from her cheeks surreptitiously, straightened her shoulders, took one last survey of the painting, and walked away.

With chin held high, she entered through the opened

glass doors, stepping around people paying the cashier, in search of Sally. Spotting her friend's raised hand, she strode forward and slipped into the roomy plastic booth with a weary sigh. The cooled air was a welcome balm on her heated cheeks. She intended to forget the painting. She had to!

"What's the matter, Joy?" Sally questioned. "Surely the sight of a stupid cow stomping a cowboy into the ground doesn't appeal to your city tastes?" She stared at Joy's pale face curiously. "I distinctly remember you telling me months ago that you detested anything to do with rodeos, so why the concern now?"

"I did say that," Joy admitted honestly. "There's something about that particular painting that fascinates me."

What a liar I've become, Joy reflected. *It's easier to prevaricate than to admit the happiest day of my entire life was associated with a rodeo.*

"Well, country life of any kind doesn't turn me on! Especially when we're late eating our lunch," Sally blurted out, looking around for a waitress.

"Didn't you know country's cool now, Sally?" Joy teased, making a brave attempt to regain some of her former sense of humor. "You'd be surprised how many single women catch 'big-hat fever.'" She remembered Jake telling her that was what they called it when a female was turned on by cowboys. She had found out the hard way that there was no known cure.

"Not this kid. I like the city. Expecially this one. Hollywood, just the way it is, suits me fine—crowded, smoggy, exorbitantly expensive, teeming with weirdos, full of attractive, unattached girls competing for every straight guy here... and all!"

Joy laughed softly, knowing Sally meant every word she said.

After their lunch was ordered, Sally blurted out, "I can understand you being fascinated with Clint Eastwood or Christopher Reeve, but not a smelly cow."

"Look again, Sally," Joy teased. "That smelly cow is obviously a bull. The artist paints so terrifyingly lifelike I could feel the animal's destructive power. I actually felt distress for the injured cowboy sprawled facedown on the arena dirt underneath the bull's heavy cloven hooves."

Sally was momentarily speechless, hushed by Joy's intensity and apparent knowledge of the sport.

Joy's voice shook, her dark lashes lowered to shield her tumultuous thoughts.

"There's blood on the fallen rider's back and leg. His clothes are torn and he's disabled. The bull's massive head is lowered sideways, ready to gore him with wicked blunt-tipped horns."

She clasped her fingers together in her lap, trying to stop their sudden trembling. It was painful to even talk about the helpless cowboy, though she knew it was only a figment of some artist's mind.

"It's such a cruel, brutal portrayal. The deep colors are realistic, the details so authentic, I can almost inhale the pungent dust of the arena and hear the shrill screams of the spectators watching helplessly from the stands."

"How come you know so much if you hate rodeos? I assumed you hadn't even been to one," Sally inquired, looking at Joy with inquisitive, hazel eyes.

"I went to one...last year," Joy whispered hesitantly. "I've never forgotten the sounds, the smell of the animals, the feverish excitement...or the contestants."

Joy's words were interrupted by the harassed waitress hurriedly placing their lunch on the table.

"Where are you and Dan going tonight, Sally?" she asked. She was genuinely interested in hearing her friend's plans despite her own inner turmoil. Stirring artificial sweetener into a tall glass of iced tea, she forced her mind to reject thoughts of the past.

"To a movie probably. I'd rather go to his place but he's afraid I'll compromise him."

"Isn't it supposed to be the other way around?" Joy smiled. "The man's the one who usually endangers the woman's reputation."

Sally shrugged her plump shoulders, taking another bite of her double cheeseburger. "Not with Dan," she complained, talking with her mouth full. "He's kind of inhibited. Are you gong out with Dr. Stevenson?"

Joy crumpled her napkin with nervous fingers, then laid it on the table. She pushed aside her untouched tuna salad before answering.

"I don't feel like male company tonight."

"Didn't he lure you into his office to ask you out?"

"He did want a date," Joy answered indifferently. "I'm in a solitary mood today and refused him."

She looked through her purse in search of her billfold.

"You're crazy. Dr. Stevenson is wild about you. He's gorgeous, intelligent, and assured of great wealth. The patients and staff fawn over him constantly, yet you ignore him as if he's a creep."

"I don't really," Joy interrupted.

"You do too! The man can't keep his eyes off you. Hands too, if you'd let him," Sally told her bluntly, not understanding Joy's reticence or refusal to respond to his overtures. "My mom would flip out if I could snag a graduate of medical school."

Joy counted out the correct change, laid a tip on the table, and prompted Sally to hurry.

"It's almost one o'clock and this is billing week. Thank gosh next month we go to computers and that I took two years of BASIC in college." Noticing Sally's quandary, Joy explained, "Beginner's All-purpose Symbolic Instruction Code. It'll take some brush-up training before I'm competent again, I imagine."

"Better you than me," Sally said dryly, unhappy she hadn't had time for a hot fudge sundae. She paid her bill, then mimicked in a high reedy voice. "'Yes, Mrs. Smith. No, Mrs. Smith. Certainly, Mrs. Smith.' Our darn phone never stops ringing."

"If it didn't, we'd be out of work," Joy reminded her with a grin as they left the café to weave their way through the crowd.

She and Sally walked briskly the two blocks to their building. After taking the elevator to the seventh-floor offices, they parted to continue their routine duties.

Joy applied fresh lipstick, smoothed her hair as much as possible, then placed her purse in the bottom drawer of her desk. She was ready to start work. Reaching toward the pile of file folders at her elbow, she opened the top folder on the pile at her elbow and checked the unpaid balance. Her fingers rapidly covered the keys as she typed.

Neat and efficient, she enjoyed her work, taking pride to see she always did an excellent job. It was her sole responsibility to see that insurance and industrial accident forms were promptly and accurately completed. In addition, she took dictation, answered private inquiries, and handled monthly billing. She was well paid, skillfully trained, and pleased to be working in pleasant surroundings. It was a direct contrast to the hectic conditions of her uncle's small general practice clinic, which she had managed so many years.

Looking up at the sound of her office door opening, she thanked Brian as he set a cup of coffee on her desktop. She glanced at the dainty gold watch strapped to her left wrist, exclaiming in surprise.

"My gosh, I had no idea it was that late, Dr. Stevenson."

She sipped the hot coffee appreciatively, before setting the cup down. Relaxing against the back of her padded chair, she wiggled her shoulders in an attempt to ease the tension from hours of uninterrupted typing.

Brian watched her, his hip propped on the corner of her cluttered desk. "You called me Doctor again, Joy," he complained with obvious annoyance. "My God, honey, I've taken you to dinner, on drives along the coast, to movies, been to your apartment, eaten at your table, and—to your chagrin—tried to hold you close. Are you always going to act this formal with me?"

Taken aback by his outburst, Joy stared at him speechlessly. *He's right*, she thought. *I've used him as a balm, when he deserves so much more*.

Brian looked boldly at her stunning, sensuous figure, telling her truthfully, "You're a passionate-looking woman, Joy, yet you always act so reserved. You dress conservatively, wear your glorious hair in a damn knot on the back of your neck, and avoid physical expression at all cost."

His voice deepened as his emotions surged forth. "My medical training helps me see below the surface. A woman with soft, kissable lips and compassionate personality like yours has to be a sensual, loving person."

He inclined his slender body forward, staring at Joy with keen, intelligent eyes. He openly admired her full, rounded breasts as she leaned back in sudden confusion, not wanting to acknowledge the passion rising in his eyes.

"You look on me as a doctor, Joy, forgetting I'm first and foremost a man. You are a beautiful, desirable, extremely troubled woman, and you stir my senses."

"Don't talk like that, please! It feels awkward to call you Brian at work and I—I feel uncomfortable when you pay me personal compliments even knowing you think I'm uptight."

She shifted uneasily. "Thank you for the coffee," she said, prompting him to leave her alone.

"I didn't come in here to supply you with caffeine, which isn't good for you anyway. I came to confirm our dinner date tonight."

He stood up, his white uniform jacket pristine, his face serious as he waited for her answer.

Joy looked at Brian's pale, smooth hands, irrationally comparing them with Jake's deeply tanned, work-roughened hands and long hard fingers that had touched her so tenderly.

She was tired, her mind weary with the unsuccessful task of holding back a maze of torturing images. Her reply was a weary rejection.

"Sorry, Brian. I don't want to take up any more of your time."

Disgruntled with Joy's answer, he paced the small room, before retorting wryly, "I refuse to take no for an answer. If you won't eat out, we'll eat in. I'll pick up some Jewish food and bring the dinner to you. You can even wash your damn hair, if you have to. See you at six!"

"No!" Suddenly changing her mind, Joy hesitated, watching as he stood in the doorway about to protest her argument.

Brian will help keep thoughts of Jake from my mind and tonight I can't bear to analyze my feelings, she concluded.

Joy smiled, her expressive eyes meeting his with a poignant plea for his understanding. "You win, Brian. Make it seven, though. I have some shopping to do on the way home."

"Fine. Lay out two large plates and some silverware." He returned to his office, shoulders held proudly straight.

Sally's happy voice calling out reminded her a short time later that it was five o'clock. Her mood always improved at the end of each workday. "Time to shove off, Joy. Did he want another date?" she questioned with envy.

"Yes," Joy admitted reluctantly, automatically clearing her desk. She covered the typewriter and gathered her light sweater. With her shoulder bag held tightly to her side, she strode from the office, eager to say good-bye to Sally and get away from her incessant chatter.

"You haven't heard a word I've said," Sally complained to Joy. "If you want my opinion, you've been acting weird since you saw that painting at lunchtime and I think you're getting the flu. Your face has been pale as a ghost all afternoon."

"I'm fine," Joy answered agreeably. "And sorry to be rude. I'm rather preoccupied today." They waved farewell, parting as Sally scooted into her car.

Joy breathed a sigh of relief at being alone, turned from the parking lot, walked back to the front of the office building, out the side doorway, and across the boulevard.

As if guided by unseen hands, she found herself in front of the gallery window, staring at the canvas that had been in the forefront of her mind all afternoon.

A feeling of pain and terror caused her nerves to pulsate wildly as she stared at the injured cowboy. It was uncanny, the feeling of compassion aroused by a scene that was purely a figment of some artist's imagination. She searched for the name, curious to see if she recognized it. She did have a limited knowledge of the old masters as well as an appreciation for more modern paintings and sculpture.

All she could find was a brandlike marking in the lower right-hand corner. Determined to seek the artist's identity, she entered the plush interior, her steps soundless on the deep carpeting.

A slender, dapper man appeared from the rear of the gallery, his pleasant smile welcoming as he approached.

"I'm Mr. Hanson, the manager. May I help you?"

Joy introduced herself and inquired about his front display.

Without answering, he motioned for her to follow, leading her to a large room separated from the rest of the gallery by ornate metal grillwork. He stood back, watching curiously as Joy caught her first glimpse of his exhibit.

She was silent as she entered the room to gaze wide-eyed at a dozen paintings. Each was brilliant, painted in rich, earth tone shades, explicit with vigorous detail and brutal in its authenticity. The artist's style was distinct and forceful. They were powerful works depicting rodeo scenes etched permanently in Joy's brain.

Bucking horses with wild flowing manes and tails reared and plunged. The riders leaned back, one arm raised, both legs outstretched with blunt spurs touching their horses' shoulders. Their faces expressed the determined fearlessness necessary to stay the limit and win.

Roping horses—with broad muscled chests straining, slender legs reaching forward, heads extended, ears flattened back—raced at top speed. The riders leaned over their withers, piggin string held between their strong teeth, swinging a wide loop as the husky calves raced frantically to get away.

Joy's heart hammered in agony as she gazed at a bulldogger slipping from his horse's back to grasp the horns of the steer at his side. The hazing horse and rider were alongside to keep the steer traveling in a straight line.

Abruptly turning away from that painting, Joy bit back the urge to cry, moving quickly to the next composition.

"Who is the artist, Mr. Hanson?"

Standing beside her with his hands clasped behind his back, he shook his head. "I don't know, Miss Sanders. I deal only through the man's agent. He implied the man is an isolationist. His logo is a brand with the letter J in the middle. His last initial, I believe."

"Is the canvas in the window sold?" Joy questioned, her voice faltering momentarily. "It's horrifying and brutal but to me it's the most compelling work. I saw a bull like that last year that frightened me so I'll never forget it."

"That painting is for display only," he told her with regret. "A shame too, since I've had several bids on it already. I held a private showing this weekend and within three hours had sold out."

"I knew they had just come in. I check your window each weekday on my way to lunch. Isn't it unusual to sell that fast?"

"Considering most were in the five figure range, it's startling," he pointed out proudly. "My customers know quality and were quick to see the appreciative value."

Joy noticed the time, thanked the manager, and rushed to her car. Within minutes she was maneuvering her bronze Volkswagen Rabbit into her West Hollywood apartment garage.

The doorbell rang as she was hurriedly slipping into a pair of comfortable green designer jeans and a cool print silk blouse.

Tucking a wayward curl behind her ear, she opened the door. Dr. Stevenson stood nonchalantly balancing a large sack in one hand and holding a bottle of wine and bouquet of flowers in the other. He looked at ease and handsome, dressed in light blue slacks and navy print sport shirt. His smooth face was freshly shaven, his hair glistening clean.

"Doctor, er, Brian, how lovely," Joy welcomed him warmly. "Come in, please. I just arrived home and haven't had time to set the table but the coffee's hot and fresh."

They talked comfortably as she got out plates and he placed cartons informally in the center of the table.

"I picked up our dinner at Brownie's Deli on La Cienega Boulevard," Brian commented pleasantly. "It's my favorite place to buy kosher food."

As Joy watched he opened a carton of fresh-made coleslaw, unwrapped a package of thin sliced corned beef, then another of lean pastrami.

"You really splurged for two people," Joy told him gently. It had been an unsettling day and she was grateful for his quiet thoughtfulness. She poured their coffee, the pungent aroma filling the small room with a homey smell.

"You bought enough for a party," Joy teased as Brian continued to pull cartons from the sack.

"A party for two," he agreed. "Sit down, honey, and let me serve you," he prompted, aware of her tensed nerves.

She relaxed, watching in amazement as he unwrapped the rest of his purchases.

There were fresh baked bagels, still warm from the oven, and cream cheese and lox to enjoy with them. Thin sliced New York-style sour rye bread and crisp green kosher pickle slices, plus a small plastic container of her favorite treat: chopped chicken livers. For dessert he had purchased *luchen kugel,* a unique noodle pudding, filled with diced fruits and spiced with cinnamon and nutmeg.

Brian sat across from Joy, his eyes filled with concern as he waited for her to begin eating. "You first, love," he urged.

Joy smiled graciously, took a spoonful of salad, a pickle slice, and some chopped chicken liver. She watched as Brian piled numerous pieces of meat between two slices of rye bread.

"What we don't eat, you have to take home," she told him. "I couldn't finish all this in a month."

"Fair enough," he admitted between mouthfuls of his tasty sandwich. "A couple midnight snacks and I'll have every container emptied."

His keen eyes took in Joy's increasing distraction but he decided to wait before questioning why.

Joy sipped her coffee, annoyed to see her hands begin to tremble. It was ridiculous, she thought uneasily. Despite Brian's easy friendship she couldn't settle down. The graphic oil paintings had made Jake's presence so real it was interfering with her ability to relax.

It's all been bottled in so long, she thought. *All the shame and all the sadness. Worst of all is the terrible unending longing for Jake's company.* At times the loneliness seemed unbearable.

Brian reached for the wine, intending to pour each of them a glass, when Joy stopped him. He looked at her quizzically.

"Don't you drink at all, Joy? You've never consumed a drop of liquor while with me."

Joy frowned in contemplation before answering. "I don't

appear to have a head for liquor. I haven't touched any alcohol for over a year now." She gave him a tender smile. "It was kind of you to bring it, though, along with the food and flowers."

Joy looked in silence at the deep red unopened petals of the rose buds for a moment. Gathering the plates, she stood up and took them to the kitchen sink. She had her hands in the sudsy dishwater when Brian came up behind her.

Her body stiffened the moment she felt his hands touch her waist. Every nerve in her body quivered with tension when his head bent and he placed his mouth on the side of her neck. Unable to bear his touch, she jerked away and, turning around, glared angrily at him.

"Stop that, Brian! Don't ever dare touch me again. I—I can't stand to be handled." Her emphatic outcry stunned him.

"I was only going to kiss you!" he exclaimed harshly. "What's the matter with you? I'm not an ogre but you won't let me get near you."

Displeased by her coldness, he pulled her roughly forward and kissed her face hungrily, holding her squirming body with fierce determination. His control left rapidly when he felt her breasts touch his chest. Moving his mouth over her tightly clenched lips, he beseeched her to respond to his passion.

Joy held herself stiff, silent, and unresponding, but he continued to kiss her with surprising force. As she strained to get away, she felt his hand move toward her breast. Repulsed by the thought of anyone but Jake fondling her intimately, she pulled away.

Brian regained control of his emotions. He looked at her with solemn eyes, his erratic breathing slowly returning to normal. His hands rose in dismay.

"Okay, Joy, you win. I seem to turn you off as much as you turn me on. If you can't respond to the man in me, maybe you'll relate to the doctor," he reflected ruefully.

She faced him, her eyes stormy with anger over his unexpected lack of restraint. She straightened her blouse, unsure what to say. She had never thought he'd force his attentions on her. Her skin still crawled from his touch, though she admired him more than any man she knew. Her actions were paranoid. Only one man had ever pierced the frigid barrier she imposed. She didn't understand her reasons so how could she make Brian understand?

"I've dated you, observed you, and wanted you since I first became a partner in the clinic. All that time you've remained unmoved by any personal advances I've made."

Avoiding Brian's eyes, Joy nodded he was right. But he wasn't finished admonishing her and demanded she hear him out.

"I know you aren't dating anyone else and frankly I'm tired of being patient with you, Joy. You act as if I'm loathesome. You didn't even realize the symbolism of the red roses I brought you," he retorted bitterly. "I love you, Joy, yet you can't see me as anything in your life but a friend and employer."

She let Brian cup her shoulders, her face lowered in shame, knowing he spoke the truth. He drew her into the living room, and she was gently seated in a comfortable easy chair.

He sat across from her, his voice calm with resignation.

"Talk to me, Joy," he coaxed gently. "Are you frightened of men? Afraid of the sexual relationship a man wants of you?"

"No...not really. I like you more than any man I've met this last year, Brian." Her eyes held his, pleading for his comprehension. "I freeze up inside when you hold me. It has nothing to do with you personally," she assured him. "I'm that way with all men. Please...please leave me alone."

She sobbed quietly, her face buried in the palms of her hands. Her body was racked with pain. Trying hard, she gained a modicum of control, raising tear-drenched eyes to him.

"Forgive me," she pleaded. "I don't know what's the matter with me today. I feel so touchy and unsettled. It's not your fault, Brian, believe me."

He gestured impatiently. "Didn't you even listen to me, Joy? I told you I loved you. I also need to know if there's a chance of it being returned. I can't go on any longer looking and not touching."

His intelligent face was strained, eyes deeply serious as he continued slowly. "It isn't normal to continue a platonic association if one or both partners care deeply for the other. You're a mature woman and must feel the need for release of your emotions through a giving relationship too. I desperately crave the satisfaction you can give me in your arms."

Unable to verbalize an answer, Joy assented with bowed head that she understood.

"Has a man mistreated you in the past?" Brian asked, each question carefully chosen to delve into her innermost feelings. "Are you a virgin, Joy?"

She raised her tear-streaked face, blanching under his intent scrutiny. "No, Brian." The pain of her answer was obvious. "I, er, I lost that, among other things, months ago," she slowly whispered, unshed tears shimmering in saddened eyes that mirrored pain.

"When did this traumatic event take place?" He waited for her answer, leaning against the back of the couch. His voice soothed in an attempt to calm her shattered nerves. "Tell me about it please. Confide in me as a doctor."

"I—I can't." She had never even confided in Rena. How could she possibly explain to Brian what happened?

"Were you raped?" She showed the same nervousness that many victims he'd treated in the past exhibited, the same fear of intimacy.

A harsh laugh was torn from her throat, her eyes meeting his boldly. "God, no! It was a totally victimless crime with equal guilt on both sides."

"Talk to me. I need to know after this outburst." It was nearly impossible to restrain his curiosity about the man she had given her virtue to. Her statement was startling, to say the least.

"It will probably help to talk with you, Brian, but it's not fair. I like you, but I could never love you," she told him truthfully. "Do you still want to hear?"

"Of course." Scanning her lovely features with regret, he implored, "Think only of me as a doctor who is interested in all things connected with the functions of the human body. Both physically and mentally.''

Joy clasped her hands together to stop their trembling. She began to speak in a soft, faltering voice.

"I've never told another soul ... and I don't know where to begin."

"At the point in time your problems commenced," he coaxed urgently. She looked so vulnerable with her slender legs curled beneath her on the soft chair, his heart was torn, broken, yet heavy with the awareness she would never be his.

Chapter Nine

"Thirteen months ago I saw Hollywood, California, for the first time."

Joy licked her lips nervously. It was going to be difficult to explain her mood prior to meeting Jake. Brian would never understand how barren her life was. Looking back, she might have been temporarily unstable. It certainly seemed crazy to her now that she had avidly sought a total stranger to be her first lover.

"I was raised from childhood by an aunt and uncle who had recently moved to Sacramento from Seattle. This unexpected move fit in with my plans perfectly. That is until I found out I was left in sole charge of establishing a new clinic while my relatives returned to their hometown on an extended vacation."

Joy raised her eyes, pleading with Brian to let her continue uninterrupted.

"By the time the third weekend came around I was climbing the walls and rebelled. I was in a lonely, reckless mood and depressed to think there wasn't a single person I could contact for company. My friends were scattered all over, intent on their own pursuit of happiness as they enjoyed their vacations."

Joy frowned, remembering her bad case of the blues at the time. She had expected to seek Jake the first weekend but the heavy work involved in setting up a new medical office had detained her day after day.

"I had an important reason for wanting to go to Reno. My car was still in Washington so I decided on the spur of the moment to take one of those bus tours advertised so often in the local papers. Its schedule fit in perfectly with my plans."

Brian listened, wishing she would quickly get to the point where she met the man. Bitterness filled his mind, thinking of her in bed with anyone other than himself. His long celibacy since meeting her was beginning to interfere with his work, yet he couldn't imagine finding release from another woman. No one would ever compare favorably. She was the most appealing woman he'd ever known.

"Within moments," Joy spoke, "a reservation was made and I was on the bus to Nevada. Though it wasn't my purpose, I couldn't believe it when I was actually in the middle of all the glitter and glamour.

She looked across at Brian with vivid eyes, her hands raised expressively.

"There was a mix-up with my hotel reservation and I was subsequently booked into a rather plain motel room on Center Street, but I didn't really care. It was close to Circus Circus and I was outside walking toward the downtown area within minutes."

It was all so lucid to Joy relating her trip. She remembered how exhilarating the clean air was and the vivid blue color of the sky. She had been so eager to find Jake.

"I was so excited, Brian. Entirely intent on my original purpose for being there, I saw only the shiny surface attractions. The depressing side street pawn shops or their reasons for being didn't touch me, nor did I bother to wonder about the occasional appearance of people with sadness and desperation etched into their faces. All cities had this and Reno was no different. The hundreds of tourists walking the sidewalks looked as excited as I felt."

Joy's hair shone in the soft light of a table lamp, her expression becoming dreamy as she continued to reflect back to the happiness at the beginning of her trip. She was unaware Brian watched with heightened interest as her look changed to despair, her thick lashes lowering in a vain attempt to stop the tears that trickled down her cheeks.

"Joy, are you okay, honey?" Brian asked, bringing her abruptly back to the present. "You've been sitting there without saying a word for several minutes and you're quivering."

Choking back sobs, Joy apologized for her behavior. "I'm sorry, Brian. I was thinking to myself. I can't bear to relate all the intimate details. They're too private." She wiped at the tears indifferently.·

"If it's too painful for you to remember the past, don't try now. Why don't you briefly outline what happened, then I'll leave you alone. Maybe an early night will benefit you better after all," he added, sympathetic to her distress.

Pleased at his empathy, Joy leaned back into the soft contours of her one easy chair, telling him calmly, "In as few words as possible, I'll tell you what happened in my life a year ago that affects my future relationship with any other man."

"Okay, Joy, that's probably best now anyway," Brian said, resting comfortably against the back of her well-cushioned couch.

Joy looked at Brian's earnest, intelligent face before continuing. She felt composed after her brief outburst and related the past in a slow, monotone voice.

"Several weeks before going to Reno, I became fascinated by a cowboy in the background of an ad for men's boots. For the first time in my life I began to have erotic dreams. Night after night I fantasized that this stranger and I were making love."

Brian leaned forward, afraid he would miss some of the remarkable story unfolding as he listened.

"It became the most important thing in my life. I couldn't get him out of my mind. He was the first man to arouse my slightest sexual interest. Intrigue mounted until I thought of nothing but finding him. I was determined he become my first lover."

"You what?" Brian blurted out unintentionally. Her tale was startling.

"I told Rena about him." Joy met Brian's incredulous gaze coolly. She knew he and her best girl friend's personalities clashed violently.

"I can imagine what she said," he muttered beneath his breath. He had met her twice and they had taken an instant dislike to each other. She was everything he hated in a woman. Too tall, too skinny, too loud, and much, much too outspoken.

"She wished me good luck. Said it was my burgeoning hormones and not to expect bells to ring."

"That figures. Just what I'd expect from a loudmouthed staunch feminist."

"Shush, Brian. She's the most loyal friend in the world and I adore her."

Brian settled back. He hadn't intended to intrude but Rena set his teeth on edge.

"I deliberately tracked him, hoping against all odds the trail wouldn't end and that I could find him in Reno."

"Why, Reno?" Brian asked. "Was he a gambler?"

"For pleasure only. His main pursuit, other than women, was bulldogging. He was a rodeo cowboy."

Words failed her as she deliberated. Could it have actually been thirteen months, seventeen days and—she checked the table clock—twelve hours since their fateful meeting?

"Don't stop now, Joy," Brian prompted gently.

"Three cowboys became a nuisance. An older cowboy, named Jake Travis, sent them on their way."

Her voice lowered, unintentionally becoming soft and loving as she spoke about Jake. "I was staggered. It seemed impossible, unbelievable really, that the man I sought had intervened."

"Implausible, to say the least," Brian readily agreed.

"It was as if I became another person when I met him. He was even more attractive in person. His rugged physical appearance brought forth an astonishing response. I was instantly overwhelmed and realized I had fallen head over heels in love from the first glimpse of his photo."

"You sound like a hopeless romantic, Joy. No wonder it didn't work out. That kind of attraction rarely lasts."

"It was more than physical appeal," she countered. "We seemed to share a mental rapport that was uniquely profound. Need I tell you the outcome of my day?" she pleaded, her hands gesturing with poignant expression.

"I was bewitched from the beginning. The man I had spent weeks seeking relentlessly pursued me from the first.

Jake bought me a western outfit, more expensive than any clothing I'd ever owned, took me to my first rodeo, and escorted me on a whirlwind tour of the casinos. I won and lost jackpots, unknowingly drank too much, and made a complete fool of myself."

"I should be so lucky," Brian mumbled jealously, glad Joy hadn't heard his whispered entreaty.

"We danced, we kissed, we caressed. It was so wonderful, Brian. My aunt and uncle loved me, but were never the least demonstrative. I craved the affection Jake offered. He was a touching person, couldn't seem to keep his hands off me, and I gloried in the warm, pleasurable feelings he aroused. I was never happier in my life."

Joy closed her eyes, reliving some of the moments with Jake.

"I can still feel the gentleness of his fingers—they were callused from the rodeo riding but so gentle. Each tender stroke was given for my pleasure. He told me bluntly how he enjoyed the feel of my body. I reveled in the fact I was a female and he a strong, compelling man chasing me with such desire."

Joy's eyes became luminous, darkening with hidden depths. Her face paled and her voice slowed as she told him the outcome of her visit to Reno.

"It was so wonderful at first. A beautiful dream that turned out to be nothing but a fanciful vision that changed into a nightmare of reality. I foolishly thought Jake returned my love."

"He's the fool, not you, Joy," Brian told her.

"Thanks, Brian, though it's not true," Joy disagreed, steeling herself for what had to be said. She groped for words to explain her shame.

"The next morning I awoke in his bed...*alone*. What I presumed to be a legal marriage ceremony was actually a cruel hoax. Needless to say, I left for California as fast as possible."

"If you were so besotted with the man, why did he go to the trouble of faking a wedding?" Something didn't add up, Brian thought.

Joy refused to meet his eyes, knowing he thought her

terribly naive for her age. She shrugged her shoulders, as perplexed as Brian.

"I don't know. I never denied him a thing when we made love," she blurted out sadly, her oval face flushed at the implication of her revelations. "He didn't force me into anything. I was eager—embarrassingly so—to have him make love to me. Jake made love to me so passionately, did things I'd never dreamed could be so arousing. Immediately afterward I either fainted or passed out—lack of sleep, no food, and too much liquor, probably."

"That still doesn't explain his deceitful nuptials."

Joy paused for a moment, then spoke in such a soft tone that Brian strained to hear.

"The only reason that I could see to pretend to marry me was that I was a virgin. He, er, he told me he'd never taken any woman's innocence before."

"What a bastard!" Brian exclaimed. He hated the man more with each word. "What happened to make you run away?"

"When I awoke the next morning, I was naked and Jake was gone. There wasn't even a note, a good-bye or anything. Instead, I was accosted by his mistress and bluntly informed that I was a stupid, gullible fool. Believe me, it didn't take long for her to convince me she was correct. I dressed hurriedly, left his suite, and was back in Sacramento within three hours."

"Are you absolutely certain the marriage wasn't legal?" Brian demanded, leaning forward with both hands clasped between his legs.

"Of course it was a hoax. It all tied in after what his mistress told me. I had fallen for the line of a practiced womanizer who bragged to her about all the trusting girls he seduced as he traveled from rodeo to rodeo."

"Why didn't you wait to hear Jake's side of the story?" he asked, amazed that Joy, who appeared so sensible and intelligent, had fallen for such a line.

"After her news, I couldn't force myself to wait until Jake returned. I—I didn't dare see him again. His appeal was too devastating. I had no control over my senses when we were together. It was so soon after he had made love to me that I was afraid I'd weaken if he asked me to stay. His Texas drawl alone could seduce me into believing he was maligned."

Her eyes brimmed with tears as she continued. "It was such a shock to find out about his perfidy. Jake was well liked by all his friends. Everywhere we went people crowded around him, sincere in their desire to talk with him. His best friend extolled his virtues endlessly."

"He sounds like a schizophrenic."

"I don't think so, Brian. Apparently, his personality quirk—his only problem—is his own passionate nature and contempt at the easy availability of women."

Joy's next words spilled forth with painful honesty. "Jake easily made me feel as if I were the only woman in the world he had ever loved." A bitter laugh was torn from her throat at his duplicity. "All I ever was was the first one he picked to seduce in Reno!"

Her voice broke, plainly in agony at her admission. "Jake forgot me instantly, but God help me, I'll never in my lifetime be able to forget him."

Joy walked toward the kitchen, her slender shoulders held proudly. She glanced sideways toward Brian, giving him a hesitant smile.

"I'll make us fresh coffee now. You deserve it for listening patiently to the sordid details of my past."

She refilled the percolator with cool water before adding fresh ground coffee. After it was plugged in, she turned, her eyes locking with Brian's, who had followed her to stand in the doorway of the compact room.

"How did you end up living in Hollywood?" he asked.

"It seemed the easiest place to hide in and rebuild my shattered life."

Joy reached for coffee cups, adding, "I didn't have the heart to tell my aunt and uncle how foolish I had been. When they returned from their vacation, I told them a college friend had a good job lined up for me and I wanted a change of location. I intended to change jobs anyway so it worked out fine."

"I'm surprised you didn't tell Rena. Her meddling was partially responsible for your problem."

"I couldn't tell her. I was too ashamed." She slanted him a friendly glance. "I did phone her as soon as I returned to California, asked to join her current tour, and spent two weeks traipsing around Italy while she tried to line me up with all the handsome men she could muster."

"Which was plenty, I presume," Brian scoffed.

"More than enough. The last thing I needed at the time was another man's attentions. She never dreamed her ploy to find me a man brought forth the finest acting I'll ever do. Inside I was ravished. I felt torn apart by grief."

"The woman's a complete fool."

"Wrong. By the time I returned to the States, closed my apartment, and moved to Hollywood my outward composure was firmly entrenched."

"No cream or sugar, Joy," Brian interjected when she reached to fill their cups with the freshly brewed coffee. He took his to the table, sat down in the brightly painted wooden chair, and sipped his hot drink before reminding her how careless she had been.

"You were lucky you didn't get pregnant, Joy. I treated several women during my internship who conceived during a permissive weekend without thought of the danger."

"There speaketh the doctor," Joy teased, sitting across from him.

"True," Brian admitted. His coffee turned cold as he thought back to the young women filled with disbelief when given the results of their lab test.

"Not one had looked ahead to the possible consequences of their impulsive actions. It's always the responsibility of both partners entering into a sexual relationship to see that the woman is protected. Sad to say, my gender is often remiss in the heat of passion."

Joy took a sip of the black liquid, enjoying the soothing effect of her favorite drink. Further astounding Brian, she told him, "I would have given anything to have gotten pregnant."

She looked at his fierce frown, adding, "I know you think me idiotic, but I loved Jake that night. Even worse is that after a year I still feel the same. A child would have at least been a part of him, a tiny replica that I could have shared my love with—not just memories that haunt me every day of my life."

Joy shrugged with resignation. "I soon found out I wasn't, so that didn't become a reality."

"Lucky for you, Joy," Brian returned. "It's wrong to want a child only for what it can do for you. Whenever possible, both loving parents are needed to care for and guide a child during its crucial years. The family unit is important."

Brian finished his coffee, glanced at his watch, and looked at Joy's expressive face. She had been through hell and he ached to help her. Unable to resist the temptation to hold her, despite knowing her love was lost to him until she forgot the man in her past, he walked forward. He drew her slender form close, inhaling the sweet fragrance of her gleaming hair.

Joy offered no resistance, but leaned gratefully into his slender strength. She raised her face, offering any solace he might find in her lips. Surprised when he gave her a gentle kiss on the forehead and gently pushed her an arm's length away, she gave him a perplexed look.

"It is late, isn't it?" She bowed her head, her soft whisper barely audible. "Thank you, Brian, for the excellent dinner, the flowers, the wine, and most of all for being so sympathetic to my depressed mood and tainted past."

"Hardly that," he chided. "Foolish would be a better description."

Pulling from Brian's arms, she walked into the living room, turning to look over her shoulder.

"I've shocked you, haven't I? I'm not the sweet, innocent woman you thought I was."

"Surprised, Joy, but certainly not shocked. I knew you were a passionate woman. What I feel most is sadness that I wasn't the person to awaken you to womanhood. I guarantee you may not be the last woman your cowboy seduces, nevertheless, no man, having held you in his arms could ever forget you. You're the loveliest woman I've ever met. I realize now that it's foolish to expect anything of you until you get over Jake." He stared at her with tender indulgence. Brian took his key ring from his slacks pocket, looked through for his car key, and, finding it, held it in his slender, capable fingers.

"I hope by sharing your problems with me, it will help you solve them. Good night."

He turned to leave, hesitated, then spun back to face her. His voice spewed forth his deep frustrations.

"God, Joy, don't you realize your Jake has to be the biggest damn fool in the world and the luckiest bastard I know?"

Joy shook her head, disputing Brian's words while tears fell unbidden from her eyes.

"If you don't feel better in the morning, don't come to work. The billing can wait or I'll have one of the other girls do it. Doctor's orders, sweet."

Joy walked forward and stood on tiptoe to give him a brief kiss on his smooth cheek, thinking his after-shave was as conventional as he was.

The soft touch of her mouth lingered, along with the quietly spoken thank you, as she walked to her kitchen then returned.

"I almost forgot," she smiled, handing him the cartons of leftover food.

"Glad you didn't," he told her, accepting them and leaving to drive home to Westwood.

From force of habit Joy straightened her living room and kitchen before taking a leisurely scented bath. Her motions were automatic as she dried herself with a fluffy, chenille bath sheet, placed it on the towel rack to dry, and pulled a wispy jade-green satin gown over her head.

She sat before the oval mirror of her dressing table, seriously contemplating her reflection. She raised her hands to deftly remove the clip holding her chignon in place. Long strands of chestnut-colored hair fell in a silken cascade down her back to far below her waist.

She picked up her hairbrush, tilting her head to one side then the other, and pulled the soft bristles through the heavy waves. Her lustrous hair soon sparkled with electricity, lying in a silken swathe around her shapely shoulders.

Her eyes were shadowed, vividly green against the pale color of her oval face. She stared at her mirrored image.

"I love you, Jake. I loved you when I first saw your photo and I still love you. Please, oh, please, release me from your hold. I need to be free of your vision in my dreams and of the thoughts that come unbidden to my mind throughout the day."

Head bowed, she clasped her face in trembling hands.

"Let me go, darling. Oh, Jake, please free me from your brand on my heart," she cried out in abject despair.

Later she lay twisting and turning in the darkened bedroom as her thoughts drifted back...back a year...back to the compelling paintings in the art gallery...back to their meeting in Reno...back to her first sight of his photo....

Once again her night's sleep was interrupted as the dreams returned to haunt her. Memories that started out as pleasant images always ended with the nightmare words of his mistress echoing over and over again.

Joy watched the hazy light of dawn filter through sheer drapes to light her bedroom with the leaden gray of another day. The long night had finally ended. After easing from the rumpled bed, she walked listlessly to her kitchen. Huddled at the table, she clasped a cup of reheated coffee between her palms, watching the minute hand slowly circle the clock face twice until it was time to prepare for work.

Promptly at eight forty-five she pulled into the underground parking lot, breathing a sigh of relief as she turned off the ignition. Driving from her apartment to work in heavy commuter traffic each day was always a dreaded necessity.

"Joy! Wait up," Sally hailed loudly, dodging around parked cars as she rushed up to her friend.

Joy locked her car before turning to smile good morning. Sally's intense gaze prepared her for the next comment.

"God, Joy, you look awful. You'd better get a prescription from Dr. Stevenson and go straight home." She scanned Joy's shadowed eyes, blurting out smugly, "I told you yesterday you were getting sick, didn't I?"

Joy dropped the car keys into her deep purse, shrugging her shoulders in a noncommittal reply. Aware of Sally's persistent stare, she smiled. "I'm fine, really. I didn't sleep too well last night, that's all."

"I don't think so, Joy. You look ghastly."

Grating on Joy's ragged nerves with her continued mention of her wan appearance, Sally was censured firmly.

"Knock it off, won't you? I'll be fine later. Right now I'm not in the mood for all this chitchat. My head's throbbing and I just want to get through today as quickly and quietly as possible."

"I can take a hint," Sally snapped. "If you don't want to talk, then I won't bother you anymore!" A deep frown revealed her displeasure at Joy's surprising ill-temper.

"Don't be mad, please?" Joy placated. "I don't want to talk about myself, but I would like to hear about your evening with Dan," she added graciously, wishing that her workday was over already.

Unaware of Joy's inner turmoil, Sally talked incessantly until Joy was able to escape into her own office at the first ringing of the reception office phone.

Joy took a large armful of files from the cabinet, looked at the first name in the *I*'s, checked the amount owed, and typed it neatly onto the billing slip. Undisturbed, she progressed gradually through the first half of the alphabet. Her fingers felt leaden and she was constantly using the correct bar to erase her errors.

With a weary sigh, she raised her face, looking straight into the intense blue eyes of Brian. "Dr. Stevenson, you surprised me!" she exclaimed, not hearing him enter.

"Dammit, Joy, you look like hell! I told you not to come to work until you had your emotions under better control," he scolded impatiently.

"You're the second person today to tell me I look terrible. I'll soon begin to believe I'm ill if this keeps up," Joy replied, a faint smile adding to her look of innocent vulnerability.

"You're temporarily depressed, Joy, and that can be as debilitating. You've always been such an excellent, efficient secretary it's a shock to see you acting lethargic. I had hoped that telling me about your problems would help you." Leaning toward her, he asked, "Do you have a bad headache?"

"A faint one," she lied flatly, rubbing her temples with

slender fingers. "I didn't sleep much last night. I imagine the pain will go away after a while."

Joy looked at Brian with solemn green eyes. "Don't you hear enough complaints from your patients without asking your secretary to cry on your shoulder too?"

"I love you, Joy, and it hurts me to see you this unhappy," he said.

Joy watched as Brian left her office, thinking how much happier she would be if she could return his love. Resting her face in her palms, she leaned her elbows on the desk, hoping a moment's rest would ease the tension headache pounding incessantly over her forehead.

At the touch of a hand on her shoulder she looked up to see Brian holding a small white pill and paper cup of water. She accepted his ministrations with gratitude.

"Thanks, Brian. Your secretary is a sluggish, pathetic mess today."

Seated on the edge of her desk, he crossed his arms over his chest, looking intently at her features. "Go home, Joy. I see you've finished a third of the billing. One of the other girls from the back can work on it or let it wait. I want you to drive straight home, go to bed, and stay there until I check on you after the office closes."

Handing her a bottle of pills, he said, "I don't want to see you back at work until you're feeling normal."

Tears of weakness flooded Joy's eyes. Turning her head away from his gaze, she told him, "I haven't felt normal for over a year, Brian. Please don't bother to come by tonight. I'll be fine once I get some rest."

Brian drew her unresisting body from the chair, took her jacket from the hanger, found her purse at her direction, and prompted her to leave. "Go through our private side door, Joy. I'll explain to Sally and the others that you're ill."

Squeezing Brian's hand in appreciation, Joy murmured thank you and left. She got off the elevator on the mezzanine floor instead of at the garage, walked out the main entrance, across the street, and up the sidewalk until she reached the art gallery.

She hugged her arms across her abdomen, staring at the

painting of the fallen bull rider. Studying each detail again, she knew beyond doubt the bull was Gravedigger. The markings on his face were identical.

Her stomach muscles clenched with anguish. She looked fixedly at the picture as tears trickled slowly down her cheeks. It was more horrifying each time she viewed it, somehow pointing out more than anything could that she would not see Jake again.

Oblivious of the stares of people walking past who noticed her stricken face, she turned and fled to the privacy of her car. In less than an hour she had arrived home, changed into a comfortable nightgown, slipped between her cool percale sheets, and was sound asleep in her darkened bedroom.

Chapter Ten

Awakened by a loud knocking on her door, Joy raised herself to a sitting position before turning on the bedside lamp to check the time.

"Seven o'clock! I can't believe it," she murmured sleepily. She groped for a flowing beige velour robe and tied it securely around her slim waist. Slipping on fluffy slippers, she marched on none too steady legs into the front room.

One hand rose to hold her unbound hair from her face. With caution she opened the chained door, peeking through the narrrow opening to see Dr. Stevenson waiting anxiously in the hallway.

"Brian! I'm sorry it took so long." She slipped the chain and stood aside to let him in. Still drowsy, she excused her appearance, unaware he found her tumbled chestnut hair hanging down her back in a thick satiny cloud beautiful. "That was some pill you gave me."

"Glad it worked so well," he told her. When she turned toward the bedroom to put on slacks and a blouse, his fingers clasped her arm. "Don't dress. I won't be very long."

"I'll make some coffee," she volunteered. His eyes hadn't left her hair and the contours of her body enfolded in the full-length robe since he'd entered the room.

"No. I'd rather look at you. I never realized your hair was so long or so beautiful. You're a gorgeous woman, Joy." With trembling fingers he touched the silky chestnut strands, annoyed when she jerked abruptly away. "Dammit, Joy, why can't you love me?"

Joy eased across the room, realizing Brian's emotions were rising. It had been silly of her to open the door until she had dressed. She faced him squarely, her words painfully honest. "I've been doing lots of thinking since last night and feel it best that we don't see each other away from work anymore. It's not fair to you or good for me. I've done nothing but take advantage of your kindness since we met."

Brian ignored her statement. They could argue about that later.

"Sit down, Joy. No good doctor leaves his patient until she's well." He watched as she curled up in the armchair, careful to wrap the robe around her limbs though an enticing glimpse of jade satin gown ruffled around the edge. "I've also been thinking about your situation. You're too intelligent to spend such a long time loving a man who betrayed you. It isn't natural. Many men and women have numerous affairs that seem intense at the time but soon fade and die without either party being any the worse off in the long run. You say you met Jake over a year ago, yet you still think you love him."

"I *do* love him, Brian!" she corrected firmly, breaking out of her lethargy. "I also realize my feelings are futile and that I need to snap out of my recurring moods of depression."

Brian looked at her vulnerable face, speaking soothingly, "Did you know scientific research has shown there's a chemistry involved in being in love other than the mystical connotation of the word?"

"No, but I'm not surprised. It's so overwhelming. So powerful," she whispered, thinking of the constant excitement she shared with Jake.

"Doctors have found love brings on a giddy response comparable to a high on amphetamines," Brian continued, speaking earnestly.

"It also brings on a low," Joy reminded him with poignant feeling.

"True," he admitted. "The crash that follows is much like the withdrawal symptoms from the same drug." His eyes were keen, the smooth features of his face expressing intelligence. "When people believe they're in love the brain pours out its own chemical correlate to amphetamine. When the person is spurned or disillusioned the brain halts production of the substance and immediately begins to suffer from the absence."

Joy listened with interest. Her personality had certainly changed.

"One doctor noted that people in his study group known for their repeated disastrous love relationships went on chocolate binges when the affairs ended. Chocolate is loaded with phenylethylamine, which is the brain's correlate for amphetamines. It seems I should have brought you a big box of chocolates," he commented wryly.

"You've done enough." Joy smiled. "I am glad to hear that lovesickness has finally been acknowledged as a genuine syndrome."

"Otherwise known as depression," he scoffed. His textbooks on psychiatry hadn't even included a paragraph on affairs of the heart.

"Good enough," Joy told him. "I get so depressed when I'm alone at night that I sometimes feel helpless with the pain of it. If I'm not depressed but suffering from lovesickness, how will I know when I'm cured?" she asked impulsively.

"Easy. You'll fall in love with me," he answered seriously. "A new romance is my prescription for a speedy recovery."

Joy's eyes closed, her mood pensive. She sat with her head leaning into the chair back, both hands clasped tightly in her lap.

"I don't feel like I could ever fall in love again. Once in my lifetime's enough." Her voice broke, thoughts withdrawing to Jake.

"At twenty-eight? That's ridiculous," he chided. "Being a healthy female, your body's needs will overcome your persistence in denying yourself male companionship eventually."

Joy stared at him, refusing to comment. No man in the world could ever touch her but Jake. The thought of it made her shudder with distaste.

"If you'll give me permission." Brian's voice altered, changing the subject abruptly. It became more obvious each day that Joy would never be interested in having an affair or marrying him despite his continued attention.

"For what?" Joy answered. She really wished Brian would leave. She was so tired.

"I'd like to talk with an attorney friend of mine and ask him to check Reno Vital Statistics Section to find out if there's a chance your marriage could have been legal and properly recorded."

"Go ahead," Joy agreed halfheartedly. "You'll both be wasting your time though."

"Maybe. Maybe not. You didn't give Jake an opportunity to explain his side of the story. If there's the remotest chance that he was sincere, you must find out." Brian's brow furrowed. Despite an obvious reason for hating the man, he did feel Joy had treated Jake unfairly too by not waiting until he returned to the room.

"I told you last night why I had to flee Reno."

"Yes, you did, but if you were legally married you've done Jake a grave injustice by not waiting for his explanation of the woman's accusations." His eyes pinned hers. "I'm surprised you haven't checked before now, Joy."

Gesturing with her hands, she replied plaintively, "I couldn't bear to inquire after the things his mistress said."

"She could have been lying. Maybe even had her own evil intent."

"That was my first thought," Joy said, her voice faltering at the remembered trauma of that morning. "She knew Jake had told me I was the only one he'd ever loved, that we'd gotten married, she knew my name, even the name of the old judge who married us. I had never met her and the only one who could have given her that information was Jake."

"You said you'd met some of his friends. Couldn't they have told her?"

"Yes, some of the things." She faced him squarely. "But not this. She told me she had come straight from her room where Jake had spent the previous hour making love to her."

"How long had he been gone from your room?" Brian inquired.

"I don't know. I was asleep when he left. Marie confronted me about a half hour after I woke up."

"Still circumstantial evidence, Joy," Brian pointed out fairly.

"Not when it's all put together. Jake nor I talked to a single person after we left the dance hall. He didn't even say good-bye to his best friend Louis and his wife Jean. He paid for the drinks and rushed me out the door to the Marriage Bureau, sped to the judge's house and back to the hotel suite."

"Someone could have seen you. You said Jake's well-known."

"Well-known by his mistress," Joy snapped. "Right down to her description of a scar in the man's groin. No casual friend would ever know about an injury on *that* part of a man's anatomy!"

"Okay," Brian agreed. "I'm convinced now. I'll let you know what my friend finds out. Maybe hearing officially you've never been married will break the final emotional ties Jake seems to have on you."

"Go ahead," Joy consented. "It's all a waste of time though. My so-called marriage was nothing but a sham!" She stood up, walking toward the door as Brian rose to leave. As they stood in front of it saying good-bye the doorbell rang, its unexpected shrill making both of them start.

Joy opened the door, crying out with happiness when she spotted Rena standing in the hall, balancing a Gucci purse strap on one slim shoulder, a foil-wrapped box in one hand, and a large canvas traveling bag clasped in the other.

They rushed into each other's arms. It had been two months since they had been together and Joy was thrilled to death to see her friend.

Brian stood aside, a deep scowl on his face as he contemplated the difference between the two women. Joy was small, beautifully curved and innocently lovely. Rena was thin and angular, barely two inches shorter than he. She met his glance over Joy's shoulder with eyes that could read his soul.

"Hi, Doc," she teased, her laugh brittle as she looked from Joy to Brian. "If I didn't know Joy, I'd suspect you two were up to no good."

"If we had been, your presence couldn't have been more unwelcome than it is now," Brian pointed out rudely. They had never minced words about their dislike for each other.

"How's the great Hollywood pill-pusher tonight?" Rena taunted, dumping her things on the carpet before settling into the corner of the couch. Her knowing eyes stared up at Brian boldly. "Bought any new Cadillacs since I was here last?"

"Not all doctors drive Cadillacs," he retorted with rising temper, watching her cross one long, elegantly slender leg over the other.

"The ones with offices on Hollywood Boulevard do," she smirked, reaching into her bag for a cigarette as Joy rushed to get her an ashtray. Lighting the foreign brand she preferred, she inhaled, blowing the smoke deliberately out her nostrils at Brian.

"Put the damned thing out," Brian demanded, furious at her defiance. When she inhaled for the second time, he leaned down and took it from her.

Joy sighed, listening as they argued while she prepared coffee, set out cups and saucers, and placed chocolate chip cookies on a plate in the center of the table. They always fought like cats and dogs. She'd never seen Rena so antagonistic toward a man before.

"Don't you know you're killing yourself, woman?" Brian questioned, stubbing the cigarette in the dirt of a potted plant. "You wouldn't be so skinny if you'd eat more and smoke less."

"A woman can never be too slender," she scoffed, ending with, "or a man too rich."

"You're not slender," he snorted, his feet planted firmly on the rug before her, arms held over his chest in a dominant stance. "You're thin as a rail. A man would have to rattle the sheets to find you."

Rena laughed up at him, her eyes filled with mischief. "Wouldn't like to try me out, would you? The first time I met you I knew immediately that you were sexually frustrated." She reached out a sandal clad foot to touch his creased slacks leg.

Brian stormed into the kitchen, a faint flush tinging his smooth face. She was the most blatantly outspoken woman he'd ever encountered.

"Simmer down, Brian," Joy soothed. "Rena's the sweetest woman in the world. If you didn't react so hostile each time you saw her she'd be purring at your feet and even let you wait on her hand and foot."

"God, perish the thought," he scorned. "The woman's unbelievable."

"Unbelievably adorable," Joy smiled. She felt so much better with Rena there. No one could ever be depressed when she was around. She was like a whirlwind. Always stirring something up, then departing without warning for another few months.

"Coffee's ready," Joy called out, laughing when Rena sauntered into the room. She never walked. Her steps were too flowing and smooth for that. Joy thought her the most elegant woman she'd ever known. She accepted the foil-wrapped box from her hands, thinking her the most generous friend too.

Joy tore off the foil, her eyes lighting with delight when she found a five-pound box of Godiva chocolates inside.

"Oh, Rena, how lovely, but so expensive!" Joy exclaimed in pleasure.

"Not in Belgium. They only set me back six dollars a pound. A mere pittance of their States price," she scoffed, not wanting praise.

"Just what Brian said I needed," Joy laughed, setting the opened box on the table for them to sample.

"Why?" Rena asked. "Does he think you're too skinny too?"

"No," Joy smiled back. "Just moody. Brian was just telling me that chocolate helps cure a dismal state of mind."

Rena shot him a taunting glance. "I should have brought you two boxes, Doc. Your mood's always dour."

"Shush, Rena," Joy scolded. "Both of you sit down and quit arguing while I pour our coffee."

They talked amiably for another hour before Brian left. He turned his back on Rena deliberately, brushed Joy's forehead with his lips, and told her he'd see her at the office in the morning.

Joy shut and latched the door, then turned to Rena. "How long are you staying this time?"

"A couple of days. Why? Are you wanting to get rid of me already?"

"You know I'm not," Joy persisted. "You couldn't come at a better time. I had a beastly headache before and now it's completely gone."

"Good." Rena laughed, unzipping her travel bag to remove a sleek pair of gold pajamas she had tailored to fit in Hong Kong. With her toothbrush in the other hand she faced Joy, asking with total seriousness, "You don't care for Doc, do you?"

"No, Rena," Joy replied softly. "He's dear to me but I could never love the man. Why? I thought you hated Brian."

Rena shrugged a narrow shoulder. "There's nothing wrong with the man that a good romp in the sack won't cure."

"Rena!" Joy exclaimed. "You couldn't." Surely her friend wouldn't consider Brian as a partner. Not after the way they fought.

"Why not? It's been two months and that's about all the celibacy I can handle and retain my peace of mind." She ignored Joy's startled gasp, took out a cigarette, lit it, then stubbed it out immediately without a puff.

"Why'd you do that?" Joy asked. Rena was a chain smoker, had been for years, and it was a shock to see her stub an unsmoked one out.

"Not sure," she called over her shoulder on the way into Joy's bathroom to prepare for bed. "It's as good a time as any to quit smoking, I guess." She removed her outer clothes, standing before the mirror in brief underwear. "Do you think I'm too skinny?"

Joy followed her in, removed bed linens from the closet, and stood looking at Rena's reflection.

"No, Rena. You're lithe and sleek as a cat. Very sexy!"

"You really think so?" Rena questioned, turning around to look at her back.

"Would I lie to my best friend?" Joy returned truthfully. "Let's go to bed. I'm bushed and I have a heavy workday tomorrow."

As she walked into the living room to make up the hide-a-bed couch, Rena asked, "Doc's not gay, is he, Joy?"

"Heavens no," Joy replied, wondering what her friend was up to.

"Good," Rena sighed in relief. "I've met some of the most gorgeous hunks of manhood only to find they were more turned on by my current lover than I was."

"Go to sleep, Rena. You must be suffering from jet lag!"

Two nights later Joy and Rena were sitting in the living room, laughing about all the things they had managed to cram into their hours together despite Joy having a full-time job: a good movie, lavish dinners, an expensive foray into a chic Beverly Hills boutique, and hours of talk. Joy had expertly avoided any comments on her past interest in Jake. She knew Rena assumed that her momentary fantasies had been forgotten a year earlier. If her friend stared at her more than usual, probed into her private life a little deeper, or suggested life was passing her by, she turned away, ignored the comment, or disagreed pleasantly. She still couldn't bear to confess what happened during her reckless weekend in Reno.

At ten thirty the doorbell rang. Joy hopped up and opened it happily when Brian identified himself. "Come in, Brian. Rena and I just returned from gorging on Kalufilet Oskar followed by an orgy of pastries that nearly emptied Scandia's dessert tray."

"Sounds decadent and delicious. I've eaten there myself. If you had invited me along I would have even picked up the undoubtedly astronomical tab." It would have been worth it to have Joy's company during the meal. His glance went back and forth between the two women. They were such opposites in looks and disposition.

"Now he tells us!" Rena exclaimed, throwing her head back in dismay.

"Aren't you about due to leave?" Brian asked Rena pointedly.

"Nine o'clock in the morning on Pan Am flight—"

"Good," he interrupted. "I haven't had a minute alone with Joy since you've been here."

"You're wasting your time, Doc. I know my friend better than you and she's not interested," Rena told him bluntly.

Joy returned from the kitchen where she had busied herself fixing Brian a tall glass of iced tea. It was hot in the apartment, even though the windows were open letting in a lazy cross breeze.

He accepted the drink with pleasure. He'd had a busy day. An exacting surgery had extended twice as long as anticipated. He had just come from the hospital, relieved to find the patient recovering well. It was some solace to know his practice was successful despite his personal life being in such shambles. He looked up to find Rena staring at him, a wide smile on her mouth. The only thing curvy and full about her, he thought, avoiding her eyes to talk with Joy.

At eleven he stood up to leave. Speaking with Joy always made him feel so much better. She listened attentively and asked intelligent, compassionate questions about his work.

Rena left them at the door, walked into Joy's bedroom, and returned with her travel bag and purse. With casual ease she spoke. "I'm going with you, Doc. I need cigarettes." He'd never find out her bag had several unopened packs inside.

Brian's voice faltered, his eyes going to her bags. "Why the suitcase, then?" Damn her! She was so forward.

"You can drive me to the airport too. No need to take a taxi when you only live fifteen miles from LAX." She reached over to give Joy a hug, thank her for the hospitality, and tell her she'd be back again in a month or so.

Brian took her travel bag, uncertain how to handle the situation. The last thing he wanted to do was chauffeur Rena around. Suddenly remembering their earlier conversation, he chided, "Your flight doesn't leave until morning."

"So? I'll be early. Let's go, Doc. I'm having a nicotine fit."

Giving Joy a wink, she took Brian's arm and rushed him down the hall before he could think up a reason to depart without her.

Joy shut the door, a bright smile lighting up her face. She wasn't certain of Rena's purpose but it didn't surprise her in the least that she left so abruptly. Ever since she opened her travel agency she had arrived and departed with startling suddenness.

After straightening the apartment, Joy prepared for bed and retired with a new best-seller she had been anxious to read. Rena had done her a world of good. Thirty minutes later she yawned. She felt dismally drowsy and couldn't keep her eyes open. The anticipated story was so boring she doubted if she could force herself to read another page. Snuggling into her favorite sleeping position, she was soon sound asleep.

After a dreamless night Joy woke early. A new day, she thought, filled with determination to do something about her life. Brian was right. It was time to stop running from Jake's haunting memory and put her life in order.

The ringing of her bedside phone interrupted an inner voice warning her that erasing Jake from her mind would be easier said than done.

"Hi, Rena," she said, recognizing her cheery voice despite the background noise. "Dare I ask what you've been up to?"

"Of course," she laughed. "Have I ever had any regrets about what I do?"

"None you'd confess to me, I imagine," Joy laughed back.

"I called to tell you to be gentle with Doc today."

"Why?"

"For starters, the poor baby's liable to be in a sour mood."

"Why?" Was she actually hearing Rena call Brian a poor baby?"

"Too much sex and too much conscience. A terrible combination."

"What happened, Rena?" Joy demanded in astonishment.

"I eased the Doc's frustrations, sweetie."

"You didn't!" Joy was stunned. They had seemed to hate each other.

"Three times," she told her, her voice lowered and filled with reverence. "The first time all he thought of was you. He loved you—past tense, hopefully—very much, Joy. The second time all he thought of was himself. Aah, but the third time"—her voice became dreamy and soft—"at my insistence he wised up and thought only of me."

"I'm stunned," Joy told her. "You always fought so, I can't picture you in bed together."

"We still fight," she chuckled. "He told me he hates skinny women, railed at me for smoking, though I only threatened to smoke to annoy him, and said he hated pushy women."

"I hate to ask what you answered," Joy teased.

"Oh, I got my licks in. I told him he was too stuffy, too intellectual, too inhibited, and I hated blond men: He promptly criticized my narrow bottom and remarked he liked full breasts."

Joy listened intently. Rena's story was better than the one she read last night.

"But Doc couldn't keep his hands off me...."

Joy listened as Rena recounted the evening, and a shudder went through her body. She could feel her nipples become erect at the thought of Jake pleasing her. Her one brief interlude had brought her so much pleasure she knew she could match Rena's years of experience with a single bout of love.

"Yes, Doc was wonderful," Rena concluded.

"I recall you told me in Seattle that making love wasn't all that special," Joy teased.

"Until now it wasn't," Rena answered huskily. "I think I hit on my problem too. I tried so damned hard to make Doc forget you I forgot my own pleasure to please him. In doing so I enjoyed it more than I ever have."

"I'm pleased for you both," Joy told her sincerely. "Brian's a wonderful man and you know I've always thought you were the best friend in the world."

"Thanks, Joy. I think he's the kind of man I need. He's

so busy with his own career he'd let me get on with mine. Meeting every two or three weeks would be ideal. We'd both be so in need of release our sex life would stay great. When we started fighting I'd arrange a tour and cut out." Laughing once again, she teased, "Of course, it'll take me a few more visits to convince him he needs *me*."

Before Joy could comment, Rena said she had to rush and hung up. Joy threw back the sheet and bedspread and stood up. She could hardly wait to see Brian. He had begun to show the strains of celibacy, she agreed with a wide smile. Rena's loving would probably steady his hands during surgery for weeks to come.

At work, Joy placed the last of the files into the cabinet, breathing a sigh of relief that she had completed the billing for another month. It was the most boring part of her job.

She knew Brian had come into work late but she hadn't talked with him yet. Apparently he was avoiding meeting her for fear Rena had mentioned their interlude in the wee morning hours. Which she had, Joy chuckled.

Sally came in promptly at noon, insisting Joy rush so they could have a full one hour for lunch. Walking with her to the café, Joy listened while she complained about her boyfriend's lack of attention.

As they approached the gallery, Sally grumbled, "I guess neither you nor I are destined to meet a tall, dark, handsome lover, Joy. I read once where every woman's ideal is a black-haired, brown-eyed hunk. Do you agree? Will we ever find one?"

Thinking of Jake's dark good looks, Joy smiled without commenting. It was much too painful to contemplate losing her one love after a single day's pleasure.

Continuing despite Joy's silence, Sally said, "I have Dan with his sandy hair and you have Dr. Stevenson with his blond waves and blue eyes."

"I don't have—nor do I want—Dr. Stevenson, Sally," Joy corrected. Rena seemed to have taken Brian in hand for the time being.

"You could if you wanted. You're a fool, Joy. The man's going places fast. I heard the nurses say he's going to teach this fall. As young as he is that's really something, especially considering this area abounds with some of the best neurosurgeons in the country."

"I'm glad to hear of his success, Sally," Joy said sincerely. "He's very deserving and devoted to his part in healing those in need of his skills, but I'm not in love with the man." She looked at her friend with an exasperated glance. "Is that all you think of? Trying to see me paired up with Dr. Stevenson or trying to pair yourself up permanently with the best you can find?"

"Well, not really," she admitted. "But I don't look like you. You can afford to wait and be a little more picky, I guess, but I don't intend to spend all my life answering telephones for overworked physicians. Dan may not be my ideal but if he asks I'm his for life."

Disagreeing with Sally's outlook, Joy smiled to herself. "I want to look in the gallery before we eat."

"Jeez, not again! You've stopped there every day this week. As usual I'll go get a booth." She walked up the sidewalk, her back stiff with anger.

"Hello, Mr. Hanson," Joy greeted the manager. "I'm back again."

"My pleasure, Joy," he told her, using her first name at her request. "I probably won't see you over the weekend, will I?" He had found out where she worked and would miss her pleasant company.

"No." Joy smiled back. "That's why I decided to take a quick peek before I eat lunch."

She walked into the side room to view the pictures that had haunted her the entire week. Walking from one painting to the next, she noticed the sold tags in the far left hand corner of each.

As Mr. Hanson joined her she lifted her eyes to him, asking, "Since they're all sold, how long will the exhibit be here?" She dreaded the thought of not being able to look at them each workday. They drew her like a magnet somehow.

"Three more weeks. I insist each exhibit be committed for a full month. Which is usually the length of time it takes to find buyers," he added as an afterthought.

Straightening the imaginary tilt of one picture, he gestured to the remaining exhibit. "Selling these the first weekend is a minor miracle considering this is the artist's first exhibit. I think their vast appeal is man's desire to get back to the basics of life, away from the plastic and steel atmosphere of our cities. An earthy entreaty."

"They certainly have a hypnotic effect on me." She glanced at her watch, bade him a hasty good-bye and rushed to the café just as Sally was finishing a thick piece of coconut cream pie.

Joy scooted into the booth, apologized for being so long, and ordered a cottage cheese and fresh fruit salad. It would be cool and light and wouldn't take long to prepare.

By quitting time she was in her office reading a memo from Dr. Tilson. Intent on its message, she didn't hear Dr. Stevenson slip into her office.

She looked up, amused that he avoided eye contact. Despite a serious frown drawing his brows together, he looked sheepish and haggard.

She greeted him brightly, her mind reeling with Rena's confession of their early morning affair. They were the last two people she would have expected to have a sexual conflagration.

"Joy, I want you to come into my office right now." His words were flat, lips thinned in a tight line.

Joy followed him down the hall to a private room at the back of the clinic. She paused uncertainly in the middle of his office. He was acting so strangely. Surely he wasn't mad at her over Rena's behavior.

He closed the door behind him, sealing them in complete privacy.

"Sit down, Joy." He walked behind his desk to a cabinet built into the paneled wall. Pulling the door open, he took a glass from the small bar and poured out two glasses of bourbon.

"Take this, Joy. I think you might need it. I know I do," he told her harshly.

Alarmed by his manner, Joy took the glass and stared at him with questioning eyes. "What's the matter, Brian? You couldn't have had time to find out anything about Jake yet, could you?" She could feel a small pulse beat start throbbing rapidly at the base of her throat, a premonition that he had something ominous to tell her.

"I have, Joy," he blurted out harshly. He downed the strong whiskey in one gulp.

She watched him. Her breath was caught in her lungs and she couldn't say a word if her life depended on it.

"My friend phoned me a minute ago." He paced the room, walking back to stop before her. "I don't know the best way to tell you this, but the fact of the matter is...you're married!" He watched his announcement sink into her mind.

Joy sat down abruptly on the chair beside his desk. All feeling left her limbs and she knew they wouldn't hold her any longer. Cupping the drink in both hands, she looked at him, her pale face reflecting the shock of his news.

"Are you certain, Brian? Oh, God, are you really certain?" she inquired in a tormented voice. She stared at him, searching his eyes for further information before setting her untouched drink on his desk.

"There's not the slightest doubt. Mr. Jake Travis was legally joined in holy matrimony to Miss Joy Sanders in Reno, Nevada, over one year ago."

Trying desperately not to reveal any of his own inner turmoil, he demanded, "What do you intend to do, Joy?"

Joy bowed her head, cupping her face in hands that trembled. Tears of shock streamed unbidden beneath her clenched eyelids as she took a minute to gather enough composure to answer his leading query. Moments later she raised her shimmering eyes to meet his curious glance head-on.

"I intend to ask him for a divorce." Her voice was calm. After months of turmoil she knew she was able to face her problems in a calm, mature manner until they were resolved.

"The fact that I still love Jake doesn't alter the circumstances. I've heard nothing from the man in over a year. If he'd wanted to, I'm certain he could have found me."

Brian eased his taut shoulder muscles restlessly. He couldn't understand why he was so tired. God, yes, he knew why, suddenly thinking of his night with Rena. The long-legged witch had seduced him as easily as Jake appeared to have Joy.

"I don't know why Jake actually married me," Joy continued, "but I intend to find out. After that I'll file for divorce. I could never live with a man who has sex with his mistress the same day he marries the only woman he professes to have ever loved."

"How will you find him, Joy? You told me you don't even know where he lives." He checked his watch. "It's too late now to contact offices in Reno to see if they have his home address."

"I know he lives in Texas," she answered calmly.

"So do approximately thirteen million other people," Dr. Stevenson remarked in a dry voice.

"I'll call his best friend, Louis Edwards. He lives in Boulder City, Nevada, and will be able to give me Jake's address and phone number."

"If you need any money or a shoulder to cry on, phone me, honey. I want to help you any way I can."

He opened the office door, looking back to tell Joy, "It appears everyone's left for the weekend already. That will save you having to explain your reddened eyes to Sally and the rest of the staff."

Joy returned to her office, gathered her things, and walked with Brian to the elevator. Separating in the garage, he strode off toward his Lincoln Continental while Joy unlocked the door to her Volkswagen.

As she prepared to get behind the steering wheel, he called out, "One last thing, Joy. Did Rena happen to mention when she'd be back?"

Chapter Eleven

Early the next morning, Joy phoned the business number the long distance operator had given her for the Louis Edwards Stock Show Company. A recorded message related the office was closed on weekends and if she would leave her name she would be contacted.

"Darn!" Joy complained bitterly. "It's the same runaround that I was given by Alfonso."

She dialed information again seeking Louis and Jeannie's home phone number in Boulder City. In tears of frustration she found their number was unlisted. Pacing the living room floor, she berated the fact it was a weekend and all city offices in Reno were closed also.

"Judge McClellan!" she exclaimed out loud. "He'll be listed in the phone book." Why hadn't she thought of him first?

Tapping her fingernails on the tabletop, she waited nervously for the operator to check the directory. She could feel her stomach churn in knots while waiting for the judge's number. Throughout the day and well into the night Joy called only to hear it ring over and over. In desperation she dialed it for the final time at midnight.

"Judge McClellan?" Joy asked anxiously, startled to hear the hesitant voice of the old man answer his phone.

"Yes...yes!" he mumbled gruffly. "Who is it? Speak up, woman, I can't hear you," he continued in a slurred voice.

"I'm Joy Sanders, Judge. I was the woman you married to...Jake Travis...last year."

"Yes, I remember you. Small girl with lots of brown hair.

What do you want?" he asked bluntly, obviously irritated at the late call.

"I was wondering if you could tell me where I could get in touch with Jake? Give me his address or something?" she begged tremulously.

"Speak up, girl! I can't hear you. Did you say you wanted Jake's address? Aren't you living with the boy?"

"No, I'm not," Joy answered in a rising voice. "I need to contact him immediately though."

"Always a rush. I don't understand you young people nowadays. Only thing I know for sure is the lad comes from a small town aways outside of Austin, Texas. Shouldn't be no problem finding the family. They're well-known in that area."

"Thank you, Judge," she answered, her spirits crest-fallen at not receiving Jake's address.

"I haven't seen Jake myself in over a year. Come to think of it, it must have been the night I married you two. Give him my regards," he muttered, adding more to himself than Joy, "Always liked that boy."

Joy replaced her receiver when the judge abruptly hung up. Austin information was another dead end. No Jake Travis, despite numerous listings with the same surname. The rooms became claustrophobic as she paced up and down. She was wretched. The day had brought her no closer to getting in touch with Jake despite hours of effort.

After a restless night with dreams tormented by his image relentlessly pursuing her and an erotic interlude in his bed, she woke with a start. Her body was covered in a light film of perspiration. She could see Marie's angry face gloating about her relationship with Jake. Why was she subject to such destructive recurring nightmares? It was as if some uncontrollable inner force was keeping Jake's memory alive. The sweet tender period of their courtship, the single passionate interlude after their marriage, and the cruel, haunting treachery afterward.

Joy walked to her stereo and placed a record on the turntable. Jerry Lee Lewis's voice soon filled the room as she listened again and again to his haunting rendition of "Help Me Make It Through the Night."

What would I have done without this record? she wondered, stepping from the shower with dark strands of freshly shampooed hair stringing down her back. She toweled it vigorously before brushing it dry with long leisurely strokes. Laying her head against the back of an easy chair, she shut her eyes, letting the music soothe her tightened nerves. Through the long, tormented year she had listened to the words, reflecting back to that moment in Jake's arms when her happiness seemed complete.

The following Monday dawned bright, the sky a vivid blue and free of its usual blanket of early morning gray smog. The surrounding hills were clearly visible out her apartment window. Too restless to sit in her spotless apartment—she had cleaned it thoroughly the day before—she dressed casually in white slacks and a comfortable yarn-dyed ruffled blouse in vivid plaid, pushed her feet into wedgies, slung a purse over her arm, and headed for her car.

The weekend traffic had lessened and soon she was pulling into the private lot behind the art gallery. She slipped quietly through the numerous people looking with interest at her paintings and stopped before the one with the least crowd blocking her vision.

If only she were as tall as Rena, she thought, trying to peer over or around a huge, heavy muscled man. She felt a soft hand on her elbow and glanced across her shoulder to see Mr. Hanson smiling broadly at her.

"Hello, Joy. I hardly recognized you without your white uniform on nor did I expect to see you here today."

"Hi, Mr. Hanson." Joy smiled back. His appearance was always so dapper; this morning's dark pin-striped suit was no exception. He looked unapproachable and stuffy until you looked into his friendly eyes. "The gallery's really packed today."

"Great for business," he whispered, looking around with pleasure. "I'm glad you dropped by. Some interesting things have happened this weekend. First, the artist's agent contacted me, deflating my pride by saying he wasn't the least surprised the exhibit sold out within three hours of the private showing. Second, a leading art critic observed a noteworthy detail about each of the paintings."

"Something I hadn't spotted?" Joy asked in surprise. She had probably looked at the works as much as the artist.

"Apparently," Mr. Hanson nodded, taking her forward to the roping picture. He pointed to a small figure in the scenery behind the horse. "I'm surprised you missed this. Look very closely and you'll note in all of the paintings a girl with her back turned to the rodeo arena. The only person depicted that way. Most noticeable is her long dark hair. Apparently this is the artist's talisman."

Joy looked at the picture as Mr. Hanson touched his finger to the background. The sight of the outline of the slender girl affected her strangely. Only a trained eye would have observed the figure; it was so subordinate to the main theme of the work. Her colors were muted, blending easily into the crowd scene. In each painting Joy noticed this same object merge into the softened tones of the spectators.

"Mr. Edwards is quite a personable gentleman," Mr. Hanson spoke.

"The artist?" Joy questioned curiously.

"The agent," he affirmed. "Louis is obviously knowledgeable about art, although I must say he looks more like an athlete."

"Louis? Louis Edwards?" Joy asked, spinning around to face him. Her heartbeat increased as she reached up a hand to touch the manager's arm. "Do you have his address and phone number?"

"Certainly, Joy," Mr. Hanson agreed, leading her toward his private office. "Do you know the man?"

"I hope so." She smiled, closing the door behind her while he looked through his file holder for a card.

Joy took the card from Mr. Hanson's outstretched hand, thanking him profusely. She was giddy with happiness at finding a lead to Jake's whereabouts. Unaware of the manager's startled expression, she rushed from his gallery in a flurry of motion.

Carelessly throwing her purse onto the couch before picking up the receiver, she swallowed in a vain attempt to catch her breath. Her nerves were still shaking from the tension of the drive home. She had had to force herself to obey the traffic laws when she wanted to disregard safety for speed.

Her finger trembled as she dialed the home phone number listed on the embossed business card. She listened to the ring of the phone, sinking into the chair the moment she heard Louis answer. Her knees had buckled as if someone had kicked her from behind.

"Edwards residence," Louis answered, his deep masculine voice husky and clear.

"Louis, this is Joy Sanders. I met you in Reno last year—"

Interrupting her, he exclaimed, "Where are you? I'd like to see you if at all possible." His friendly tone changed to one of cool contempt when he recognized who it was.

"I'm in Hollywood. I called to find out where Jake is. I—I, er, want to see him and I don't know where he lives."

Louis paused. "Have you heard anything about Jake since you left him in Reno?" His voice was disapproving and aloof.

"No, of course not," Joy answered, taken back by his coldness to her. "Until Mr. Hanson at the gallery gave me your card I was stymied in my attempt to locate either a phone number or an address."

"Mr. Hanson, huh?" Louis pondered. "So you saw the paintings, did you? Did you like them?" he inquired harshly, his mood still distant.

"Oh, yes," Joy cried out truthfully. "I've been going there each day. I think they're the most compelling paintings I've ever seen. Why do you ask?"

"No particular reason," he lied, his voice rising to chastise. "Since you seemed so opposed to have anything lasting to do with rodeos or cowboys, I naturally assumed you'd detest western paintings too."

"You misunderstand..." Joy whispered, trailing off in silence. There was no need to explain to Louis. He was Jake's best friend and from their close friendship it was clear neither man would tolerate criticism of the other.

"This is Jake's parents' home," he told her, repeating the address and phone number slowly so she could write it down. "I don't think you should disturb them, although they can advise you better than I about Jake's whereabouts. I haven't seen him for several months myself."

His voice was still strangely contemptuous as he bade her good-bye with one final comment, "If you have any idea of seeing Jake now I suggest you reconsider. He's not the man you met in Reno, Miss Sanders." He hung up the phone, rudely disconnecting the call.

Joy was stunned at the change in Louis's amiable manner: she could not fathom the cause. After all, Jake had betrayed her, not the other way around. Not heeding Louis's advice, Joy dialed the number of Jake's parents' home at once.

"Travis residence. Who's calling, please?" a pleasant male voice answered, the deep drawl unmistakably Texan.

"This is Joy Sanders," she whispered wistfully. "I—I—"

"My God, I can't believe it! Where are you, girl? Are you here in Texas?" he gasped. Joy could still hear his deep voice as he turned from the phone and called, "Mother, it's Joy on the phone. Come quick! For God's sake, tell us where you are!" he demanded harshly.

"I'm calling from Hollywood, California. I'm trying to locate Jake. Could you tell me where he is now?" she pleaded, her voice breaking with the depth of her feelings. It would be such a relief to get everything settled and to confront the renegade who had torn her life apart since she first saw his photo.

Jake's father heard her sobs and answered kindly. "Don't cry, honey. Give me your address and I'll reserve you a ticket and wire you some money to close out your apartment. I want you to catch the next flight from Los Angeles to Dallas-Fort Worth. I've business up there tomorrow and we'll fly back to the ranch together."

"Is Jake staying with you?" Joy asked, remembering he had told her he had been on his own for too many years to recall.

"Not on our home ranch, but when you get here I'll see you're taken to him without delay."

After Louis's unexpected anger Jake's father's kindness touched her heart. It was what she needed after the constant upheaval trying to contact his son. When he told her which airline to reserve, Joy stopped him firmly.

"I don't need financial help, Mr. Travis. I always pay my own way, but I would appreciate you meeting me at the airport. I'll phone you if I can arrange time off from work tomorrow."

"Fine, Joy. Now don't hang up. Mother, er, Jake's mother wants to talk with you a minute."

A soft feminine voice broke in. "Oh, Joy, I'm so happy you phoned us. Please come see my boy," she pleaded. "He's changed so this past year. He told us you and he were married but that's all he would say." Her voice broke mysteriously. "We've been desperate to understand our son these last few months." Crying with happiness at hearing from Jake's wife, she took Joy's number down and hung up the phone.

Restless after the phone call, Joy went to the kitchen to fix a glass of iced tea. As she stirred in artificial sweetener, she heard the doorbell ring. Hoping it wouldn't be Sally, who had a bad habit of dropping in at the most inopportune times, she walked to the door.

"Brian! How nice." She welcomed him, motioning to him to sit on the couch while she got him a glass of iced tea. Dropping ice cubes into a tall glass, she noticed him out of the corner of her eye. She poured in the fresh-brewed amber liquid, added sugar, a squeeze of lemon, and handed it to him.

He sipped the cold drink with obvious pleasure and eased into a small kitchen chair. "Exactly what I needed," he told her. "I just finished with the hospital calls and was anxious to see if you found out anything about Jake yet."

"Your timing is perfect, Brian. I wanted to see if you thought I could take my vacation starting tomorrow. I talked with Jake's parents a few moments ago and they want me to fly to Texas immediately."

"No problem, Joy. I'll explain your absence to the others first thing in the morning." He emptied the glass, set it down, and looked at Joy. A deep frown crinkled his smooth brow. "Did you talk to the great man himself?"

"No. Only his mother and father, who invited me to

their home. They were so kind and promised to take me to Jake as soon as I got there."

Noticing Brian's mutinous expression, Joy realized he was jealous that she would soon see the man she had hastily married.

"Don't be unhappy, Brian. I have to see Jake." She paused, swallowing to ease the tightness in her throat. "It's not a romantic reunion." Saying the next words was the hardest thing she had ever done. "My sole purpose is to seek a divorce," she blurted out, her voice breaking at the thought that her ties with Jake would be irrevocably severed. She blinked back tears before continuing sadly.

"Don't you see, Brian? I still love Jake but I have to ask him for a divorce." Her gem-colored eyes raised, pleading with him to understand. "I couldn't have managed without your help these last few months. You're the only one who knows I've even been married or that I've been running away from the heartbreak of a twenty-four-hour trip to Reno."

Brian's scowl eased as he reached across to clasp her trembling fingertips. "Dammit, Joy, it hurts to see the urgency with which you're anticipating a trip to ask Jake for a divorce. You never looked like you do now when we started out on a date. Your eyes are shining, your body's tense with excitement, your voice throaty and soft."

His grip became painful as he leaned across in anger. "Don't you realize how much I love you?"

Joy lowered her lashes, pulled her hands from his grip, and toyed with her frosty glass of tea. Unable to retain her comments any longer she met his glance, her words filled with open reproof.

"You don't love me, Brian. You just think you do."

"How the hell do you know how I feel about you?" he retorted dryly.

"If you had, you wouldn't have taken Rena to bed last Thursday."

"She told you about that?" His face paled, a look of embarrassment showing in his eyes. "It was sex. Nothing more."

"Maybe so. Maybe not, Brian. I don't care but I do know

I love Jake and with that love comes a commitment that won't ever allow me to tolerate another man's touch. In return, I'd expect the same from my partner."

"Touché. Perhaps you really are one in a million, honey." He refilled both their glasses with iced tea. "Too bad your choice is totally immoral and a despicable liar too."

"That's hitting below the belt, Brian," she admonished him. "Don't you think I'm not aware of that and haunted continuously by it?"

Brian shook his head, trying hard to conceal his remorse. "I know. Forgive me, honey, please. I've been questioning my feelings too. I love you." His voice lowered, became husky and plaintive. "I know I do. Yet Rena was like a drug. I'm not even certain I like her, though she was the most exciting woman I've ever been to bed with."

"She said the same of you, Brian," Joy told him, observing his sudden interest. "She's honest, hardworking, and totally true to the man she loves. When her feelings change, she tells him so and moves on. You need never worry she'll play around behind your back. You have her intrigued now and she'll be all the woman you'll ever need."

"Probably too much," he moaned with a harsh chuckle. Yet he had to be honest. He had thought of her more than he wanted.

"Who knows, Joy, what the future holds for either of us." His own was certainly in a period of change.

"I'm taking mine one day at a time." Joy smiled, her eyes filled with friendship. She knew she was better able to handle any trauma with Jake because of Brian's constant support and would always be thankful for his concern.

"Have you thought how drastically Jake may have changed in the last year? You've changed and matured during these past months and time won't have stood still for Jake either."

"I know, Brian. I'll probably wonder what I ever saw in him in the first place," she lied, trying to ease the temporary friction brought on by talking about Rena.

"Do you need any money, Joy?" He leaned forward,

eager to help in any way she would let him. "I'd be happy
to pay your expenses."

Joy, overcome by his thoughtfulness, stared at him with
tears gathering in her eyes. "No, thank you. I've managed
to save some money this year. That's the least of my problems."

Brian stood up, gently pulling her to her feet. He
gathered her into his arms, his capable fingers pressing her
face into his chest to comfort her. He knew it would be the
last time he'd ever hold her and the thought hurt. He raised
her face and met her lips in a farewell kiss.

Pulling herself from his arms, she placed their glasses in
the sink before turning to face him. She decided it would be
better to leave the clinic and look elsewhere for a job when
she returned from Texas.

"I'll mail you my resignation tomorrow, Brian. It's really
best I quit. I've thought a lot lately about returning to
Seattle, where most of my best friends live."

Seeing the benefit of her decision, despite his feeling of
loss, he reluctantly agreed she was right. He walked with
her to the door of her apartment. "Without you in the office I'll feel more inclined to accept an offer to do neurosur-
gical research and even teach. Seeing you each day ruined
any hopes I had of total concentration on my work."

Joy smiled at his earnest face. "You're sweet, Brian,"
she told him. "You're everything Jake is not. Honest, faithful—you were until Rena anyway—and kind. The ideal of
any woman with the slightest amount of intelligence."

"That sounds like an eulogy," he told her, reflecting that
it was. A taking away of herself forever. A giving of her
friend Rena. Not an equal exchange yet, but possibly one
of growing importance.

After Brian left, Joy wrote out a letter of resignation to
her employers, explaining briefly that she was moving from
the area. She dropped a card to Sally, apologizing for her
abrupt departure without detailing the reasons. She left a
note on the coffee table for Rena, who had her own key,
telling her to call Doc for the details of her hasty trip. She
had a hunch her friend would make an appearance before
she returned from Texas. If Rena really liked Doc she'd see

he clearly understood it was to his best interests to forget anyone else stat!

The following morning Joy made reservations for a flight that was leaving in two hours. She rapidly packed her suitcase, unthinkingly putting in too many clothes for a short trip. A quick conversation with Jake's parents told them of her estimated arrival time. In the taxi she watched the traffic go by in a blur as the driver sped down the busy freeway to LAX.

She tipped him quickly, balanced a suitcase in each hand, and still managed to adjust the large shoulder bag over her shoulder as she wended her way into the busy terminal to the ticket counter.

When she was finally relieved of her suitcases she walked around, looking with interest at the people traveling. Her stomach churned with pain at the reason for her journey. Walking into the gift shop, her shapely figure was shown to advantage in a slim-cut beige skirt tightly belted over a kelly-green print blouse in whisper thin silk. Knee-high boots matched her leather shoulder bag and chic little vest. She looked elegant as she placed a package of mints on the counter to purchase.

Taking the escalator to the upper level, she checked the time, impatient to board the plane for the two-and-a-half-hour flight to Texas. As the steady drone of the jet engines drummed into her mind, she relaxed in the soft seat. Her eyes were drawn to the professional drawings by the beautiful auburn-haired woman sitting beside her.

"Those are lovely," Joy told her. "That is definitely a happy person."

"I certainly hope so. It's my husband." The woman laughed before introducing herself as De-Ann Howell.

"I'm Joy...Travis," she responded, thinking she might as well use her proper married name once at least. "He's a very good-looking man."

De-Ann concentrated on her pen sketch, outlining her husband's smiling mouth with great care. "The most handsome, dearest husband in the world. This is the first time we've been separated since the end of our honeymoon and I'm about out of my mind I miss him so."

She looked up at Joy, smiling with easy rapport. "I always have to do something with my hands," she explained. "My favorite occupation when Derek's working is to put his likeness on paper."

Joy noticed without envy that her clothes were not off the rack, and her dainty high heels and purse would have cost a half month's salary.

De-Ann immediately turned the finished page over and began another drawing. This time it was of a darling baby boy with his father's eyes and wisps of unruly hair.

"Is that your son?" asked Joy, stricken with sorrow to think she would never bear a child for Jake. Life seemed determined to cheat her of a fulfilling lasting love like De-Ann's.

The flight attendants started beverage service and Joy accepted a cola, De-Ann orange juice.

"Either that or daughter," De-Ann added softly, adding a bow and dainty smile to the baby she was drawing. "Do I look pregnant to you?"

Joy looked over her narrow waist. "Not yet."

"I guess you don't start showing at six weeks." De-Ann chuckled. "It's quite funny really. My best friend, Carlyn Sandini, and her husband, Nick, took an extended vacation in northern California about the same time Derek and I did and she called last week to tell me she's pregnant too. It must be the climate." She smiled at Joy. "Either that or the balmy nights and foggy mornings."

Tears filled Joy's eyes forcing her to turn from De-Ann's wistful face. She clasped her hands together trying to still her trembling fingers. It was suddenly impossible to listen to De-Ann extol her happy life. Filled with shame over her lack of control, she lowered her face into her palms, sobbing softly while De-Ann looked on in silence.

She took Joy's cola and her unfinished orange juice and handed the glasses to the flight attendant. Her words were soft and touched with sympathy as she asked, "We have a long flight ahead, Joy. Why don't you tell me why you're so sad?"

Joy glanced at De-Ann's concerned face. She was prepared to tell her no, but the entire story spilled out, including the surprise marriage and Jake's unfaithfulness. The need to purge herself of their relationship was too great to contain any longer.

"At least he married you," De-Ann told her thoughtfully. "Derek wanted no part of any legal commitment. He even went so far as to have his attorney search for a surrogate mother rather than tie himself to any woman."

"But that's not my problem," Joy told her. "It's Jake's adulterous life-style I can't tolerate."

"Joy, Derek went through most every single woman in San Francisco, each state, and several countries too!" De-Ann pointed out with exaggerated emphasis. "But since we've been married he's totally devoted. I will never doubt the man's fidelity."

Joy thought about the woman's comment as she checked to see that her eyes weren't obviously red from her outburst.

"If our stormy courtship, without the offer of marriage, could end so perfect, then yours," De-Ann added, "with a legal offer on the first day, should run smooth as glass! How could you stay away so long? I'd die if Derek and I had to be apart more than a few days."

Joy bowed her head, whispering, "Jake was unfaithful to me the day of our marriage. Right after making love to me for the first time."

"Well, that would give a woman second thoughts," De-Ann admitted. "I'd probably have killed Derek instead of running off."

She groped inside her purse, taking out a Smokey Bear stuffed toy. "Isn't this little devil cute in his forest ranger—outfit?"

Joy smiled, raising her eyes to De-Ann's. It was her new friend's way of saying it was time to forget her troubles. "Is that for the baby?"

"No." De-Ann chuckled softly. "It's for my big brawny husband." From her purse she pulled out a brochure on a Dallas project he was building. "My husband's a contractor, but more than that he's a staunch conservationist. You can tell his projects. They look more like parks than malls, housing tracts, or businesses."

"The artwork is exquisite," Joy remarked, scanning the colorful brochure with interest.

"That's my imprint. I do Derek's advertising and illustrations."

Lunch service interrupted them, but they spent the rest of the flight talking about various interests they shared. As the plane circled to land, they hastily exchanged addresses and phone numbers. De-Ann insisted that Joy write her after seeing Jake.

"Don't give up your heart's desire easily, Joy. Pride can be an awfully poor bedmate. I gave Derek an ultimatum and worried myself ill while awaiting his decision. If I had it all to do over I'd have gone to him with open arms on any terms he wanted. I truly believe the end result would have been the same. All I did was waste precious time that could have been spent together."

"I'll think about what you said," Joy told her. Their situations were too different to compare.

"Take time to listen to him, Joy. Jake's version of what occurred might be altogether different from what you think happened."

Joy thanked her, and later watched enviously as she was swung up into the arms of a handsome man who had pushed his way through a crowd to greet his wife as she exited the plane.

Chapter Twelve

Joy picked up her luggage and waited uneasily for her name to be paged. After a light application of lipgloss, she checked in her compact mirror to assure that her hair was still neatly confined in a smooth chignon. All were ploys to kill time and hide her nervousness.

She looked around, immediately drawn by the sight of a tall man walking with determined strides in her direction. His western suit and creased hat were similar to those Jake wore the night they were married.

The stranger approached, removed his hat courteously, and inquired.

"Joy?" His eyes were the same warm brown as Jake's though his features showed marked maturity. He was a strikingly handsome man for his age. "I'm Jake's father, Walter Travis."

"Yes, I'm Joy," she whispered, sudden tears blinding her eyes. Instantly crushed in a bear hug, her fragile body was held close to his with tender affection.

God, she cried inwardly, *how could this gentle man sire a rake of a son like Jake?*

He released her from his hold, his keen eyes knowing as they scanned her lovely face for the first time. "I knew you without having ever met you before, Joy," he drawled in the deep Texas accent she had admired so in her husband. "Come with me, dear. Mother's waiting anxiously in the plane to meet you. You're exactly as Jake described."

Joy followed obediently, her arm clasped firmly in the hand of the man at her side. His warmth acted like a balm to her troubled heart. "I appreciate your kindness, Mr. Travis." She owed him some kind of explanation but preferred to wait until after she had talked to Jake.

Aware of her inner turmoil, he told her, "Don't worry your mind, honey, Mother and I don't intend to pry into your relationship with our son. That's not our way. Your lives will straighten out soon, I know."

Joy's steps faltered as they crossed the runway to the ultra-sleek Beechcraft Baron 58TC. The twin engine passenger plane gleamed brightly, its red and white exterior reflecting the sun's rays in the clear air.

"I came here to ask Jake for a divorce. I have no plans to stay."

"I'm disappointed, Joy," Walter told her with honest warmth. "Whatever happens between you and Jake, we love you because our son cared for you enough to make you his wife."

"Jake doesn't love me, Mr. Travis," Joy cried out, her short steps having trouble matching his long strides. "I don't know why he married me, but I do know it wasn't for that reason."

"Hush now, honey. Don't you cry," he soothed her. "I think you are very much mistaken about my son."

Walter placed her luggage in the carrier after assisting Joy into the plane. Her jade-green eyes were held by the vivid blue gaze of a slender dark-haired woman watching anxiously as she seated herself in one of the forward passenger seats.

Mrs. Travis introduced herself, clasping Joy's fingers with trembling hands. "Joy, my dear, how glad we are that you came. Walter and I have been beside ourselves with happiness since your phone call."

She scrutinized the younger woman thoroughly before smiling. "I knew my Jake would marry a lovely girl, Joy. You're everything I could ever want in a daughter. Welcome to our family, dear."

Secure in the pilot's seat, Mr. Travis glanced over his shoulder to smile at Joy reassuringly, then speak to his wife.

"Don't press Joy with our wishes, darlin'. Most important now is Jake and Joy talk to each other alone." Love glimmered in his eyes as he smiled at his wife before turning to the controls of the luxurious private plane.

As the engines revved up, Mr. Travis checked with the air controller for clearance to take off. Joy listened intently. She could feel the steady drone, hear it change to a low roar as he taxied down the runway. She clenched her fists tightly around the secured seat belt, closed her eyelids tight together, and held her breath until she realized they had smoothly lifted into the cloudless sky.

Slowly opening her eyes, she smiled shyly at Mrs. Travis. "I've never flown in a private plane before."

"Don't feel frightened, dear. Walter's flown for years." She leaned forward, talking to her husband. "Does Joy know?" She sat back, her eyes darting toward her daughter-in-law as he shook his head no.

Joy observed the changing scenery for a while. "Am I going to see Jake today?" she inquired reluctantly, hating to dwell on the traumatic meeting ahead. She turned to Dolly, her eyes plaintive and wide.

"Yes, love." Jake's mother patted Joy's arm gently. "Walter has some supplies to deliver later and will take you with him."

"Where is Jake, Mrs. Travis?" Joy asked.

"Please, dear, don't call us anything other than Walter and Dolly, although we would both prefer you use Mother and Father."

Joy smiled at the elegantly dressed woman sitting across from her, wishing with all her heart that her marriage had worked out happily and she could look on these kindly people as her in-laws.

Dolly took one well-manicured fingernail and smoothed an imaginary wrinkle from her dress. "Jake's at the cabin, dear. He's been staying there since he came home from the—his travels. We have a large property, Joy, and our son owns a similar sized ranch adjoining ours. In one of the more rugged areas of his property he's fixed up a line cabin to suit his current needs."

"I'm afraid I know very little about Jake," Joy explained in shame, though she listened avidly to each word. She was eager to learn anything about her husband. Maybe some small detail would explain his actions. She yearned desperately for insight into his personality.

"Jake has a lovely ranch home, dear. Quite elegant, in fact. Much too large for a couple. Like our home, it needs the laughter of young children."

Deliberately interrupting when Dolly spoke wistfully of children, Joy asked, "How does he care for a home when he's away so much?"

"He has an excellent foreman and plenty of hands to work his ranch. A devoted couple run his home." She paused, her voice weary with calm resignation. "Walter and I rarely see him since he's seemed determined to isolate himself in the outer reaches of his ranch these past six months. Fresh supplies are delivered every couple of weeks since the cabin lacks many of the modern comforts of his main house."

Dolly changed the subject, asking Joy about her flight from Los Angeles and her job at the medical clinic. She was entranced by the exquisite young woman her son had married and curious to learn more about her early life. She knew Walter would chastise her if he overheard her asking anything about her relationship with Jake.

Walter taxied the plane to a smooth stop on the paved landing strip adjoining a large cluster of ranch buildings.

"We've arrived at the ranch, Joy. If you like, you can freshen up in the room Mother has prepared for you, then after a bit of supper I'll drive you to the cabin. It's quite some distance. It'll take over an hour to get to."

Assisting the two women from the plane, Mr. Travis smiled at Joy and drawled softly. "Welcome to the Double Bar T, Joy. May your visit be a permanent one."

Joy swallowed back tears at the sincerity of his welcome. She glanced curiously at the wide expanse of open countryside visible beyond the tree-shaded ranch buildings and the hangar for the plane. The immense size and condition of the buildings were impressive, momentarily leaving her aphonic. Joy was accustomed to a middle-class existence, and the wealth of her surroundings and the ease with which Jake's parents accepted their affluent standard of living was disconcerting.

Joy stepped into the rear seat of a Cadillac and seated herself next to Dolly. Sinking into the deep beige-colored cushions of the custom automobile, she looked about with admiration.

"Do you like the car, love?" Mrs. Travis asked, noticing Joy's changing expression. "Jake will buy you one like it if you wish, my dear. He's like his father in that respect."

"No," Joy corrected firmly. "I wouldn't let him if he wanted." She met her eyes, admitting sincerely, "I had no idea things here would be this lavish. Jake told me he owned a tiny spread in Texas with a small herd of cattle."

Walter laughed deeply, turning back to smile at Dolly and Joy. "Honey, our son has one of the finest herds of registered Santa Gertrudes outside the King ranch. We argue their merits versus my Herefords all the time. You have married a very wealthy young man, my dear."

"That isn't why I married Jake," she told them softly. "He was very generous to me and his friends but I assumed it was from his rodeo winnings at Reno."

"Your innocence is a delight, Joy," Dolly laughed. "Jake is a man of many talents and like most Texans manages to make a profit on all of them. The Beechcraft Baron is Jake's; he purchased it to follow the rodeo circuit."

"Money, or rather the lack of it, isn't one of our family's problems, dear," Walter interrupted.

"Agreed," Dolly said. "But the men in the family have always worked harder than any of their employees to add to the family fortune. It's we women"—she smiled at Joy—"who lead a life of luxury, my dear. Jake is his father's son and there has never been a more generous man born. I've been showered with gifts since Walter's whirlwind courtship over forty years ago." She chuckled, looking at the large solitaire diamond ring Walter had given her for their engagement. "Learn to accept graciously, Joy, or you'll be a source of dismay to my menfolk."

"Please, Dolly, don't talk as if Jake and I will be living together. That isn't why I'm here." Joy gazed out the car window in amazement as Mr. Travis turned the car into a large circular driveway and stopped before a two-story colonial home in the midst of a parklike lawn. Its wide polished doors welcomed above the flagstone walkway and wide stairs.

"This is a gorgeous home, Dolly," Joy told her as they stepped out of the car. "You're very fortunate to live here."

"Let Jake show you how pleasurable it is being married to a Texan," Walter returned proudly, before glancing at Joy's stricken face.

"Please don't talk about it," Joy protested, her face trying to hide the pain that was revealed in her expressive eyes.

"Forgive me, Joy," he pleaded, moving forward to place an arm around her slender shoulders. "It's impossible to believe you and Jake won't work out your problems amicably. You have to, Joy," he added intensely, "you just have to if Jake is to have any future."

Joy swallowed quickly, trying to contain the tears that threatened to spill. As they entered the wide entrance hall her love of beautiful things gave her the poise she needed to enjoy the luxurious home and its priceless antique decor mingling with modern pieces in a comforting blend.

A robust, gray-haired woman emerged from a side door, staring with curious, impassive eyes at Joy. Both arms crossed over her buxom figure as she stood in the hallway. Her lips were thin, her eyes dark and unwelcoming as she announced, "Lunch will be ready in fifteen minutes, ma'am. I set the table in the sun room as you requested."

"Thank you, Miriam. I'd like you to meet Joy, Jake's wife. I expect you to see she lacks for nothing while she's our guest." Dolly Travis spoke with affection, obviously regarding her housekeeper as a friend of the family also.

"You're a lucky young woman to marry my Jake. He was just knee high to a grasshopper when I come here and I helped raise him, didn't I, Mrs. Travis?"

"You certainly did, Miriam," Dolly chuckled. "It took all of us to keep him in line at times. It's been so hard this last year not to be able to offer him advice or solace." Her voice was torn as she turned into her husband's waiting arms for comfort.

"Everything will be fine now, darlin'. Just you wait and see."

Walter turned to Joy, telling her pleasantly, "Miriam will show you to your room, honey. I'm well aware you're anxious to see Jake. As soon as I change and we eat some of Miriam's excellent cooking, we'll be on our way." Reassuring Dolly, he guided her through a wide hallway to the rear of the house.

"Follow me, miss," the housekeeper commanded. Her voice was cold and strident. It was obvious she was reserving her affection until Joy had proven herself in some way. "I've been head housekeeper here for over thirty-two years and I guarantee you there's not a finer family anywhere."

The older woman motioned for Joy to precede her into an upper bedroom, standing back to look over the woman Jake married. She was blunt and outspoken and had never hesitated to speak her mind.

"You're a beauty, I'll grant you that, which is certainly to be expected. My Jake spent his entire life surrounded by beautiful things, including a constant stream of fine-looking doting women." She pointed toward a bright, feminine-looking bathroom, larger than any Joy had seen.

"I won't question your reason for deserting Jake now, though I do know you caused him much pain." The housekeeper's eyes turned frosty black and hard as stone. "That, young woman, I find impossible to tolerate! If having you at his side eases his problems, then I welcome you. If he receives another setback, I'll be only too pleased to see you leave for good!"

Taken aback by the housekeeper's angry outburst, Joy turned quickly away from her uneasy survey of the guest suite to stare at the face of the woman standing stiffly in the doorway.

"You don't understand." Her hands rose helplessly. "I didn't abandon Jake . . . at least not intentionally."

Joy's shoulders quivered at the unexpected chastisement. It seemed unjust. There were so many misjudgments and puzzling revelations the last few days, she shook her head in dismay. Her fingers clenched at her hips and her face lifted proudly when she questioned the woman.

"Why does everyone seem to misunderstand my part in Jake's life?"

"Do you love the boy?" the housekeeper bluntly asked, unabashed at the personal nature of her interrogation.

Joy's eyes shimmered with unshed tears, mirroring the pain of her inner feelings. Love was too common a word to explain how she cared for Jake. It had been from the first and probably would be to the end.

"Hmmph! So that's how it is," Miriam retorted. "I'm pleased to see you're devoted. Now that my mind's eased in that way I hope you'll be comfortable during your stay."

"I didn't say I loved Jake," Joy whispered, meeting her glance.

Miriam moved forward, wrapping her arms around Joy's shoulders.

"You didn't have to, girl," she told her sympathetically. "Doing so, though, makes you one of the family now in every possible way." A smile lit her homey face and softened the coldness in her black eyes. "I'll be here for confidences, child. I don't gossip and I care like he's a son, though I admit he's always been a person who keeps his innermost feelings to himself."

Miriam patted Joy and eased away self-consciously. "You look young and innocent and he might have overwhelmed you with his audacious ways. When he acts arrogant I remember back to when he was young and I paddled his backside and his haughtiness don't seem quite so bad."

Joy smiled tremulously, astonished by the quick change in Miriam's attitude. "I'm glad we'll be friends for the little time I'm here. You see," she admitted, "you're only the second person who knows that I love my husband. I can't tell you why we parted so shortly after our marriage, but it wasn't because I felt passionately indifferent."

"Well, I should hope not!" the older woman scoffed. "No one could have anything to do with my Jake and not care." She removed a fluffy guest towel from a rack and handed it out, advising forcefully, "Dry your eyes, girl, and freshen up a bit while I serve the lunch. Come down the stairway and turn to your left. You'll find the sun room easily."

She smiled broadly at Joy and walked from the room, not the least concerned she had rudely asked questions that were none of her business.

Crossing the hall to the kitchen, Miriam spotted Mr. and Mrs. Travis talking together in his den. She went up to them and blurted out, "Don't you two worry about Joy and our Jake. That young lady totally adores him and as far as I'm concerned they'll work out their problems."

Walter looked at his housekeeper with amusement, inquiring, "How did you find that out, Miriam?"

"I asked! If more people come right out with what's on their mind instead of pussyfooting around, this whole world would be in better shape today," she retorted boldly.

"Did you tell her about Jake?" Dolly asked with concern.

"No need to. I could tell by the girl's eyes that it won't make any difference in how she feels. Her face just glows with rapture and the concern she feels for Jake." She stormed away telling them if they expected to get any lunch before dark to let her get on with her work.

"Another thing," she called back. "I'd advise no further questions until she's seen Jake. She's trying hard to keep her emotions under control and I think it best lunch talk be kept impersonal."

"Can you believe Miriam?" Walter laughed before sipping from a small glass of whiskey. Swirling the amber liquid around the cubes of ice, he gazed with amused eyes at his wife.

"She's incurable, sweetheart," Dolly agreed, looking at her husband with love-filled eyes. "I was dying to quiz Joy but felt it impolite. Miriam comes right out as soon as they're alone."

She smoothed her gleaming black hair, noting her husband had changed into faded denims and a western shirt exactly as his ranch hands wore. "Do you think it will be all right, Walter? I couldn't bear it if our Jake was caused more pain. He's suffered so much during this last year."

"I know, darlin', and agree totally. Do you feel better now, love?"

"Yes," Dolly told him, stepping forward to lay her head

affectionately on his sleeve. "I was embarrassed at breaking down in front of Joy. I can't understand what could have possibly separated them so soon after their wedding. Jake wouldn't tell me a thing!"

"That shouldn't have surprised you. Our son keeps his own counsel."

Walter glanced toward the doorway at the sound of Joy's boot heels as she walked across the polished wood floors into the den. Smiling his welcome, he asked, "Would you like a sherry before lunch?"

"No, thank you. I don't drink," she answered, her eyes covering the vast room slowly. It was so unlike the rest of the house it was startling. Obviously a man's room, it was furnished with deep leather sofas, heavy coffee tables, and western memorabilia that hung on the walls. Over the back of the long bar hung a painting of a polled Hereford bull standing on a grassy knoll with cows and calves grazing in the background. The quality of the painting reminded her of the ones hanging in Mr. Hanson's gallery.

Miriam called them to lunch, checking Joy's inspection of the large oil painting. She followed Walter and Dolly, thinking the sun room was aptly named. In a bright, airy location it overlooked a broad flagstone patio surrounding a swimming pool, whose water shimmered a cool blue in the afternoon light.

Coming to Joy, Walter pulled out a cushioned chair after seating his wife at the glass-topped wrought iron table.

"Come on, Miriam!" he shouted to his housekeeper. "Joy and I want to get traveling. It's a long, hard drive to the cabin and back."

Miriam pushed a serving cart into the room, ignoring Walter's remark to place a tureen of soup on the center trivet. She added a large platter of relishes, sliced meats, and assorted cheeses. Next came a tray of delicious-looking tiny tarts. A bowl of crackers and freshly brewed coffee completed the late lunch.

"This looks delicious, Miriam," Joy remarked, smiling at the woman.

"It is and see that you eat plenty, girl. You're much too thin to my way of thinking," she scolded. Scooting the dessert tray close to Joy, she told her, "I especially want you to eat some of my tarts. They're Jake's favorite sweet and are filled with coconut and Texas paper-shell pecans, the best pecans in the world."

Joy looked around the table. Everything was beautifully prepared.

Standing with both hands outspread on her ample hips, Miriam remarked pointedly, "I suppose you thought all Texans ate was chili beans and barbecued beef!"

"No, I didn't." Joy chuckled with sudden humor, her eyes twinkling. "Though I must admit I'm crazy about chili and barbecue."

"Serves you right for being smart with our guest," Walter laughed, noticing his housekeeper's raised eyebrow at Joy's pert reply. He dished up the hot vegetable beef soup in large man-size servings.

The tantalizing aroma was lost on Joy as she wished the late afternoon lunch would end soon and they could get to Jake's cabin and back before dark.

Toying with her food, she listened, trying to act attentive as Walter and Dolly explained about the ranch. She knew it was their way of attempting to make her feel comfortable as the meal passed.

Walter stood up, looking at Joy with sympathy in his warm eyes.

"Come on, honey. The Jeep's loaded with supplies by now. Since I dislike putting off things that are bothering me any longer than I have to I can understand your impatience."

Joy thanked Dolly for the meal and her gracious hospitality, reached for her purse, and followed Walter to the Jeep waiting at the rear entrance.

Dolly hugged Joy to her briefly, kissed her husband good-bye and waved as they stepped into the covered Jeep, whose back was heavily loaded with large cartons of supplies. Her eyes filled with tears as she prayed that everything would be all right with her son and the lovely young woman she already loved as the daughter she'd yearned for.

Joy clambered awkwardly into the bucket seat. Her tight

skirt was definitely not meant for Jeep travel. She balanced herself the best she could as Walter pulled away from the main ranch area, across a bumpy cattle guard, and onto a rough dirt trail leading to the outer edges of the vast ranch property.

The rutted road was no deterrent to the sturdy Jeep, though Joy felt as if her spine was broken as she was bounced along. Dust swirled inside, coating everything with a fine red film. It was evident she should have changed into old jeans and a cotton T-shirt at the house.

Cattle grazed on heavy bladed grass in the valleys, their red coats and white faces attractive against the landscape. She noticed several windmills dotting the land, their blades turning slowly in the soft breeze to pump the pure water from deep within the earth into large circular troughs for the cattle to drink.

Walter pointed off to the right, showing Joy where his foreman and crew were vaccinating calves. The holding pens seemed filled with the milling animals as the cowboys systematically went on with their chores.

"Those are Jake's cattle, Joy." He pointed out the reddish-toned animals. "The dividing line between our ranches was that barbed wire fence we passed several miles back."

"I never dreamed there was this much unpopulated land left in the United States," Joy exclaimed. She felt like she'd been in the Jeep for hours already.

"You've barely seen a portion of our properties, child," he told her gravely. "Naturally one day Jake will own both places and in turn one day his sons will inherit the ranches from him. Jake's veins are filled with generations of ranching blood. He loves this land as his forebears did before him and you will learn to in the years ahead."

At her plaintive gasp he patted her hand. "It will work out fine, honey. Don't you worry your pretty little head about a thing."

Joy clearly remembered Jake asking her to have his son. He told her he would fill a bunkhouse with their children. A pain knifed through her stomach at the thought that some other woman would bear sons and daughters that had the same deep love for the land that previous generations of Travises had.

Joy wondered sadly what quirk in a man's nature made some faithful, devoted, and loving to their wives with total commitment while others seemed to be incapable of forming lasting relationships with women.

"How long will I have to talk with Jake alone before we have to start back to the ranch? This road doesn't look like it would be too safe to drive on after dark."

"Give me a few minutes to unload the supplies and see how my son is, then you can talk as long as you want."

"I'd prefer to be alone, if you don't mind," she said, knowing he would understand.

"I've thought about that," he told her seriously, braking to avoid hitting a ground squirrel who darted across the road. "I'll drop you off out of sight near the cabin until I'm finished. I won't even tell Jake you're with me. When I come back with the Jeep you can walk to the cabin."

Walter's kind words soothed her taut nerves as he competently eased the sturdy car around the worst of the ruts in the road. The Jeep climbed steadily upward after crossing several streams. The land was beautiful in its rugged state. Small pines dotted the landscape on the high elevations, growing more profuse as the road twisted back and forth in numerous tortuous turns.

Walter geared the Jeep down as the climb steepened abruptly. He glanced at Joy's profile as she waited impatiently for them to get to their destination.

"Are you getting tired?" he asked gently when she glanced at her watch again. "We've traveled a little over thirty miles. Since most of that has been over switchbacks it's taken a long time to get here."

"Are we almost there, Walter?" she queried tremulously. Her stomach churned so badly she could hardly speak. It was all she could do to keep from pleading that he return her to the ranch. She didn't think she could bear to see Jake in person. So many terrible things had happened since the night of their marriage. Everything had seemed so perfect. Too perfect to end so bitterly, she cried inwardly.

"About a mile farther. I think you'll find the location

appealing. It's set among a thick stand of pines above a grove of tall cottonwoods growing along the edge of a meandering creek with lush green banks. It's very picturesque."

"It sounds beautiful," she whispered, trying hard to keep her hands from trembling. She had loved the woods around Seattle.

"I fixed the cabin up with a few modernizations several years ago for Dolly's and my own comfort. There's no electricity but Jake did concede to letting me have a propane stove and refrigerator installed along with a small indoor bathroom. Fresh spring water's piped to the inside but the only heat is supplied from the fireplace or the old wood cook stove in the kitchen alcove."

"Does it have a bedroom?" Why had she asked that? Joy wondered, her face tinged with a soft flush.

"The single bedroom holds a queen-size bed Mother and I put in. We like to come here once or twice a year for a few days away from telephones, television, and ranch business. It's good to get out among God's great outdoors."

Joy envied the lasting love that could carry a couple through nearly forty years of marriage and still be a thing of beauty to both partners.

"Jake's seemed to feel the need for privacy these last few months," Walter said simply, despite the sorrow that crossed his face for a brief, unguarded moment.

He pulled the Jeep to a stop before a sharp bend in the road. Looking with compassion at Joy's trembling fingers as she clasped them in her lap, he soothed. "If you wait in this thick grove of pines I promise not to be too long. Usually one of Jake's hands delivers his supplies, but Mother and I haven't seen our son for a month now and get worried about him, even though he hasn't lived in our home for many, many years."

Walter stepped down from the Jeep, walked around to the side, opened the door for Joy, and assisted her out.

Stiffly easing her tautened muscles, Joy groaned. "Jake called me a city slicker, Walter, and I guess this ride proved it. I feel all shook up." Stretching her stiff shoulder muscles, she added, "I can't believe I actually woke up in

Hollywood early this morning and now here I am deep in the heart of Texas."

"Much to my pleasure," he told her. He bent his tall frame to place a brief kiss on her forehead. "You'll be safe here, honey," he whispered in his soft drawl. Hugging her tightly to his broad frame so like his own son's, he supplied comfortingly, "The cabin's only a few yards around the corner so don't worry about waiting here alone in strange territory." He patted her slender shoulder gently, smiled in encouragement, and stepped back into the Jeep and drove rapidly out of sight.

A feeling of overwhelming sadness overcame Joy after Walter left her, an unbearable loneliness, as if her last link with the security of a helping hand had been cleaved.

She listened to the loud motor of the Jeep as it strained around the bend, surprised to hear the sound of brakes and the motor cease so soon. Shocked at the closeness of the cabin, she listened intently as the slightest sound carried clearly in the mountain air.

The slamming of the Jeep door was immediately followed by the noise of a cabin door squeaking as Walter Travis climbed the steps to greet his only son.

Joy's stomach lurched with pain as she heard Jake's firm voice resound through the woods. If she didn't panic, the trauma would soon end.

"Help me, Lord," she whispered in despair. "I still love him so much that the sound of his voice after all these months brings pleasure to my heart."

She eased up the road, walking closer to the cabin, afraid to miss a single word her husband said.

"Hello, Dad," Jake greeted Walter. "I thought I heard the Jeep stop for a couple minutes before you arrived. Didn't have any problems, did you?"

"No, son. The Jeep's fine," he answered as he looked at his son with deep concern.

"I thought Hank would drive up today. It's good to see you though. How's Mom?" Jake's deep voice carried easily to Joy across the few yards of woods that separated them.

"Mother's fine, son, but you don't look too good. Still not shaving, I see." He laughed as he looked at Jake's heavy beard. "You still need to put on several more pounds to be back to your normal weight...about twenty-five I'd guess. Why don't you come home, son? Let Mother and I take care of you for a while," his father pleaded as Joy listened transfixed by the conversation.

Why had Jake lost weight? Had he been ill? Was that why he was spending time alone in the mountain cabin? Was he recuperating from something? All the puzzling actions and discussions during the last few hours came back to haunt her as she stood impatiently waiting for Walter to return.

"I'll unload the Jeep while you get me a glass of water. I have to get back to the ranch. Mother and I are going to an auction and entertaining at dinner. It'll take some doing to get all this Texas dust off and me into my evening suit," he explained with good humor.

The sound of their voices blurred, becoming indistinguishable until Jake spoke briefly. "Why all the extra boxes, Dad? You know I don't need much. You have enough goods here to feed a branding camp for a month. Good whiskey and our own prime beef will satisfy most of my needs."

"Most of this is Miriam's idea and your mother's so quit complaining. You know I don't have any choice when those two take things into their own hands. What you don't want feed to the squirrels," he advised.

The sound of the cabin door slamming shut stopped any further eavesdropping.

Joy set her purse on a tree stump, propped a mirror open, and glanced at her reflection. With great care she wiped all the dust from her face, thankful she had some moist towelettes in her bag. Pursing her lips she applied fresh lipgloss to her bare mouth. She avoided the reason for her excited, shining eyes as her image was revealed in the bright light. She sprayed her wrists and throat with a light mist of the perfume Jake had liked. She tried to smooth several tendrils of hair that escaped her hastily redone chignon after the quick brushing, but gave up in exasperation as they refused to lie smoothly.

The slamming of the cabin door jarred her from her contemplation of the past few months. Glancing at her watch, she was stunned to see that well over a half hour had passed while she'd been waiting alongside the rutted dirt road.

The Jeep swung around the corner seconds after Joy heard the good-byes exchanged between Jake and his father. Walter stopped the vehicle, opened the door as Joy walked around to greet him, and listened to her breathless inquiry.

"You didn't tell Jake I was here, did you, Mr. Travis?" she whispered.

"No, Joy. I promised I wouldn't tell my son." He pointed up the road to the bend. "Follow that around the big pine and you'll see the cabin clearly." He took her hand in his, squeezing it gently. "Go to my son, honey. He needs you, Joy, no matter what you might have thought to the contrary."

He released her hand, urging her to go to Jake when she held back. She was reluctant to confront him despite the effort of the last few days to find where he lived.

Walter's sympathetic look gave her the final impetus to face her husband. Smiling courageously, she told Walter she'd be back within the hour.

The rutted road went unnoticed as Joy's thoughts were on the quick completion of her confrontation with Jake and the return to the waiting Jeep. The less time in Jake's presence the fewer chances there would be that he'd realize she still loved him. She hoped to leave with some pride intact despite De-Ann's warning what little solace there would be in a future without the man you cared for more than any in the world.

Chapter Thirteen

The cabin came into view, its wood exterior and shingled roof blending naturally with the woods surrounding it. Its primitive beauty appealed to her senses. Knowing Jake had lived there the past few months touched her heart.

Joy walked forward cautiously, her body tense with the expectation that Jake might loom up before her. A lonely silence continued as she crossed a pine-needle-strewn path toward the front porch.

Her boot heels echoed loudly on the rough wood porch with each determined step forward. Her hesitant knock went unanswered. She rapped louder, starting involuntarily when Jake's deep voice boomed into the still air.

"Come on in, Dad. I'm hooking up the propane tank; I can't leave it yet." His voice was strained as he concentrated on his work. "Did you forget something?"

The heavy front door scraped noisily, partially smothering the sound of the Jeep's engine starting. Joy paused to listen, but assumed it was the wild pounding of her own heart and walked inside.

The cabin's interior registered automatically during a cursory glance around the roomy living area. Faded Indian rugs were the only color in front of a worn leather couch and armchair pulled before a stone fireplace whose hearth was scattered with ashes. She could see two doors. One at the rear of the room and the other beneath a steep stairway leading to an attic.

Moving into the kitchen, divided by a low knotty pine wall from the living room, she observed a small wood kitchen table with two plain chairs placed in front of a dirty, fly-specked window.

A large refrigerator with a cross-top freezer gleamed, its modern exterior out of place in the old-fashioned room. She grimaced at the narrow stove flanking the other side of a stainless steel sink overflowing with dirty dishes and un-scrubbed pots and pans. A mammoth wood cook stove took up most of the third wall.

The bare tabletop held a crumpled bag of sugar, salt and pepper in their store containers, and a half-emptied bottle of ketchup. The gross untidiness of Jake's existence regis-tered on Joy's mind as she passed through toward a narrow screened door that stood open.

Sharp metallic scraping sounds took all her concentra-tion. She walked outside, took a deep breath, and called out. "Jake." Her voice broke, sounding unfamiliar to her own ears.

"What the hell!" he exclaimed, pulling himself stiffly up from the ground where he had been kneeling behind a wood box tightening the newly filled propane tank to the outside pipe connections. His tone was brusque, matching the deep frown that creased his brow.

Brushing the palms of his hands down the sides of his jeans, he scrutinized her from the top of her glistening hair to the dainty toes of her high-fashion boots.

She stood before him nervously. Her breath was caught in her throat and she couldn't say a word though her eyes devoured the man she had married. He was leaner by many pounds; his face was etched with deep lines from suffering and long nights of solitary drinking. Several strands of silver were visible in the shiny ebony waves of hair around his temples. He looked older, harder, and totally relentless as he faced her trembling body with narrowed eyes and an arrogant, formidable expression.

Faltering at the change in him, she hesitated before speaking.

Completely gone was the laughing, warm, loving look of the tender passionate man who had declared his love for her over and over during their brief encounter so many months ago.

His eyes glittered, darkened from soft velvety brown to pitch black and were granite hard as he glared at her. Cold hostility emanated from their depths while he stood still as death before her. Smoothing his hair back with one hand brought attention to the short clipped beard that covered his lean face and stubbornly raised chin.

"Why did you come?" he spat out harshly. "Did my father hunt you down and force you here, thinking that your soft little hands would soothe my worried brow?"

Despite the drastic change to his physical appearance she was filled with compassion. Love pounded through her body ceaselessly. She yearned to bring him comfort and to cradle his head to her soft breast. A craving possessed her. An aching to be held in return. Deep prayer that the magic of their earlier relationship be restored. With newly gained insight her continued caring had been for a purpose. It was her soul telling her only he could create the rapture and enchantment she needed from the man she loved. No other would do.

"No," she answered in a faint whisper. "I found you through the help of the doctor I work for." She tried to face him bravely, despite the shock of seeing him in this condition.

"Why?" he demanded brutally. 'Why the hell did you come back into my life now?" Each word was torn from him with brooding hostility.

Joy turned her back, fearing Jake could see the pain in her eyes. She bowed her head, filled with sorrow and torn with pity for his debilitated state. Suffering had always bothered her. To see her husband in distress made her tender heart grieve with the need to ease his pain.

But suddenly she remembered his cruel perfidy and she stepped into the kitchen and spun around, bluntly pointing out, "I came here to ask you for a divorce." Her gem-colored eyes were large, trying vainly to put up a brave front while she challenged his superior control. She hoped he couldn't see the imperceptible shaking of her upraised chin or the trembling of her fingers held stiffly at her side.

Jake followed her into the kitchen and slammed the flimsy door shut so forcefully its hinges vibrated dangerously.

"You want a divorce? You've got a damn lot of nerve! My God, woman, there hasn't even been a marriage!" he retorted cruelly, his face set in a hard, uncompromising line.

Shifting his body uncomfortably, he limped to the cupboard. He took a whiskey bottle from the near empty shelf, checked to see how much was inside, and, raising it crudely, drank it straight from the glass container. Throwing the empty bottle carelessly into the filled trash can beside the stove, he wiped the back of his hand across his lips as if deeply satisfied, then turned to look for more.

"Don't drink any more," Joy cried out. "Please, Jake, stop it or you'll kill yourself."

He ignored her request and reached for an unopened bottle on the shelf, tore off the label, and unscrewed the cap in preparation for taking another drink.

"Quit that!" Joy demanded, feeling her temper rise to meet his.

"You look like you've been drinking for weeks."

Pausing with the bottle at his lips, Jake stared with cool arrogance before drawling sarcastically, "Thirteen months, twenty-four days and several hours to be exact."

"Don't you care about those who love you?" she insisted boldly. Her brave front was rapidly disappearing at the closeness of his lean frame. The small kitchen ringed them with an implied intimacy that brought all the passionate memories flooding back into the forefront of her mind again.

"Those who love me?" he mocked bitterly. "That's a laugh! Who do you mean? My mother? My father? Miriam the housekeeper?" His lips thinned, cutting the drawl into razor-sharp clarity. "Surely that doesn't include you... *my wife!*"

Placing the unopened bottle back into the cupboard, he leaned against the edge of the kitchen counter staring with eyes cold as steel.

Anxious to secure his promise not to fight the dissolution of their marriage and return to Walter waiting in the Jeep, a cry was wrenched from her throat. It was imperative that she leave his presence before she lost all pride and begged him to allow her to stay under any conditions he wanted.

"Let me have my freedom, Jake. Please!"

"Why is your freedom suddenly so important to you?" he asked lazily. He sensed her impatience and would do nothing to feed it. "You've been away for over a year and apparently you and the doctor took considerable trouble to find me. Why now?" he demanded in frozen anger, his speech harsh and withdrawn. "Why not six months ago or two years hence? Why the hell did you pick this moment in time?"

Unafraid, Joy stared at him with eyes that reflected her pain like windows on her soul.

"I have to be freed from your bondage, Jake. I just have to!"

"You're pregnant, aren't you?" he growled bitterly. "That's why the rush, isn't it?"

Joy recoiled from his brutal accusations. She felt shocked speechless by his erroneous implication.

"I was afraid of that," he stormed, not giving her a chance to deny his blatant insinuation. "You're so damned passionate I knew it wouldn't be long before another man took you." His speech slowed, the inherent drawl shockingly heavy. "I couldn't sleep nights knowing some bastard was enjoying your soft body before I recuperated enough to claim you."

How dare he! Joy thought silently. How dare Jake accuse her of doing the very thing he gloated doing at each rodeo he competed in.

"My God!" he continued, his face raised to berate her without waiting for an explanation. "It was that damned doctor, wasn't it? While I lay in the hospital dying the fool held you beneath him, slaking his libidinous needs in your sweet flesh."

He moved forward, threatening with the force of his bitterness.

"I'll kill him." He gripped her trembling shoulders in a painful hold. "But first, my unfaithful little wife, I'll take what I've agonized over missing." His hands raised, cupping her chin upward. "Starting with this." His head lowered, his thinned lips taking hers with months of pent-up passion.

Joy's body trembled uncontrollably as she felt the first touch of his firmed mouth. The burning contact of his hard, masculine physique was met with her soft form melting into his. She cried inwardly, instantly opening her traitorous mouth to him in response to a hungry kiss that left her aware of his touch on every inch of her skin. His heavy whiskers were painful for only a moment, their abrasiveness surprisingly sensual as the stormy kiss continued on and on.

Her hands groped upward, clinging to his broad shoulders helplessly. His effect on her was even more powerful after the painful months of separation. Drowning in harsh possession by his mouth, she moaned, a deep sound of excitement that stopped him.

His steely grip encircling her body relaxed, and he pushed her an arm's length away.

"Why did you lay with another man, Joy?" he demanded. "Tell me why."

"I didn't!" she stormed back, refusing to be intimidated by his false charge. "How dare you accuse me of such a thing when your...mistress Marie told me you've practiced seducing women at every rodeo you competed in for years. No wonder you were All-Around Champion!"

"No one in their right mind would believe anything that bitch said," he snorted, unconcerned about her comments on his actions. His only interest was in dealing with Joy's relationship with the doctor.

"I did!" she pointed out painfully, consumed by feelings of outrage.

"More the fool you," he laughed hoarsely, determined to pursue her relationship since they were apart. "When did you first go to bed with the man? The first day after you left Reno? A week later? Or did you wait one full month?"

Incensed by his continued pressure regarding Brian, Joy faced him fearlessly. She rarely lost her temper but when she did she was a match for anyone.

"What the hell do you care, Mr. Travis? After our episode when you initiated me you lost all claims on my body!" That should give him something to think about, she thought furiously. That arrogant beast!

"Initiated you!" he laughed scornfully. "That sounds like you joined a club. Hardly the proper way to describe what I did to you that night, my dear little wife."

She pulled back, challenging him with eyes that were dilated and sparkling. "So I used the wrong word. The point is you used me once then cast me aside!"

A shiver ran across her sensitive skin as she recalled her wild response to him after their marriage. Tears welled beneath lids that rapidly closed. She turned away, clenching her hands until her fingernails dug deeply into her soft palms. Would the force of those vivid memories always return to haunt her?

Misunderstanding the reason for her sudden dejection, Jake continued his diatribe. "I didn't use you, sweetheart," he drawled, letting his eyes linger suggestively on her breasts straining against the thin material of her blouse when she spun forward at his continued chastisement.

"I made love to you, yes, but you, my dear, made love to me too! Oh, yes, I remember everything about that night. You were as hot for me as I was for you. You couldn't keep your eager little hands off my body."

Jake's words were painfully true, Joy admitted. She had acted like a wanton, as if there would never be another opportunity in her life to experience a man's erotic touch.

Beads of sweat broke out on his brow at the thought of the past. His words were as much for her as a reminder how foolish he had been to give her his trust.

"You helped me undress," he added emphatically. "Do you remember that?" Not waiting for her reply, he continued. "I've never forgotten the sight of your face and responsive body or the feel of your silky limbs clinging to my hips. You may have been innocent that night, but your unequaled responses were those of an experienced woman."

He took her shoulders into his palms, demanding she look at him. "If for no other reason than that, there will be no divorce!"

Joy's lashes closed, fighting for control as her head spun with the thought she would be tied to a man so changed he felt only bitterness. She would be married to a person who wanted her solely for his memories of her abilities in his much used bed.

My God, she cried inside. *How deserving since I originally sought him solely for the same thing!*

"I've been to hell and back this last year, Joy," he warned her in an ominously low voice. "For my next trip I intend we go together!"

Raising her face to his, he bent down, kissing her over and over. The hunger for the taste of her mouth seemed insatiable. The onslaught continued, his touch searing her skin like a hot brand straight to her heart.

She felt as if her rib cage would break from his tight hold. A murmur was torn from her throat as her soft lips accepted his need to exorcise his hurt. Tears slid beneath her closed lids. He was not alone in needing to rid his past of haunting memories.

She responded, her love the driving force as she moved, her body arching upward to let her breasts press against him. The image of his hair-covered chest filled her mind. She took one inquisitive hand and worked her way to the front of his shirt. With tentative strokes she caressed his lean throat before unbuttoning his shirt and splaying her fingers over his upper body.

His kiss changed the moment he felt her responsive fingers. It became gentle, searching her mouth with a tongue that left her breathing as ragged and harsh as his. His hands trembled, as they wandered over her back and downward to her rounded hips, pressing her close.

Joy felt the hardening muscles of his aroused body imprinted on her own. Her breath caught in her throat at Jake's sensual expertise. As her hand trailed downward through his chest hair she could feel his muscles contract involuntarily. Elated, she continued lower, the hair suddenly sparse as she touched a raised weal crossing his stomach to his hip.

She jerked her mouth from his searching kiss, pulling back to stare at a long scar crossing his tanned midriff beneath his opened shirt.

"Oh, no," she cried out in pain. She couldn't bear it to see him hurt. Shocked at the sight of her husband's healing wound, she turned away, bowing her head into shaking hands.

"What happened, Jake? Was that the reason for your hospitalization? Is that why you're so much thinner and limp when you walk? Tell me!"

Her heart was in agony at the glimpse of his terrible scars. She swallowed back tears, determined he wouldn't see the depth of her sympathy and horrified pain.

She felt the room shift as her mind tried to handle the sudden shock of finding him after all the months of loneliness and the trauma of seeing his scarred side.

Silently Jake enfolded Joy within his powerful clasp, swinging her up into his arms to carry her into the small bedroom. He laid her gently on the rumpled covers of his unmade bed. Stiffly he lowered his aching body to the bed, encircling her with arms that were tender as he listened to her murmur his name over and over.

Joy's lashes fluttered open, her glance locking with his. One unguarded moment revealed a glimpse of desire and love expressed like that she cherished in Reno, but just as quickly he lowered his lids to conceal his response to having her on his bed.

"How did it happen, Jake? Please tell me," she asked softly, touching his hair-roughened face.

Her eyes shimmered with tears of empathy as she lay beside her proud husband. There was so much bitterness that needed soothing, so many questions to be asked, numerous problems to be resolved.

"Don't pity me, Joy. I don't need that from you," he warned her, his voice ragged with anguish.

"I don't pity you, Jake. You wouldn't accept it if I did. I do ache for you. Let me see your wound, please?" she asked compassionately.

Bitter and unsure, he studied her face. "It will only repulse you. The first time we made love I only had one small scar. Then I wasn't a crippled cowboy. I couldn't bear to see you cringe."

"Scars don't bother me. Your pain does," she told him truthfully. She raised herself from the bed and pulled his opened shirt aside.

He lay on his back beside her, resting his head on a crumpled pillow, arms crossed beneath his neck in casual repose.

She stared at him, her eyes lingering as they scrutinized his torso thoroughly. His muscles were leaner but still powerful and sharply defined. He smelled so good to her as she inhaled daintily. It was a warm, masculine odor. His cabin may have been a mess but his body and clothes were immaculate.

With tender fingers, Joy touched his scar. Her stomach knotted with anguish, knowing the excruciating pain he must have suffered when he got injured. The long jagged scar crossed his rib cage diagonally over his midriff, toward his hip bone, before disappearing beneath the waistband of his low riding jeans.

She looked down at his bearded face. "Let me see all of it, Jake."

His eyes narrowed. "I warn you it's not a pretty sight. My own mother cringed in horror when she saw me in the hospital the first time."

He raised himself stiffly from the bed, turning his back to her while shrugging out of his cotton shirt. He unbuckled his belt, the muscles in his broad back rippling with each movement.

As he lowered his jeans, Joy sat with her heart in her throat, slender legs drawn beside her as she leaned on the bed. Her eyes filled with distress as she looked at the long scar running down the spine of his lower back.

Clad in snug navy-blue briefs, he turned, slowly exposing his left thigh where another scar ran from the back of his knee upward for several inches. His powerful chest rose and fell rapidly as he stood up before her.

Joy loved the way his muscles moved under his skin and the tanned beauty of his finely honed body. With or without scars he was the most appealing man she would ever hope to meet. Her pulses throbbed uncontrollably at his physical appeal. She looked upward to his impassive face, his body held in tight control as he watched her for the slightest sign of rejection.

Staring at her face, he refused to soften. His faith and

trust had been stretched beyond his limits with the traumatic events of the past year. The repulsion he expected to see was not there. His wife looked at him with such longing it took his breath away yet he refused to yield. It was too soon. Bitterness filled him, overpowering his wish to give credence to her gentle eyes.

Joy was puzzled as Jake held back. Sliding her legs off the side of the bed, she swung around to sit on the edge of his bed. She clasped his lean hips tenderly, holding him with fingers that yearned to soothe. Lowering her face, she rained slow, featherlight kisses down the length of the healing scars, across his flat quivering stomach, ever lower as she followed their paths.

"Stop that," Jake ordered in a clipped voice as he roughly pulled Joy from the bed. "You're a woman of experience now and you should know what that does to a man. Unlike you, I've not been held in someone's arms this last year. I spent three lousy months in a damn hospital while you and your doctor became lovers."

"You're wrong, Jake," Joy told him simply. "That was your idea and there's not a bit of truth to it at all."

"You're lying! Why else would you insist on a divorce?"

"Ask that damn blond witch Marie," Joy shot back. She was getting increasingly annoyed by his accusations and black mood.

"I have better things to do with my mouth," he groaned harshly. Hoping to ease his painful months of forced abstinence, he kissed her greedily. Aching to touch the remembered lushness of her breasts, he reached up to unbutton the barrier between his fingers and her flesh. He inhaled, his nostrils filled with the scent of a perfume that had haunted him night and day. She couldn't be pregnant. He believed that, but what, then?

Joy stopped his questing fingers with her hand and pulled away at the sudden horrifying remembrance that Walter was waiting for her in his Jeep. How could she have ever forgotten anything so important?

"What now?" Jake demanded, reaching to pull her back into his arms. He was just beginning to slake his needs and had no desire to stop.

"Your father's waiting outside in the Jeep." She turned her head in sudden confusion. "I—I forgot all about him until now."

Jake swore angrily, pulled on his jeans, and stormed out of the small bedroom without a single glance. The front door slammed behind him as he called for his father.

Joy slumped weakly onto the edge of the bed. He was so bitter. She waited for several minutes, letting the tears that had been threatening all day fall freely down her cheeks. Hearing the door slam, she raised herself from the bed and walked into the living room. It made no difference that her face was streaked with tears and her clothes crumpled from their passionate embrace.

Jake looked at her contemptuously before limping heavily to the overstuffed chair in front of the corner fireplace. He threw himself into its deep cushions, stretching his long legs out before him. His face was pale beneath its heavy tan with the pain of rushing over the uneven road to find his father.

"Don't look so frightened. I couldn't continue with our previous lovemaking if I wanted to. That hike looking for Dad is the farthest I've traveled since I left the hospital. Consider yourself temporarily safe from my depravities," he told her bluntly, his naked chest rising and falling unevenly with the effort of his recent exertions.

"Remember," he continued before she could retort. "This is just a delay in the starting time. When I regain some of my strength, be warned, I'll break all barriers to get you beneath me. When I do, it'll be a longer ride than any damn eight seconds, I'll guarantee you now!"

Blood rushed from Joy's face at Jake's crude choice of words. She refused to give him the pleasure of acting shocked, asking calmly again about his physical disability. She was curious to see if her experience as a medical assistant or her year's nursing training could help ease his injured back and leg.

"Were you in an accident, Jake?"

"You might say so," he answered noncommittally. "But one of my own making," he added as an afterthought.

"Where did it happen and when? I want to know before I leave."

"You weren't listening too good. I said there would be no divorce. That means, my dear devoted wife, that you'll remain with your husband for the rest of your life. Or mine, which from the way I feel now will probably end shortly."

He leaned forward, rubbing his left leg in an attempt to alleviate the pain that traveled down the back of his thigh, behind his knee, and along the outside of his calf to the ball of his foot.

"When will I be able to leave here?" Joy persisted.

"You can't go anywhere until Dad decides to come back. He left you stranded, sweetheart. The only way out of here is to walk. I can't and I sure as hell won't let you try."

He looked her over, his eyes lingering on her shapely figure with obvious interest.

"A man's instincts become more base the longer he's without a woman. Heightened by living a primitive existence, he begins to think like one of his breeding animals. If the doctor couldn't impregnate you, I will!"

"Be quiet, Jake. Your coarse words don't frighten me a bit," Joy admonished him. Moving forward, she sat on the couch. She bent down to unzip her boots and slip them off. They were uncomfortably warm. Wiggling her toes, she laughed devilishly, much to his annoyance. "If nothing else, I could easily outrun you."

"You didn't let me finish," he cautioned. "I've been thinking your appearance isn't without some merit. I should put your talents to good use."

"Your cabin is a filthy mess," she misunderstood, looking at the thick dust covering everything. "I suppose I could tidy it up."

"My needs are more basic than a clean place to live. I've decided to use you like a prize broodmare. Service you. Settle you. And pamper you until you foal me a bellering black-haired stud colt to inherit his sire's ranch as I will inherit my sire's."

Joy threw up both hands. Jake was talking ridiculous. "Isn't there something Freudian about a man likening himself to a stallion?"

"Possibly," he admitted arrogantly. "If so, then I must

warn you that a young stallion if given the opportunity will service a mare over and over. He'd be no more satisfied with one breeding than I would.''

"I should have brought my track shoes then," Joy sassed. She stood up, removed her short vest and rolled up the sleeves of her blouse, then stormed off toward the kitchen.

"Where the hell are you going?"

Calling over one shoulder, she answered impudently. No big cowboy was going to intimidate her. "Into the kitchen to clear up your mess. Something my feminist sisters would have a heart attack rather than do. Since I detest filth, I'll swallow my pride and get to it."

"Enjoy yourself," he called out sarcastically. Damned witch!

"I intend to." She surveyed the room, planning her attack when she heard his boot heels as he climbed the stairs to the attic.

Pausing on the top step, he yelled down to her. "This area is out of bounds to you. No one enters this room. Not my folks, not my foreman, and especially not my wife!"

"Fair enough," she retorted. "If it's as filthy as your kitchen it probably won't hold over one at a time anyway." That should deflate his ego, she thought. By the time Walter returned she expected to be well experienced in dealing with obstreperous males. Little did Jake know his sexual threats held no fear at all. In fact, she'd relish showing him some of the things she'd thought of during their separation. He wasn't the only innovative bed partner! Stallion indeed!

She rooted through the cartons of supplies sitting in the corner where Walter had placed them. She was awed by the assorted goodies. It was better than Christmas. There were fruits and vegetables, potted meats, imported puddings, pies and breads, fresh milk and eggs, and marked packages of home-butchered beef.

The bareness of the shelves made them easy to clean and fill. She refrigerated the perishables and then found large canning jars with tight-fitting lids and filled them with flour, sugar, and coffee beans. The only break she took

came when she inhaled the aroma of fresh fried chicken in
one carton and stopped to nibble a crisp drumstick.

Two cartons were too large for Joy to move. They were
filled with clean linens and Jake's laundered clothing. Soft
percale sheets and pillowcases, thick bath towels and wash-
cloths, kitchen towels and tablecloths. The bottom was
bursting with bars of soap, liquid detergent and scouring
powder. Just what she needed!

The last and largest box had a new blanket on the top as
soft to her fingers as a lover's caress. She removed it, looking amazed at her suitcase and makeup kit lying inside. For
the first time she realized that Jake's father had never intended to wait for her.

He had deliberately left her with Jake in hopes of them
working out their problems. A long envelope lay in the bottom of the box with her name hastily scrawled on the outside. Opening it, she read:

> Joy
> Forgive me, child, for misleading you. I've
> found through the years that when children don't
> get along that if you leave them alone and don't
> interfere they will often work out their problems,
> easier than if you offer parental advice.
> Hopefully this will happen with you and my son.
> Our loving concern is with you.
>
> Mother and Father Travis

Joy crushed the letter to her breast, standing motionless
while she thought over its contents. The note, written with
love by her in-laws, gave her added courage to face Jake's
attitude.

She carried her cases into the bedroom, thrilled to death
to be able to change into casual clothes. By dusk she had
the kitchen spotlessly clean. Jake's trash was deposited in
covered containers, the vast number of empty whiskey
bottles verifying her fears that Jake had been drinking
heavily for months. The living room had been straightened
easily, due to the lack of furnishings. Plainly utilitarian, it
served as a functional room in a bachelor cabin. The bed-

room looked more inviting made up with fragrant linens and a smooth spread. She glanced around the room with its knotty pine walls, visualizing Jake living in the Spartan conditions during the last months. Scouring the tiny bathroom sink back to its original shiny white porcelain from a dingy gray took lots of elbow grease but the results were worth it.

With the cabin in order she took time to admire the simplicity of its rugged interior. The fireplace was stained with the smoke of many fires, yet secure and welcoming. The windows were bare of curtains and none too clean. Inside and out it blended with its rugged hillside setting. A welcome appealing warmth that beckoned to her innate love of nature—unlike its owner who treated her with anger and scornful criticism in addition to blatant threats.

Pouring herself a second cup of coffee from the blue granite pot, Joy stepped outside into the rapidly darkening evening. She inhaled, her nostrils flaring at the heady scent of pure mountain air heavily laced with pine.

Freshly showered and wrapped securely in her favorite velour robe, she knew it would be no hardship to spend the rest of her life in the tiny cabin. Entranced by the total silence of the late evening, she gloried in the quiet Texas countryside. Could it be possible this was her proper niche in life?

The first stars began to appear, warning her it was time to go inside before it was too dark to see. Overcome by tiredness after an endless day, she cleaned the cup and walked into the dimly lit living room.

She took one of Jake's bed pillows and the new blanket and padded barefoot to the couch. Wrapped warmly, she settled, snuggling comfortably into the deep cushions. Within moments she was sound asleep, her long chestnut brown hair spread over the pillow and blanket in a glistening sheen of seductive disarray.

Chapter Fourteen

Jake slowly descended the steep stairway from his attic. He held himself stiffly, grimacing at the pain knifing from his hip to the toes of his left leg as he walked into the room. Holding a coal oil lantern high, its yellowish light illuminated the room enough for him to observe Joy's slender form as she slept soundly on the wide leather couch.

He set the lamp on the room divider, his look perplexed as he scanned his neat kitchen. Rubbing his beard with tanned fingers, he leaned his weight wearily against the wrought iron stove. Brooding bitterly, he was stunned by the impact his wife had made in her short time at his cabin.

The small table was covered with a red and white checked cloth. Instead of the unsightly condiments there was a broad wooden bowl filled with fruit and a heavy pottery plate containing his favorite kind of tart beneath its plastic wrap. She had even tried a hand at decorating, he thought, noticing a wide copper bucket filled with fat pine cones sitting on the back of an old-fashioned wood cook stove that would fetch a premium price in any antique shop.

Joy's unexpected desertion so soon after their marriage was still puzzling. What the hell could Marie have possibly said that made Joy believe her over his declarations of love? Dammit, he was irritated. Had been for months. As much for his foolishness in many ways as his wife's renunciation. God, he had agonized over her absence.

He limped to the couch, his love for her eating at his insides. He had found out the hard way that a man's broken heart, unlike his body, did not heal. Kneeling down, he suppressed the urge to gather her into his arms. She looked so innocent, as sweet and appealing as the day they met. It was obvious the months apart had left no outward sign of torment on his wife. He felt far older, his body as ravished as his soul.

With callused fingers that trembled with checked desire, he gently smoothed the long silky strands of hair about the blanket. Inhaling its clean fragrance, he raised it to his lips so he could touch the lustrous chestnut waves with a mouth that was as tender as a child's. His dark head bowed in confusion, trying desperately to surmount their seemingly irreconcilable differences.

With a heavy heart he walked to the lamp, turned the wick down, and leaned over to blow out the tiny flickering flame. In his fresh smelling bedroom he shrugged carelessly out of his clothes. Sliding his naked body between the cool sheets he thought of the hours of pain ahead before sleep would overtake him. It was always the same. Each night was more a test of his physical endurance than the tranquil healing intended.

Drifting deeply into a restless sleep, he tossed and turned as the nightmare returned to haunt him once again. His breathing became ragged as he was returned subconsciously to the rodeo arena where his horror began.

Despite the warning of his friends, Jake was insistent on riding in his last event at the Houston Livestock Show. The mammoth Astrodome was filled to capacity on the final night. Spectators cheered wildly for cowboys in fierce competition for a quarter of a million dollars in prize money.

Three months of sleepless nights trying to forget Joy, miles of travel—Pendleton Round-up, Calgary Stampede, Denver, Cheyenne—and numerous emptied whiskey bottles, all took their toll as Jake eased onto the broad back of the bull below him, a bull supposedly purchased for breeding purposes because of its vicious temperament in the arena.

Feeling the loose skin of the enraged animal between his legs, Jake settled behind its hump, his booted feet with their dull spurs forward on the shoulder. He pulled the heavy bull rope over his palm with a final wrap, gripping it tightly in his gloved left hand.

His hat was pulled down low over his forehead, unnoticed as he concentrated his undivided attention on the power of the bull transmitted through the muscles of his legs and hips. Nodding to the anxious chute crew, he raised his right arm high over his head.

The chute gate clanged open as the immense gray bull exploded into the arena. Enraged at the feel of a cowboy on his back, the animal twisted its massive body, landing heavily from its first leap with both powerful hooves on the arena turf. Fury surged through the bull's body as it twisted sharply before reversing into a quick spin so intent on unseating its rider that it didn't feel the rowels of Jake's spurs raking its thick hide.

Jake put the iron to it, determined to give the spectators a show they would never forget. By conquering Gravedigger, he hoped to gain the strength to control his bitter unending need for his treacherous wife's company. It was not just man against beast, but man against his own inner torment as well.

Jake's strongly muscled arm and innate superior sense of balance enabled him to remain astride the two thousand-pound bull as it went into a tight spin. The bull's muscular hindquarters twisted high off the ground, writhing at each turn. An eternity passed as Jake remained atop the bull, an eternity in eight seconds... eight seconds to hell.

The crowd rose to their feet in unison, cheering the cowboy's talent and determination when the whistle sounded a completed ride. For over three years Gravedigger had remained unridden. Spectators' cries of excitement for the bull's defeat turned to screams of terror when they realized Jake was in trouble.

His only thought was to get safely off the back of the ton of contorted dynamite between his legs. Releasing his rope, he was thrown forward, knocked down in the well with his rigging hung up, pitched into the dangerous inside of the animal's spin. The loud cries for his safety didn't register as the bull continued its lightning revolutions, its massive horned head sideswiping repeatedly at the rider's helpless body being flung in circles with arm-wrenching force.

Rodeo clowns raced to distract the bull, fearless in their attempt to help Jake. Endless seconds passed before the rigging came loose and his battered body was flung to the ground beneath massive front hooves.

With lowered head, the enraged bull bellowed, gouging a blunt-tipped horn into the flesh of Jake's abdomen. Gravedigger's hind hooves caught his side as it bucked over the fallen figure. Spinning around, the animal further damaged Jake, its great weight digging into his leg as it shook its massive gray head, goring its horn through the denim pants. Even leather chaps were no protection against the force of a maddened bull who ripped long tears in flesh that matched those on the stilled cowboy's belly.

Blood flowed freely, absorbed by the trampled dirt of the arena, as a fearless clown leaped gallantly forward flapping his ragged cape in front of the bull's head. Pickup men galloped up in vain, hoping to herd the crazed bull away from their injured comrade.

Pausing, Gravedigger lowered his head to paw the ground, his small black eyes seeing nothing but the daring of a standing man waving a cape in front of his face. As the bull charged, the clown leaped nimbly into his protective barrel while another bravely grabbed at its switching tail.

Uncaring for their own safety, cowboys rushed forward, placing their friend's crushed body on a stretcher, which they carefully carried to the waiting ambulance.

Across the arena Gravedigger viciously battered the sturdy barrel over and over. Head rising, he sniffed the air dominantly before trotting back to the holding pens. Even in defeat he still looked awesome as he swept out of the bloodstained arena.

Jake was the first cowboy to ride Gravedigger the full eight seconds, but in the end it was the bull who had the final victory. As the ambulance, with sirens screaming, sped away to the hospital with Jake's unconscious form, the gray bull was placidly looking for hay, his job for that night finished.

"Stop! Dammit, stop!" Jake's powerful shoulder muscles glistened with the sheen of perspiration as he yelled out in his sleep.

Awakened by the heart-wrenching sounds of Jake's terrible moaning, Joy tried desperately to remember where she was. Her instincts to help her husband were instantaneous as she stumbled toward the bedroom.

Moonlight filtered through the unadorned window, outlining Jake's figure clearly as he lay groaning with the top sheet tightly wrapped around his slender hips.

He flung his arm about, moaning harshly. A pitiful sound much like an animal in pain coming to the end of its endurance.

"God help me ... aaaagh!"

Joy knelt on the edge of the bed, desperate to clasp her arms around him and stop his tormented writhing. She tried to waken him from his terrible nightmare, tried to ease his awful pain. She managed with difficulty to still his great body, cradling him with love while softly crooning as he slowly awakened from his bad dream. With soft fingers she wiped his fevered brow, all the time raining gentle kisses on his beloved face. The sound of her voice reached his subconscious.

Her touch broke the gruesome image in his mind. Crushing her within his hold, he sought and found relief in her arms—the first alleviation after months of excruciating pain.

Partially awake, he pleaded harshly, "Don't leave me tonight, Joy. Oh, God, don't leave!" His breath fanned her mouth, his gasped request coming straight from his soul. "I've prayed for this moment. God in heaven, how much I've prayed."

Tears streaked down her face as she strained to give him succor from his suffering. "I'll never leave you, my darling. Never," she cried into the darkened room. She cradled him to her soft breasts, murmuring over and over the abundant love she had to offer.

Jake's world was replete as he gathered her into the curve of his body. Leaving the heavenly softness of her breasts, he pulled her close, tossing the sheet aside. He wanted no barriers between his flesh and that of his wife.

With fierce urgency his hands moved over her curves, peeling her wispy nightgown over her head so they could blend their bodies as one.

Unerringly his lips found her mouth in the moonlit room. He couldn't get enough of their sweetness after his long celibate existence. He devoured her with deep kisses, his tongue urgent in retracing paths it had explored before: the edge of her teeth, the soft inner lip, and even softer interior where it was met by her fierce tongue rubbing sensuously against his.

"God, Joy. You kiss so damned good," he gasped, his thick lazy words drawled with the Texas accent that always went right through her body. He had no idea she thought he had the sexiest voice in the world.

"How damn good?" she murmured, playing with his mouth with lips that were as urgent in their pursuit as his.

"This damn good," he moaned. His mouth claimed hers in a passionate kiss that left her trembling from head to toe.

The bold insistence of his lips ignited her entire being as she returned caress for caress. Her body arched with anticipation for fulfillment. Her limbs felt the abrasiveness of his. Like the whiskers on his face they brought forth an erotic reaction created by the very difference in their gender. Her silky smoothness gloried in his well-defined muscular hardness.

Dreamlike, Joy responded as Jake ran his parted lips along the side of her neck until he reached her ear. The masculine scent of his damp body heightened her responses shamelessly. His exploring tongue brought her an agony of pleasure.

"I love you," she called out in the quiet of the night.

"Say it again!" he demanded huskily. "Say it until I tell you to stop!" he gasped, nibbling the sensitive area behind her ear before probing inside with his firm tongue.

It had been so long yet it seemed like only yesterday since Joy had received satisfaction in his arms. He was giving her again what she had learned to crave after one act.

"I love you, Jake. I love you so very, very much!"

Easing her down on to the cool sheet, Jake cupped one of her breasts in his hand and raised it to meet his parted lips.

His beard rubbed her skin while he ravished the tender nipple hungrily. His mouth was attentive to each, hot and moist as it sought to coax the tips into hardened buds of sensitivity.

"Do you know how often I've thought of doing this?" he whispered against her body. "How many times I've ached to taste you? How many nights I've remembered the feel of your nipples hardening beneath my tongue?" Between each word he stroked his tongue along the flesh that overflowed his cupped palm.

"No," she murmured, a purr of pleasure escaping her throat. "But I'd love to know."

"Every damn day, night, or hour since you've been gone!" he exclaimed.

Joy's hands clasped the smooth, rippling skin of his back, shocked to feel how little flesh there was between it and his bones.

"You're so thin," she cried out.

"Then feed me," he growled low in his throat, his mouth intent on caressing the smooth skin beneath her full breasts, en route to the cushiony softness of her quivering abdomen.

"Feed me with your body first," he told her, nibbling around his wife's navel before sliding lower to bury his warm lips in the alluring triangle of silken hair below.

"Like this." His mouth explored intimately, his tongue actively relearning what strokes brought her the most torturous pleasure.

"And this," he urged, continuing his ardent investigation.

"Oh, Jake." Joy cried out. She could feel desire deep within her body. Excitement was mirrored in her dilated eyes and the breathy murmurs of love that escaped from the depth of her pulsating throat. Helpless in her passion, she beseeched him to enter her.

"Now, Jake. I want you now!" she cried in a soft, panting voice. How could she have lived without his touch? she wondered.

Jake ached to possess her. Lifting his body, he placed his knees between hers, glorying in the texture of satin flesh clinging to his hips. When he entered her, he knew it was a dream, but one experienced while awake.

Joy's mind swam, overwhelmed with increasing passion as he moved. He was like a drug, his body's thrusting motion touching the very essence of her being.

"I'll never get enough of you," he cried out. The words were torn from deep in his throat, filling the small bedroom. "You're my love, Joy."

She reveled in his blatant declaration. Each word healed the hurt she'd borne in the long barren months past. Her arms tightened around his back and she clung to his damp body as she was overcome by the fulfilling sensation only Jake could make her feel.

With a final shudder that brought goose bumps to his heated flesh, Jake buried his face in the strands of hair lying across Joy's shoulder. Clasped within her arms, he was free of all pain at last.

Joy lay quietly, exulting in satisfaction handed out generously by the only man she could ever love. Cradled in the strength of his arms, she listened to his breathing become even, feeling immense bliss in knowing she had been able to bring him solace. Her body was languorous with the glorious beauty of his lovemaking, his warmth still inside her while he slept.

The moon shone bright through the simple, uncurtained window, and somehow that was right too. To come together, resolve all their differences in an old log cabin, was idyllic. From the first she had been attracted to his earthy virility. Her inner needs had surged forward, as basic as the man she loved.

She neither needed nor coveted the material trappings offered by the successful men she had dated before Jake. Finding his wealth far exceeded theirs made no difference. Real happiness, she had learned the hard way, had nothing to do with one's surroundings. It was dependent on that one person in the vast world that was made for you. The other half of your heart, your soul, and your life. With soft fingertips she reached out to caress him, drifting slowly off to sleep.

The gray light of dawn awakened Joy. Stretching her

naked body luxuriously she flushed at the reason for the lethargic feeling in limbs that were still entwined with her husband's. Tenderly she scanned his features as he slept, watching fascinated as his great chest rose and fell. The scattered gray hairs at his temples were the most visible sign of the trauma he had faced alone. His weight loss she could rapidly take care of with regular meals. With his mouth relaxed he looked younger, more like the man she had fallen in love with so long ago.

Gently she eased away from his limbs, pausing to make certain he didn't wake up. With more difficulty she pulled out from under the weight of his arm and slid out of bed. She was eager to start the day. There were many questions to be answered. After last night there would be no problems they couldn't surmount.

Hoping not to wake him, she stepped under the shower and shivered as the icy water rushed over her warm flesh. A hot water heater wouldn't be amiss, she giggled, thinking longingly of a leisurely bath, then scolding herself for being a real city slicker. Thank God it was summer!

She dressed and stood before the bathroom mirror as she brushed her hair until it lay like spun silk down the length of her spine. No chignon today. She swung her head back and forth, enjoying the weight of her hair as it flowed free before settling back in deep waves.

Restlessly waiting for Jake to wake up so they could talk, she paced the living room. Her eyes were drawn to the stairway. Surely after their passionate interlude that morning he wouldn't object if she snooped. After all, it might need cleaning, she thought as an excuse for disobeying his earlier admonition to keep out.

As she ascended the wood stairs a shiver of fear crossed her mind, a sudden awareness that his tenderness of last night might have been caused by his need of a woman and the long months of celibacy.

Cautiously she pushed open the door to enter his private domain. Shock surged through her body as she was hit with blinding sunshine from two overhead skylights that exposed easels and paintings in brilliant clarity. The crowded room contained dozens of canvases.

In disbelief she knew the answers to many questions that had bothered her the last two weeks. Jake was her artist, the creator of the compelling artwork that hung in the Hollywood gallery. His artistic genius, his love, and his talented creations had reached out to her across the miles that had separated them and was the direct cause of her being there now.

One partially completed painting showed a young girl with flying black hair leaning sideways with her horse as it rounded a barrel competing in the popular timed ladies' event on the rodeo circuit. A brief look, the bitter memory that Marie was a barrel racer too, made her move quickly to the next painting.

Overwhelmed, Joy stared with wide, astonished eyes at the large, unframed paintings hanging around the primitive attic studio. Each was lifelike and intimately detailed, expressing the artist's love for his subject. They were paintings of happiness, of innocence, of love, and of hope. Intimate, heart-wrenching paintings. Paintings so exact it was like looking in a mirror. Joy walked slowly to each one, seeing her image painted with Jake's gifted hands. Awestruck by her husband's loving tribute to her, Joy saw herself as she first arrived in Reno. Her eyes were wide as she looked with wonder at the casinos and the colorful gamblers, her hair confined in a neat chignon.

Another showed her smiling as she proudly displayed her new western suit and boots. A serious study depicted her with the rodeo livestock, her unbound hair flowing free and easy, one booted foot resting on a fence rung. A picture with passion-hazed eyes as she sat across from Jake at the dining table. There was even one of her with shining eyes, tumbled hair, and an undulating body when she spun out alone while dancing to a country music tune.

As she progressed around the room, the paintings became increasingly intimate until the final pictures depicted her golden body lying unclothed on Jake's hotel bed after they were married. Her chestnut hair was splayed over the pillow, gem-toned eyes dilated with passion and desire, soft mouth parted and inviting. There were a half dozen large works of her naked, each beautifully composed. Erotic portrayals of a woman replete with her lover's attention. Numerous smaller sketches in charcoal excellently executed showed the artist remembered his subject with detailed intimacy.

The larger oils all depicted her jade-green eyes alive with excitement. They revealed strong passion while never detracting from the innocence of her oval face. Her golden toned body looked slender and shapely, breasts full and high as she reclined in various, sensual positions on the wide bed. Had she really looked that wanton?

The final painting was a view of her back turned, her abundant hair hanging below her waist in a dark cloud. The deep waves ended just above the rounded swell of her buttocks, emphasizing her smooth thighs and curved calves. Across this painting Jake had etched a black slash from corner to corner as if hoping to cross her from his mind as he crossed her off the canvas.

On a small table lay her western suit and boots, protected by a plastic case. Next to the case rested a miniature wrought iron brand in the shape of a perfect heart circling the initial *J*.

Interrupted by the scraping sound of the door being pushed back, Joy spun around. Jake loomed in the doorway, his size dwarfing the entrance to his studio. His wide chest was bare above his jeans, his face clean shaven. She stared bravely, uncertain what he was thinking behind the enigmatic mask of his features as he looked at her with an unwavering glance. Never would he intimidate her again. Not after the deep insight into his personality revealed by his art.

She ran to him, tears shimmering in her eyes as she clasped him around the waist. Burrowing her face into the warmth of his hair-roughened chest, she sobbed with happiness before lifting her face to his.

"You really care, don't you? No man could portray a woman with the genius that you have without feeling love." Tears slid down her cheeks as she bowed her head in shame. "Oh, my darling, Jake, have I misjudged you all these months?"

"If you thought I could ever be unfaithful to you, you

did," he whispered hoarsely, cradling her soft body to his chest. "God, Joy, how could you believe I was capable of holding another woman in my arms after meeting you?"

Threading his fingers through her hair, he raised her shiny mouth to his searching lips intending once and for all to assure her he would never, never in his lifetime want anyone else. Joy responded instantly, but Jake pulled away, his dark brows furrowed in a threatening scowl.

"Now, tell me what that bitch told you."

With both hands clasped behind her back, he rested his chin on the top of her head, listening with astonishment to his wife's tale.

"How could you have ever believed such rubbish?" he scolded bitterly afterward.

"Why not?" she stormed back, miffed at his easy condemnation of her gullibility. "A *casual* friend would hardly know about the scar in your groin!" Hands on hips, she pulled back to stare at him with her chin raised, ready to pin him down. "Start explaining, cowboy!"

His deep laughter only increased the sparks shooting from eyes that the moment before had been filled with tears of happiness.

"How the hell should I know how Marie knew about it? I certainly didn't show it to her."

"Keep talking!" Joy warned him impudently. "I'm not satisfied yet!"

"Neither am I!" He grabbed her, capturing her mouth in a forceful, ardent kiss that left her squirming.

"I didn't mean that way and you know it," she said, seriously.

"Okay," he elaborated. "She probably overheard some of the guys teasing me years ago. They used to rib me about the injury darn near ruining my love life completely as well as raising my voice to that of a high soprano."

Joy believed him, and she reached to put her arms around his back. She pressed her face tight against his chest. "I'm sorry, Jake. So, so sorry," she whispered slowly, each word filled with regret.

She could feel his rapid heartbeat beneath her ear. His body's warmth and clean scent brought raw, aching guilt over the time apart and the heartbreak her lack of faith had caused. She raised her eyes, letting him glimpse the promise of happiness in their shimmering depths.

"I'll spend the rest of my life making it up to you," she promised.

"Good," he chuckled. Life was too precious to worry about carrying a grudge for her lack of faith. "You can start right now by rustling me up some grub."

"My gosh, you cowboys really do talk funny, don't you?" she scoffed.

With arms around each other they walked down the stairway, laughing as they tried to keep their balance on its narrow width. In the kitchen Joy immediately got busy, placing bacon strips in a big iron skillet, grabbing plates and silverware, making coffee in a blue granite pot, and reaching for large brown eggs in the refrigerator. She had removed three from the carton and started to return it when Jake stopped her.

"Better put a couple more out," he advised, munching on his second coconut-pecan tart. He chewed with relish as he watched Joy deftly fix their breakfast.

"Why on earth would you need four eggs? I only want one," she chided, scowling as he reached for another small sweet.

"A man needs lots of fuel if he's expected to keep up with a young wife."

"That will be the day!" Joy shot back, slanting him an amused glance. "You're the most virile man I've ever heard of."

She walked over, removed the third tart from his hand and put it back on the plate, making certain to cover them securely with the plastic wrap.

"Quit snacking! Your breakfast is just about ready."

"Good. I need energy fast since I'm intending to use up another two hundred calories in about sixty minutes."

"Two hundred?" Surely he wasn't going to work their first day alone.

"Yep!" he remarked smugly, placing plates, butter, and an uncut loaf of Miriam's homemade bread on the table. "I have it on good authority that's what one, er, loving burns up."

"If you don't want your breakfast burned, quit talking foolish and open a jar of strawberry jam for us."

True to his word, in an hour they were both replete with food, the best either had remembered eating in months, and were cleaning up. Joy was washing while Jake dried, surprising his wife by not having to be asked.

Jake threw the dish towel carelessly over a rack, gave Joy a leering gleam, and reached with both hands to draw her forward. While she leaned back he ran his hands familiarly over her curves.

"Hmmm," she crooned, as eager as he for affection. "Your hands feel pretty good, cowboy." She tossed her long hair and squirmed closer.

Placing one big hand over her breast, emphasized in the snug T-shirt, he cupped the weight tenderly, his thumb stroking back and forth across the responsive nipple.

"Don't you know, woman, that ranch hands feel better!" He squeezed her with delicate care for emphasis on his play on words.

"My Lord," she scoffed, catching on to his meaning and withdrawing promptly from his touch. "You really are corny!"

With sparkling, mischievous eyes Joy shot Jake an enticing glance. She fluttered her lustrous lashes for added appeal before asking, "Shall we mosey on down the trail to your bedroll, partner?"

He grabbed her waist, heading through the living room, his deep laughter filling the small area. "Now who's being trite?"

Before she could think of a proper retort, he stiffened, reaching for his back. A sudden look of severe discomfort clouded his warm eyes.

Immediately dismissing the purpose for going to the bedroom, Joy was filled with deep compassion for her husband's injured spine. She took his arm, hoping to assist him, as her eyes searched his face.

"Let me massage your body, Jake. It will help your muscles relax and ease the pain. We'll forget all about making love today."

"The hell we will!" he warned, guiding her with a decided effort to keep from limping into the bedroom. He sat on the edge of the unmade bed to remove his boots and his eyes pinned hers.

"I'm *dis*abled, woman. Not *un*able." His words were meant to be taken seriously. Next came his socks and, facing her without any embarrassment, his jeans.

When his hands slid to remove his briefs, Joy told him in a professional voice used for obstreperous patients, "Lie down on your stomach in the middle of the bed."

"Well, well, little Miss Florence Nightingale speaks," he griped, all the time doing as she asked without further coaxing.

Joy knelt on the mattress beside his hips, her training coming back with the first touch. Her fingers were gentle on tender flesh, firm on muscles that weren't sore. On and on she massaged his body, exultant when she felt the taut bunched muscles relax. From his neck to his feet, her gentle ministrations brought him release from agony.

When he felt the spasms leave his spine, he could no longer control his deep physical needs. It had been all he could do to tamp them despite the pain anyway.

"Roll over, Jake. I'm going to massage your chest now," she told him, flexing her shoulders briefly.

With surprising agility he turned over, unashamed of his partially aroused body as he reached to draw her on top of him.

"It's my turn now," he drawled, his eyes dilating with desire.

"Stay still! I'm not finished yet," she scolded, trying to avoid looking at him as other than a patient. A shudder ran through her stomach. It was impossible to remain detached. Not when his body was obviously intent on finding satisfaction deep within hers.

"Better make it quick then," he threatened. "I'm not inclined at the moment to wait much longer to make love to my wife."

"Shush!" Joy censured. As she reached to rub the muscles of his upper chest he raised up, kissing her wrists while trying to pull her down.

"Take your clothes off. You've far too much on."

She obliged. It was obvious his mood had changed and

her attempts to heal were no more on his mind than they were on hers. When he sat up, trying to take her in his arms, she thought only of the many wanton desires that had haunted her night after night. She touched his hip.

"Let me love you, Jake," Joy whispered, her gentle fingers giving him succor from the constant pain in his injured back. "Lie back, my darling, and let me bring you a hint of the satisfaction you gave me earlier."

Her hands lazily stroked the hair-roughened skin of his limbs until they reached his aroused manhood. She was encouraged by his sudden moans of excitement, and passion flowed from her fingertips guiding her intuitively when he quivered within her grip. Her face lowered, allowing her hair to cover his hips in a silken swathe that hid the perfection of her profile. Her mouth touched him boldly, without embarrassment, eager to show her love in this intimate act.

She felt his broad palms cup her head gently, his fingers twining through her hair in reaction to the unexpected pleasure of the warm moistness of her mouth. Words of love were torn from his throat, spilled forth unbidden, over and over.

With urgency nearly out of control he rolled her beneath him and shuddered with the beauty of her passion-flushed body.

"I want to please you, darling," Joy crooned, clasping his face in her hands. She was no more ashamed to express her love in a filtered sunny bedroom than she had been in the moonlit darkness. She took him into the warmth he sought, with arms and legs that clung.

Giving pleasure was returned as he held back, his body stroking hard and hot inside her until she arched upward and a low groan was torn from her throat. When he was certain Joy had reached her heights, he plunged deeper, quivering as he gave himself over to her in the final act of love.

Joy lay cradled in Jake's arms, her body still tremulous from his ardent loving. She couldn't believe her response. Would it always be like this? Would she always feel the unbearable aching for release that left her thighs trembling and the surge of emotion overwhelming consciousness itself?

Her thoughts were dreamy as she placed kisses on the dark mat of hair across his strong chest. Each time was so perfect she couldn't think of words to express her feelings.

Her husband's tenderness in the aftermath was becoming her favorite time. She felt so replete, glorying in his gentle caresses as he stroked her sensitive flesh with tender regard.

At no loss for words, he whispered over and over how he cherished her. When she blushed at the blatant way he voiced the additional ways he intended to pleasure her, he raised her mouth to his. His sweet, urgent kisses assured her that she'd like each and every one.

With gentle fingers she traced the outline of his healing abdominal scar. Tears of sadness that he had endured so much suffering alone filled her eyes.

"Jake, I know you were gored by Gravedigger, but why are you taking so long to recuperate?"

He stopped her questing fingers as they slid lower, his chin nuzzling her brow before answering. "My doctors could detail what happened better than I. For three weeks they didn't even think I'd survive. When it looked like I'd make it, they told me I'd never walk."

"Oh, no," she cried. She could feel his pain as if it was her own.

"They forgot to take into consideration I was a Texan," he told her seriously. "That gave me the determination to prove them wrong. In a month I was ready to come searching for you again, when infection set in. That was one of the most bitter delays in my life." His body shuddered at the memory.

"God, Joy, if you only knew how frantic I was when I returned from the jeweler's with your rings to find you had left. I didn't even know the name of your damn motel. I tore Reno apart looking for you, checked with the bus depot, the airlines, even the taxi service. If I had realized that Marie had accosted you, lying about our past relationship, I would have killed her with my bare hands."

"I might have done that for you," Joy told him, aware of the trauma in two lives her words had caused.

"I didn't know your uncle's name, where you worked, or anything about you. I advertised in the Sacramento papers, searched the city, even hired a private investigator. It was as if you had never existed other than in my dreams."

"How can you ever forgive my lack of faith in you?" she sobbed.

Licking the streaming tears from her cheeks, he covered her face with kisses then took her mouth in a long, searching caress that helped heal the wounds they had each received.

"Don't cry, Joy. It's all in the past now. You'd have regretted ever knowing me if you'd seen me during the first three months after you left. I was bitter, angry, and totally impossible to live with. My only friends were Louis and a quart of Jack Daniel's. Both gave me the courage to face another day. When I look back through that nightmare, I realize that without experiencing such closeness to death, I'd never have taken the time to find the talent for art within me."

Smoothing her tumbled hair from her forehead, he eased around, pulling her with him as he lay on his back.

"While I was still in the hospital, Mom realized I needed to rid my soul of the devils that haunted me day and night. She brought me paper, charcoals, oil paints, and canvases, telling me to let all my bitterness flow from my body. She encouraged me to put down on canvas and paper what was bothering me the most. After I was released from the hospital I came to my cabin like a wounded animal to lick my wounds alone. I wasn't fit company for man nor beast. All my energies were devoted to painting. By sunlight during the day and propane lanterns at night. I rarely slept but I did create picture after picture as you know."

Joy listened attentively as Jake spewed forth his months of frustration, knowing the telling would cause the final healing.

"I painted the series of you first, hanging them in my studio where I could see you whenever I raised my eyes. With your image beside me I did canvases of rodeo scenes. Scenes that I knew intimately and events that I knew I would never compete in again."

"Was I the long-haired girl?" she asked, snuggling to get closer.

"You noticed?" he asked with surprise.

"No," she told him honestly. "An art critic pointed it out to the gallery manager."

"That was you turning your back to me, rejecting my love. Even my signature was you. The brand was my heart with your initial inside."

"What about the picture of Gravedigger? Why won't you sell it?"

"That's my catharsis, what I always relived in my nightmares. That was the final rodeo event I'll compete in and more important the one that almost separated us permanently. I need it to remind myself how foolish it is to think you can show so little regard for life without eventually paying a severe penalty."

"That painting is what brought me to you. God must have guided me after I first saw it. I felt compelled to view it over and over."

With tears streaming from her eyes, she sobbed at the terrifying thought she might never have found her husband.

"If Louis hadn't sent your exhibit to Hollywood and I hadn't had the strong obsession to examine them, would you have found me?"

"Hush, love, of course I would have. Our problems are over for good," he told her, one hand cradling her damp face to his chest.

"Jake, I worked for a brilliant neurosurgeon. I could phone Brian and ask him to examine you. He's talented and innovative."

Excited at the thought of helping Jake, she drew away, propping herself on one elbow while she studied his face.

But Jake was bitterly jealous at the knowledge that Brian had shared some part of Joy's life he would never be able to. He was adamant in his refusal to let her call.

"Don't mention it any further," he told her emphatically, his arrogance coming forth in obvious clarity.

"All right, for now," Joy told him, not the least intimidated. "If you continue to experience pain in your back and legs despite my daily massages, I'll have to take matters into my own hands."

"My darling, misguided wife. I shall *never* need your doctor! In addition to everything else, Texas has the finest physicians in the world."

"I can see that not being a born and bred Texan is going to be a handicap. It will probably take me years to acquire a heavy drawl and learn to brag like you," she teased.

Rolling her onto her back, he pinned her hands overhead, deep laughter escaping his throat. "Stay just the way you are. I've developed quite a preference for city slickers."

His mouth captured hers to end any further questioning, and his broad chest pressed her wiggling body deep into the innerspring mattress, one hand sliding down to fondle her breast.

Not about to be silenced, Joy turned her face to taunt him saucily between kisses. "You're right. Ranch hands really do feel better."

Seven glorious days followed. Sunny days filled with love, laughter, and delight in each other's company. Heavenly long nights with hours of lovemaking as Jake's desire slaked itself on the equally responsive body of his eager bride. Joy's excellent meals and daily massages worked miracles on her husband's physical well-being.

They relaxed in the big leather chair, spending hours curled together watching logs burn in the corner fireplace. It was idyllic and they both dreaded the time when it would end.

On the eighth day Joy walked alone to a tree-shaded pool Jake had formed by damming a shallow creek that ran behind his cabin. It was her favorite spot. In total privacy, she never worried about stripping her clothes off and playing in the sun-warmed pool.

Luxuriating in the water, her hastily discarded jeans and T-shirt in a heap on the grass, she played like a child. She still hadn't told Jake about her erotic fantasies of him. Perhaps she never would.

She glanced up with a start, a guilty look giving her lovely face an impish touch when she saw her husband approach. She had always come down alone while he was resting after a relaxing afternoon massage. It shocked her to see the gleam in his eyes while scanning her golden body. She waited, standing boldly in the center of the hip-high pool.

Jake removed his clothes and dove into the water after her. Squeals of laughter permeated the air as they frolicked, turning into the silence of awareness when he stretched his arms out to draw her close.

His eyes were filled with love and tenderness as he held her without comment. She reveled in the warmth of his nude body touching hers from breast to knee. She was pliant, yielding as always to his greater strength. With a gentleness that she had learned to expect, he threaded his hands through her unbound hair, stroking the glistening strands while whispering words of love over and over.

Rising on tiptoes, she kissed his passionate mouth. She was dizzy with the magic of his touch. Always they were hungry for each other, one as insatiable as the other. She arched upward, pressing closer to her husband.

He swept her into his arms, his mouth imprinting hers with ardent kisses as he carried her from the shallow pool to the flat grassy bank. Hands that knew her body as well as his own stroked her compliant body.

"Make love to me, darling. Make love to me right here."

"That was my intention from the moment I first glimpsed you naked in the pond. You're a temptress again," he drawled, lazily working his hands from the fullness of her breasts to her smooth buttocks. Her wet flesh excited him and he drew her closer to feel the imprint of his arousal.

Burying his face in the lustrous waves of hair that fell about her shoulders, he moaned. "You have the loveliest hair in the world, Joy. I will never tire of touching it."

With grace he eased upward, placing himself between her silken limbs. He paused, watching her eyes change to luminescent jade as she beseeched him, arching upward in a silent invitation. He was overcome with an unquenchable thirst to savor the sweetness of her body again.

Jake fused their bodies together so perfectly it far exceeded her past fantasy. This time she would not wake up frustrated. This was real. Tears blurred her vision as she called out his name with feverish intensity until they reached the heights of love one more time.

They lay temporarily fulfilled, listening to the treetops whisper in a soft breeze while they clung together in the awesome peacefulness of their outdoor bed.

Joy's eyes closed, her limbs outstretched, her body replete as she drifted into a drowsy state of total contentment in the balmy air.

Jake pulled from her side, holding his head up to listen. On his haunches he peered through the trees a moment.

"Move it, honey. Here come Mom and Dad." He reached a hand down to help pull her to her feet.

"Oh, Jake, no!" she cried with embarrassment, frantically fumbling to pick up her clothes.

"No time to dress," he told her, taking hold of her fingers.

"They won't believe their son was playing Adam in the grass with his Eve," Joy giggled, trying desperately to keep up with her husband's long strides.

"Don't you believe it, darling. It won't surprise them at all," he laughed as they bent low to dash breathlessly inside the cabin's back door just as the Jeep braked to a stop out front.

Tooting the horn for the first time since Jake had built his cabin, Walter and Dolly smiled at each other, instinctively knowing all was well at last.

Epilogue

Joy's eyes met Jake's across the width of their luxurious master bedroom. She adored the way he always sought her out before a party to caress her and tell her in his low, stomach churning drawl how much he loved her. The sight of his beloved face still affected her the same as it had when she first saw his photo so long ago. God, how she loved him.

Her long hair was coiffed in an upswept style accentuating the beauty of her profile. Jake wouldn't let her cut it and she was glad. A soft flush tinged her cheeks at the memory of the many nights they had lain in each other's arms while he fondled the chestnut strands with tender fingers, often laying the weight of it seductively across his naked chest in the aftermath of love.

She walked forward, her elegant silk gown swirling in green folds around tiny evening sandals. The fabric matched the emerald stones in her jewelry. Raising her lips for his kiss, she felt pampered. Physically and materially as well. Everything in her wardrobe, her jewelry, and her home were the finest her husband's money could buy. She was still awed to be surrounded with such wealth.

Taking his arm, she smiled at his indulgent, love-filled expression as he led her from their room to meet their guests. It was their second anniversary and Jake was determined it would make up for not being together on their first.

Without warning he pulled her into the library, then closed the door behind him with obvious intent.

"One more kiss," he demanded, his lips pursuing hers

with an ease of motion gained from the knowledge she could never bear to resist him.

Joy raised on tiptoe, clasping his head with perfectly manicured fingernails. Her mouth parted to accept his.

"It seems unnatural that a man should still desire his wife after just making love to her for the third time today," she taunted impudently.

"You're forgetting I'm a Texan, woman," he teased.

"Never, my darling," she laughed. "Never could I forget that! Though I never dreamed *my* Texas cowboy could be so easily aroused after all this time. You're an insatiable beast!"

"*Me* insatiable!" he drawled huskily. "You're the wanton female who pursued me from state to state. Little did I dream you had plans to do wild and wicked things to my body way back in Nevada."

Joy flushed softly, scolding his devilry. "Shush, Jake!"

Early that morning while still languorous with the glowing feeling of her husband's lovemaking she had confessed why she had been in Reno and all the trouble she had gone through to find him after seeing his photo in the boot ad. Maybe she should have kept it a secret after all, she chuckled to herself.

"Your blatant chase would have put off a lesser man. You're damn lucky it was me you were hunting," he told her with amused arrogance.

"Be quiet, Jake," Joy admonished saucily. "I need no reminder that it was the best thing I ever did in my life. You're quite a turn-on for a man of your great age."

"Are you calling me a stove-up old man?" Jake teased, pursuing the enticing swell and cleavage of her soft breasts exposed in a décolleté gown.

"Hardly stove-up," Joy returned, suddenly serious. "You're doing remarkably well since the surgery on your back. You rarely ever limp now."

She examined his features closely. He was tanned and healthy-looking and so handsome in his dark evening suit she found it hard to tear her glance away. She lowered her lashes, admitting she preferred him wearing tight-fitting jeans with his bare chest exposed to her eager gaze. In fact, at her insistence he often let his beard grow so she could feel its abrasiveness against the smooth skin of her body. She had never forgotten the night in the cabin when he had brushed his lips over every inch of her body. His beard had stimulated senses long denied release during their months apart.

He looked so fit since he had gained weight and quit drinking. He had taught her to ride and despite his doctor's adamant orders not to had taken her on long horseback rides over his ranch. Stubbornly tough, he was determined to oversee his property. His painting had suffered a serious setback despite her pleas and those of the gallery owner. With autocratic indifference he had explained that for the time being his only interest was painting his wife and that those works of art would never be for sale.

"It wasn't the surgery that made the difference," Jake enthused with sincerity breaking into her thoughts. "It was the therapy of your loving hands daily massaging my limbs and back."

"I still don't know why you didn't let Brian operate on you," Joy said earnestly.

"Let Rena take care of the doctor," Jake complained sharply. "I hate the man."

Pulling back from his touch, Joy laughed at his peevish attitude.

Rena had brought Brian to the ranch on a return trip from a vacation in Greece. Her best friend confided that she and Doc would soon marry despite still fighting a lot. It seemed they couldn't live without each other now.

"You're terrible!" Joy reprimanded her husband firmly. After eleven months sparks still flew when she mentioned her former employer's name. Jake and Brian had taken an instant dislike to each other.

"I'm not," Jake insisted, nipping her neck in a reminder not to mention the man's name again. He'd never forget the way Brian's eyes had followed Joy throughout their visit. It still galled him to think his own wife insisted Rena and the doctor spend several days as houseguests when there were perfectly adequate motels a mere twenty miles away.

Joy tugged Jake's hair, knowing it best to change the subject. Removing her left hand from his neck she checked her watch. A low chuckle escaped her throat when her husband read her thoughts accurately.

"Only four hours to go," he drawled suggestively. "One for cocktails, one for dinner, and two to round up the entire herd and cut them out the door so we can get on our way."

One of Jake's Jeeps was packed and parked by the back door of their plush ranch home for the nighttime trip to the cabin. It was their fourth trip there in the last eleven months. Even the three-week honeymoon in Tahiti while Jake recuperated from surgery hadn't surpassed the memories of making love in the simple cabin in the woods.

"Now that I know I was the object of your shameful, lust-filled fantasies I can understand why you're always trying to seduce me into taking you to my cabin to make love to you on the grass," he taunted, nuzzling his lips against the scented skin of her neck.

"Shush, you fool," Joy admonished breathlessly, trying hard to answer his mischievous teasing with an intelligent explanation for her unceasing desire when the weather was suitable for nude bathing in their hidden pool.

"Replacement recreation only," she clarified brightly, her hands lowering to rest on the warmth of his broad chest.

"Replacement recreation? I don't understand," he questioned, cupping her splayed fingers beneath his callused palms.

"Since you can't bulldog steers anymore it seemed only fair that my wifely duties include the offer of a satisfactory substitute for your energies."

"The hell you say." His tongue traced a path around the sensitive skin of her ear. "I hate to admit it but this Texas cowboy's damn glad to switch sports."

"Me too, my darling. Me too," Joy told him softly while she held his head still to place her parted lips with their own potent brand of magic over his—an imprint as permanent as the one he branded her heart with from the moment of first contact.

Get this book FREE!

Mail to:

Harlequin Reader Service

In the U.S.
2504 West Southern Avenue
Tempe, AZ 85282

In Canada
649 Ontario Street
Stratford, Ontario N5A 6W2

YES! I want to be one of the first to discover

Harlequin American Romance. Send me FREE and without obligation *Twice in a Lifetime.* If you do not hear from me after I have examined my FREE book, please send me the 4 new **Harlequin American Romances** each month as soon as they come off the presses. I understand that I will be billed only $2.25 for each book (total $9.00). There are no shipping or handling charges. There is no minimum number of books that I have to purchase. In fact, I may cancel this arrangement at any time. *Twice in a Lifetime* is mine to keep as a FREE gift, even if I do not buy any additional books.

Name _____ (please print)

Address _____ Apt. no. _____

City _____ State/Prov. _____ Zip/Postal Code _____

Signature (If under 18, parent or guardian must sign.)